THE ASSASSIN
IN THE MARAIS

Also by Claude Izner

Murder on the Eiffel Tower

The Disappearance at Père-Lachaise

The Montmartre Investigation

THE ASSASSIN IN THE MARAIS

CLAUDE IZNER

Translated by Lorenza Garcia and Isabel Reid

Minotaur Books ⚓ New York

THE ASSASSIN IN THE MARAIS. Copyright © 2004 by Éditions 10/18, Département d'Univers Poche. English translation copyright © 2009 by Gallic Books. All rights reserved. Printed in the United States of America. For information, address St. Martin's Press, 175 Fifth Avenue, New York, N.Y. 10010.

www.minotaurbooks.com

The Library of Congress has cataloged the hardcover edition as follows:

Izner, Claude.
  The Assassin in the Marais : A Victor Legris Mystery / Claude Izner. ; translated by Lorenza Garcia and Isabel Reid.—1st U.S. ed.
    p. cm.
  ISBN 978-0-312-66215-8
  1. Legris, Victor (Fictitious character)—Fiction. 2. Murder—France—Paris—Fiction. 3. Booksellers and bookselling—France—Paris—Fiction. 4. Paris (France)—History—1870–1940—Fiction. I. Title.
  PQ2709.Z64 S4313 2011
  843'.—dc92

                                                        2011284521

ISBN 978-1-250-00754-4 (trade paperback)

First published in France as *Le secret des Enfants-Rouges* by Éditions 10/18

First Minotaur Books Paperback Edition: July 2012

10 9 8 7 6 5 4 3 2 1

To Emmanuelle Heurtebize

To our nearest and dearest, with special mention of B and J,
our American expert and our Moscow expert

To Anna, Valentina and Enrico

Et tu coules toujours, Seine, et tout en rampant,
Tu traînes dans Paris ton corps de vieux serpent,
De vieux serpent boueux, emportant vers tes havres
Tes cargaisons de bois, de houille et de cadavers!

Paul Verlaine
(*Poèmes saturniens, 'Caprices'*)

And the Seine flows, crawls, drags itself
Always the muddy serpent of Paris
Bearing towards Le Havre its cargoes
Of wood, of coal – and corpses

Translated by C.K. Stead

Le Marché des Enfants-Rouges was to be found behind a gate at 39 Rue de Bretagne. It opened in 1628 and took its name from the children's home nearby, which was founded by Marguerite de Navarre, housing orphans who wore red uniforms.

All the characters in *The Marais Assassin* are imaginary with the exception of Paul Verlaine, Paul Fort, Jean Moréas, Albert Gaudry, Eugène Dubois, Ravachol, Alphonse Bertillon, Trimouillat, Ma Gueule, Cazals, Caubel de la Ville Ingan and, of course, Henri de Toulouse-Lautrec.

We would like to thank all the team at 10/18 for their kindness and support.

CONTENTS

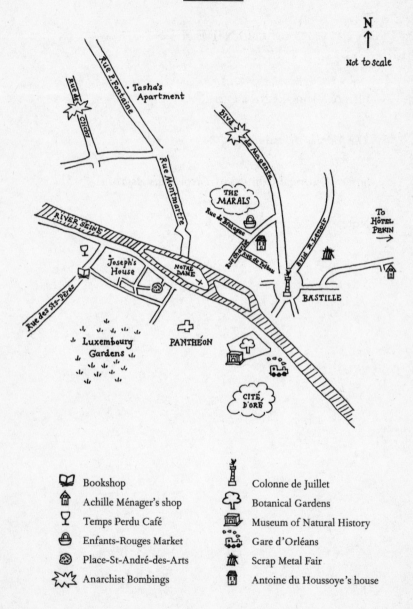

THE ASSASSIN
IN THE MARAIS

PROLOGUE

THE clock of the Église Trinité had just struck eight o'clock in the morning when, without warning, an ear-splitting explosion ripped through the district. A building on Rue de Clichy rocked on its foundations, and within seconds its staircase had collapsed from top to bottom and its windows had shattered.

His body vibrated with the shock of the blast and he thought only: *Apocalypse*. The street began to dance before his eyes. The dust pricked his nostrils, but what invaded him was something other than its bitter odour, something that seemed to emerge as a long-suppressed memory of a past experience. It was the echo of what had happened long ago. A sign.

His ardent belief in the existence of Divine decision, his respect for the Scriptures and his terror of the sacraments all stirred in him the memory of his guardian pointing rigidly towards the dark sky. It had returned, his voice growled. Always the same words:

'And there was a great trembling of the earth, the sun darkened like sackcloth, the moon turned blood red . . . Wallowing in heresy leads to damnation. You shall be punished! Punished!'

Glass fragments littered the roads. An old man sat on the

edge of the pavement, trembling all over. A woman, her clothes torn and her hair covered in plaster, was screaming. Help was already arriving.

The bedroom was a refuge in the dead of night, reassuring, comfortable, protected by its wood-panelled walls. On the desk, the pale pink lampshade created rainbows on the side of a carafe of water. A hand picked up the inkwell. The only thing to break the silence was the scratching of the pen as it conscientiously traced upstrokes and down strokes on a piece of squared paper.

This morning, the wrath of God resonated once more, piercing my eardrums and shaking my bones to the marrow. The cohort of wolves in sheep's clothing spread lies and uncertainty amongst the flock. I was there. My gorge rose; I thought my brain was exploding. I was blinded by the dazzling light. The sky beat down on us. A thousand hammers shattered my head. God reminded me what I must accomplish. I felt triumphant, for God created man in his own image bearing his likeness, and he created all things on earth and he has placed his confidence in me. As I have discovered what is being plotted, it is my duty to act. I am the arm of God. I will achieve my end; no one will take possession of that abomination. I will use extreme means. Humanity has taken a wrong turn. I must separate the wheat from the chaff; that is my solemn oath. Oh, Lord, arm your emissary.

CHAPTER 1

The Highlands of Scotland, 5 April 1892

STATIONED on the low branch of a beech tree, a Siamese cat, muscles tensed, claws at the ready, kept a close watch on a bush where a field mouse had taken refuge. White storm clouds scudded across the sky, blown by the north wind that battered the trees in the park. A red moon, alternately veiled then unveiled, feebly lit the countryside. The cat could barely make out the heather shrouded in mist where his victim was hiding. Beyond a clump of maple trees the outline of Brougham House could be seen, sitting on the hill like a sentry surveying the road that snaked up from the foot of the glen.

The cat passed a wet paw over the dark patch on his face and flattened himself against the bark of the tree. Down below, a dark shape burst out from behind a fan of bracken. The cat pounced. Just as his mouth was closing around the frail creature, a muted trembling shook the ground. The vibration surprised the cat, and he hesitated for a moment, long enough for his prey to disappear between two rocks. Disappointed, the cat abandoned the chase. Rising up full length on his hind legs, he sharpened his claws against the tree trunk and went back over to the drive, moving nonchalantly like an old gentleman taking his postprandial stroll. Suddenly a furious mass, dragged by the combined effort of horses with mad eyes, erupted before him. Panic-stricken, the cat scuttled to the top of a scrub oak, from where he observed the four-wheeled monster rolling towards the gates of Brougham House.

The cat waited with trembling ears, his nostrils filled with the odour of horse, until his heart had regained its normal rhythm. When he thought it was safe to do so, he cautiously left his refuge. Then a new fear rooted him to the spot. Something else was coming up the glen: horse and rider emerged round the bend. The cat hissed, puffing himself up, and the horse swerved. A whip cracked, nearly taking out the eye of the Siamese, who fled deep into the shrubbery.

Jennings had forgotten to stoke up the fire. Seated near the window, Lady Frances Stone was about to pull the servant's bell when the sight of a Victoria coming up the central drive stayed her hand. Who could be visiting at such a late hour? Since the death of Lord Stone, the only visitors she received were Dr Barley and Reverend Anthony, and they always came in the morning. Lady Stone drew the edges of her shawl together over her thin chest and resolved to throw some logs on the fire. A feeble mewing caught her attention. That rascal of a cat! Clamped against the window, he looked like a gargoyle, with his phosphorescent pupils and his triangular face split in a rictus. Lady Stone had scarcely opened the window when the Siamese leapt on to her knee, causing her to cry out as he drew his paws across her skirt.

'What are you purring like that for? You sound like a little motor. It's not like you to be so affectionate – have you had a brush with the poacher's dogs? Shh! Be quiet so that I can hear . . . Jennings has let someone in.'

Jennings, in light blue livery, with breeches, white stockings and buckled shoes, his powdered hair knotted on the nape of his neck with a wide black ribbon, was straight out of a Hogarth painting. Astonished by this garb, Antoine du Houssoye followed him as far as a drawing room filled with dusty furniture, massive bookcases and armour. Jennings turned on his heel without a word.

'Charming welcome,' muttered Antoine du Houssoye. 'It's freezing in here. Who was singing the praises of Scottish hospitality? In any case their thrift is not a myth! No fire even though it's so cold . . .'

In the faint light of the candelabrum left by the manservant, he made out the titles of the books lining the shelves: bibles, missals and theological treatises. He shrugged his shoulders and, taking a notebook from the pocket of his frock coat, scribbled a few lines.

I'm actually here, I will finally know if the trail indicated by the Emperor of Surabaya is the correct one. Is it possible that I will succeed in catching up with D? If I do, I will be the first to prove the existence of that . . .

He interrupted himself, struck by the thought that had taken root the previous evening in the Balmoral Hotel: where was his precious file of notes that he had gathered in Java? Had he mislaid them?

No, they must be at the bottom of one of the drawers of his trunk, or in his bag of . . .

A concealed door opened and a tiny woman in a pink muslin dress and an old-fashioned frilled bonnet entered. Antoine felt as if he had gone back in time; surely this fragile little person had been born during the reign of George III? In a voice like a hissing kettle, she informed him that Lady Stone was ready to receive him. She seized the candelabrum and without looking back trotted along a dark corridor in which he glimpsed a series of forbidding portraits. Looking up, he discovered an imposing gallery accessed by a grand staircase that the little person in the bonnet was climbing as nimbly as a squirrel. Antoine, disorientated by the gloom, his eyes riveted to the pink dress, scrambled up the steps trying desperately not to stumble, and found himself before double doors that had just opened.

A boudoir dominated by Chippendale and old porcelain and lit by the dancing flames of a blazing fire was the backdrop for a wheelchair in which a lady sat, stroking the Siamese cat ensconced on her lap. An oil lamp glowed on a pedestal table beside a pile of journals and books. The lady dismissed the wizened centenarian and slowly swivelled her chair round. Antoine was disconcerted by the sight of the pallid, angular face, all its energy concentrated in the blazing eyes, which locked on his, giving him the impression that they saw into the depths of his soul. After studying him for a long moment, she blinked and the crumpled mouth stretched into a smile. She motioned him towards her. Her emaciated body was wrapped in black lace, with a flower-patterned shawl and a wool skirt. An openwork mantilla with a garland of flowers covered her hair and a large pearl on a velvet band hung between her eyebrows. Her fingers caressed the cat's fur. She looked like one of the bas-reliefs on the Buddhist temple of Borobudur.

Lady Stone looked appraisingly at the wiry, tanned man before her. His short beard and pointed moustache were worthy of the hero of one of her childhood novels, the musketeer D'Artagnan. She pictured herself young, beautiful and eligible on the arm of this seductive individual, but his image was immediately replaced in her mind by the stout silhouette of Lord Stone.

How ridiculous I'm being. He's forty and I'm sixty-five. He could be my son. I'm acting like a young shop girl, when actually I'm an over-the-hill . . .

'I rarely receive visitors,' she said. 'I agreed to honour your request in memory of my deceased brother. Please be brief.'

She addressed him composedly in good French. She did not invite him to sit down and he shifted from one foot to another.

'As I indicated in my letter, I have come to . . .'

'In that case, alas, I very much fear that I must disappoint you. That object is no longer in my possession. As sole beneficiary, I respected the wishes of my brother and distributed his legacies to museums . . .'

She broke off and addressed the cat. 'What is it now?'

Suddenly rigid, the cat was staring at the window. A gust of wind had brought a scent to his nostrils, unexpected and hostile. He jumped on to the window sill and froze, confused by the shadows. He listened, trying to locate the intruder, and eventually made out a tall, thin figure hanging on to some toothing at the edge of the wall. Terrified, the cat ran to hide near the hearth. Lady Stone concluded that the rats must have returned and made a mental note to tell Jennings to have them exterminated.

'Where was I?'

'You made gifts to museums . . . .'

'Oh yes, museums, and the numerous accounts written by my brother and his collection of herbariums were given to scientific institutions. As for the private pieces, I bequeathed them to his closest friends.'

'Do you have the name of the friend who received the item mentioned in my letter? It's extremely important,' insisted Antoine.

'Assuredly I know the identity of the beneficiary. He lives in Paris; you can try to contact him. I've written down his address for you.'

She held out an envelope and pulled the bell.

'And now, dear Monsieur, my maid will show you out.'

He took his leave, torn between jubilation at the idea that his quest might be nearly at an end and disappointment. He had hoped to spend the night at Brougham House and now he would have to make his way back to Edinburgh on those impossible roads!

Adieu, handsome D'Artagnan, thought Lady Stone, moving to the fireplace. What can you want with that ugly object? Johnny warned me that it brought misfortune, even though he didn't believe in such superstitions. Poor Johnny, his life cut off in its prime . . .

She lost herself in contemplation of the flames, in which strange shapes danced. The cat, his fur on end, his eyes gleaming, watched a hazy apparition slip through the window, first black-gloved hands, then a foot, legs, a torso . . . Noiselessly, it landed on the carpet and approached Lady Stone from behind. The cat saw the pearly flash of the handle of a revolver and a gunshot rent the silence. Mewing raucously, he shot under a chest of drawers.

London, Thursday, 7 April

Iris had sore feet, but dared not tell Kenji. They had been wandering for half an hour among the graves of Highgate Cemetery, swept by an icy breeze. They finally halted before a pink marble tombstone engraved in gold lettering with a simple inscription:

DAPHNÉ LEGRIS

1839–1878

Rest in Peace

Kenji was unprepared for the emotion that overcame him. His eyes filled with tears, his shoulders trembled. He turned quickly away and removed the top hat that he forced himself to wear during his trips to London. He pictured Daphné's graceful form in the bookshop in Sloane Square when he was still only her husband's shop assistant. He recalled their platonic passion, the furtive smiles, the rare moments when their hands touched. Six or seven months after the death of Monsieur Legris, Daphné had given herself to him. Their secret liaison, crowned by the birth of Iris, had lasted ten years.

He surreptitiously wiped away his tears and looked proudly at his daughter, wrapped up warmly in her cloak, as she scattered rose petals over the grave. He reflected that her atypical beauty perpetuated the union between him and Daphné: East and West are fused in her. I want her to be happy and to have a glittering future.

Had he been aware that at precisely that moment Iris was thinking of a certain blond, slightly hunchbacked young man, employed in his own bookshop in Paris, Kenji would not only have been disappointed, he would have been furious.

'Why was my mother not buried at Kensal Green with her family?'

'We were very fond of Highgate. We dreamed of buying a house here, because of the purity of the air and the view of London. Daphné worshipped Coleridge, who is buried in a school chapel nearby. One day we were walking here and she made me promise that if she died first I would accommodate her – that was her expression, accommodate – in the east cemetery.'

The Egyptian-style tombs, watched over by the dark flame of the cypress trees, were vaguely reminiscent of the Père-Lachaise Cemetery in Paris. They paused in front of the last resting place of the chemist Faraday, then at the grave of Mary Ann Evans, better known as George Eliot.

'You must read *The Mill on the Floss*,' said Kenji.

'You know I'm not very keen on reading,' retorted Iris.

Except Joseph's serial, she thought to herself.

Bother! Her father was stopping again. She read out:

KARL MARX
1818–1883

'The son of a lawyer who converted to Protestantism since it wasn't wise to be Jewish in the Prussia of Frederick William III.'

'A friend of yours?' she asked, stifling a laugh.

Kenji started. She had Daphné's laugh.

'No, a friend of the working classes. The stone he threw into the political pond has not yet finished making ripples. I find him particularly sympathetic because of the answers he gave to a questionnaire put to him by his daughters:

' "What is your favourite saying?"

' "Question everything."

' "What is your favourite occupation?"

' "Reading." '

Reading! That's all they talk about! Iris said to herself in exasperation as she stood on the terrace and looked out at the magnificent view. The dome of St Paul's Cathedral resembled a gigantic mushroom. She imagined it transformed into a hot-air balloon, floating over fields sewn together like a green and yellow chessboard. Kenji interrupted her reverie by declaring in a learned tone: 'Fourteen miles from east to west, eight from north to south. London is home to more Catholics than Rome, more Irish than Dublin and more Scots than Edinburgh . . .'

'You're better than Baedeker! Last one to the Archway tavern pays a forfeit!' she cried, speeding off, holding her hat on with one hand.

'No! Iris, wait!'

He joined her, out of breath and fractious, as she hailed an omnibus.

'I want to take the tube . . . Let's go to Islington!'

It was a command.

Resignedly Kenji slumped against the window of the onmibus, trying to forget his age and his fatigue.

They took a lift down to the platform, in which Iris imagined herself plunging to the bottom of a mine. Pink with pleasure she all but burst out laughing in the coach of the City and South London Railway, where she attracted the admiring glances of the male passengers. Kenji's pride in his daughter was mixed with tenderness – she was full of youthful exuberance.

I'm in love, Iris thought as the carriage rumbled along. I'm a woman now. He kissed me four times the day I left. By now he will have received the letter I posted at Victoria station. I wonder if he blushed. When I told him I found him attractive, he turned bright red!

'Let's get out at London Bridge – we can catch a cab from there.'

She hailed one of the new hansom cabs, with its carriage suspended between two huge wheels and the driver seated at the back. Aghast at this new caprice, Kenji shouted, 'Sloane Square!' through the opening in the hood.

As they strolled round Sloane Square, the sight of the bookshop stirred up painful memories. An image rose up before him: the extremely corpulent Monsieur Legris, stick in hand, threatening Victor as he hid behind his mother. What minor misdemeanour had the boy committed? Only Kenji had not feared the bookseller. He knew how to calm him by coolly reeling off one of his made-up proverbs; he had probably declared something like, 'Of the Great Fire of London not a single cinder remains,' and Monsieur Legris would have retreated from the charge and lowered his stick.

'Has the shop changed?' asked Iris.

'It's been repainted and the windows . . .'

He stopped to listen to a newspaper seller yelling out the headlines:

'Scotland Yard still questioning staff of the murdered Lady Frances . . .'

The surname was drowned by the noise of a passing carriage.

'. . . in her home, Brougham House. Police seek identity of visitor on the evening of her murder!'

'The windows have smaller panes now,' finished Kenji.

'Shall we go in?'

'No need to stir up ghosts.'

'I like Chelsea. If I had to live in London, it would be here . . . Or else Westminster or Regent's Park.'

'Your mother and I liked to meet under the cedar tree in the Chelsea Physic Garden. We also liked the Reading Room in Cromwell Road. Shall we go there?'

'I would rather finish my purchases. I promised Tasha I'd go to Twinings on the Strand to get her some tea. And Victor would like catalogues from Quaritch the bookseller and Eastman the photographic shop. That will take me as far as Oxford Street and I'd like to see the ladies' rooms at DH Evans. Father, could I have some money?'

Kenji sighed. Iris would be the ruin of him. And if she were not, Eudoxie Allard, alias Fifi Bas-Rhin, would be. Eudoxie had tired of her Russian Archduke and had taken up with Kenji again the month before. He was planning to buy her something in one of the jewellers in New Bond Street.

Kenji enjoyed his encounters with Eudoxie, which provided agreeable interludes and satisfied his virile needs. They were careful not to introduce any elements of their day-to-day lives into their relationship, offering each other only the best of themselves. Their relationship, limited to eroticism, remained casual, because Kenji's heart would always belong to Daphné.

'We're dining at seven thirty in the hotel restaurant and I've reserved a box at the Royal Opera House in Covent Garden. I think I'll stay here for a while. Don't be late now!'

Iris nodded politely, although she detested opera and knew she would be bored to tears. I'll think about Joseph, she decided, climbing up to the upper deck of a brown omnibus. In the meantime I'll buy him a tiepin.

Paris, Friday 8 April, five o'clock in the morning
It had become a routine. He would get up quietly, listening for Gabrielle's regular breathing, grab the clothes discarded the night before from the chair and dress in the adjoining bathroom. He would light an oil lamp so that he could see his way down the hall, at the end of which he would quickly duck into the pantry, just long enough to drink a glass of water and cut himself a slice of bread. He would creep down the stairs, grateful that the old man's ancient dog had finally kicked the

bucket and would not give him away by barking. Then he would go carefully down the stone steps, snuff out the lamp and leave it outside the concierge's lodge.

He opened the door slowly so that it would not creak and crossed the courtyard, taking care that his boots did not clatter on the cobblestones. With four strides he was out in the street, filled with the intoxicating sense of freedom he felt each time he escaped the family circle.

At first he had disliked his bouts of insomnia, but he had cultivated the affliction until gradually it became chronic. Night was his kingdom. When he could not sleep, he had the time to write up notes on his conferences and plan the quest that would culminate in his magnum opus. But normally what happened, as this morning, was that after three or four hours of restless sleep, he would awake at dawn and take advantage of the early hour to wander along the slumbering narrow streets, before joining Boulevard de Sébastopol, where he would sip coffee at the counter of a bar, among the market gardeners who brought their produce to Les Halles. Then he would head for the museum.

The inhabitants of the Enfants-Rouges quarter were sleeping, shut away from the biting cold. His breath turned to vapour in the dim light of the street-lamps. He made his way into the gloom, along the wet pavements of the narrow Rue Pastourelle, then through the milky gap of Rue du Temple, which he left reluctantly, slipping quietly long Rue des Gravilliers. The game of hide-and-seek between shadow and light reminded him of his escapades in the equatorial rainforest long ago, where sun and stars were hidden by the thick mass of vegetation. The river of Rue de Turbigo flowed peacefully; the door of the Église Saint-Nicolas-des-Champs was like a rock stemming the tide. In the square, workmen in blue smocks and cotton caps accompanied by their wives in knotted headscarves were returning from Les Halles, where they had delivered their vegetables. Once the horses were unhitched they went off to put their carts back in Rue Greneta, where glorious chaos reigned under the flickering light of the street-lamps.

As the man walked past the vast hangar of a toy factory, the entrance to which was blocked off by carts, he heard someone call his name. He stopped, trying to make out where the voice had come from – it seemed to reverberate from beyond the greyish mass of a dray. A sharp crack rang out. The man made a vague gesture towards his chest, a fleeting expression of bemusement crossed his face, his legs gave way and he toppled over some bundles of wadding.

By the time he had been dragged behind a pile of crates and a hand had patted his frock coat in search of his wallet, he was dead.

Paris, same day, seven o'clock in the morning.
A pale light filtered between the curtains and the murmurings of the city could be heard in the distance. The fingers holding the pen moved rapidly across the paper:

The seven thunders have made their voices heard. I am the emissary. I have eliminated the two witnesses. Now I must destroy the abomination before false prophets get hold of it and seduce those who bear the mark of the beast and worship his image.

The emissary put down his pen, closed his notebook and went to bury it in the depths of his wardrobe. The carafe of water on the desk acted like a prism, multiplying the pinkish light of the lamp many times over in miniature.

CHAPTER 2

Friday, 8 April, nine o'clock in the morning

WHEN Tasha was asleep, the pillow squashed beneath her cheek, Victor was free from anxiety. Even though her dreams carried her out of reach, she was his. No matter how much he reproached himself for and tried to suppress his possessiveness, it always crept insidiously back. For several months he had believed that he had conquered it, but recently it had reappeared. Tasha seemed to be hiding something from him and was often preoccupied. Moreover, he had caught her one evening reading a letter that she had hastily whisked out of sight when she saw him. Since then he had been eaten up by doubt.

He snuggled up against her, fitting himself to the outline of her naked form, but still he could not relax. His mind was like an attic in which a jumble of experiences, anxieties and hopes was piled high. It was impossible to get a wink of sleep. One thought led to another . . . He was obsessed with the temptation of finding that letter; he had to know what was in it. Unable to bear it any more, he got up and began methodically going through her drawing boxes, drawers and pockets. Finally, finding nothing, he went back to bed and lay still, eyes open, staring at the window.

Where was the fulfilment and harmony he had assumed would

characterise living as a couple? Could they be called a couple? Two apartments on either side of a courtyard, two careers . . .

'We've loved each other for almost three years, and we've hardly progressed . . . And *you've* hardly progressed . . .' he said to himself, flattening a tuft of hair.

He sat up and kissed her on the forehead, neck and throat. Languorously she touched his chest and her leg slid between his. They let themselves go until they had passed the point of no return.

'Young man, you have an annoying habit of procrastinating!' barked the Comtesse de Salignac.

'What on earth? Why is the battleaxe talking to me about procreation?' wondered Joseph, engaged in tying up the parcel for the Comtesse, his first customer of the morning.

'You've been promising me George de Peyrebrune's[1] *Dairy of a Blue-stocking* from Ollendorf for an eternity. Some hope! How much do I owe you?'

The Comtesse de Salignac glared at Joseph from behind her lorgnette. She leant forward a little to study the book that he was trying to hide under his newspaper.

'Fenimore Cooper . . . The young today simply revel in violence! And people wonder at the rising tide of crime!' she exclaimed, her mouth formed in the disapproving shape of a parrot's beak.

She paid for the Jules Mary,[2] with which she had had to make do, as furious as a victim of the rabies that the newspapers indicated had returned to Paris.

'Good riddance,' snarled Joseph, unfolding Iris's letter again.

My dearest Joseph,

Dare I say 'my beloved'? Yes, your kisses permit me to. Consider this letter a pledge by which I promise myself to you. I will be yours when you have succeeded in convincing my father and in demonstrating the brilliance of your talent. Until then I swear fidelity to you . . .

'Fidelity,' he murmured. 'That's beautiful. A little chaste, but beautiful. She's shy . . . As for convincing her father . . .'

Kenji's stern face superimposed itself on the figure of the Red Indian brandishing a tomahawk on the colourful jacket of *The Last of the Mohicans*.

Surprised by the jangling of the door bell, Joseph tucked the letter in his pocket and donned his bookseller's smile.

'I'd like to see the bookshop owner, Monsieur Kenji Mori.'

The man, who had tinted glasses and wore a black wool double-breasted overcoat and a dented bowler hat, made his request calmly yet forcefully. Alarmed, Joseph imagined that the man was an officer of the moral police, come to warn Kenji that his assistant was compromising the virtue of his daughter.

'One of the owners,' he corrected. 'His associate, Monsieur Legris, won't be long. He'll be here at about ten o'clock. I'm the one who . . .'

'In that case, I'll go and see Monsieur Mori at home – where does he live?'

'He lives in the adjoining building, number 18, but he's travelling at the moment. Can I take a message?'

The man adjusted his bowler hat with a nonchalant gesture that was belied by his frown.

'That's most unfortunate. Here's my address. Please give it to him and ask him to contact me. When will he be back?'

'Tomorrow.'

The man scribbled rapidly on the back of his visiting card, put it on the counter and made for the door without saying goodbye.

'What does he think I am, that fellow?' muttered Joseph. 'Part of the furniture? I'll show them all, when I'm as famous as Émile Gaboriau!'

He had been disappointed that the publication of his serial *'The Strange Affair at Colombines'*[3] had brought him neither fame nor fortune, although thanks to him the circulation of *Le Passe-partout* had increased. According to Antonin Clusel, the editor of the newspaper, he would have to publish one or two more novels of the same sort before he could expect any recognition. 'So better get writing, old chap, and make it good!'

'I'd like to see him at it. I'm as dry of ideas as a squeezed lemon!'

Frozen in the middle of the courtyard of 18 Rue des Saints-Pères, the man with the tinted glasses stared first at the concierge, who was wielding her broom, then up at the closed shutters of the first floor of the four-storey building, before turning on his heel and leaving. He strode off down Rue des Saints-Pères.

On Quai Malaquais, a woman seated on the terrace of the Temps Perdu café lowered the menu she had been pretending to study and joined him near the cab rank.

Resisting the urge to re-read Iris's letter, Joseph picked up the notebook in which he stuck newspaper articles about crimes or unusual occurrences. He did not notice the visiting card left by the man in the bowler hat flutter down to the bottom of the umbrella stand. The last pages of his notebook were exclusively devoted to the anarchist bombings the previous month and the arrest on the 30 March, at the Restaurant Véry,[4] of their perpetrator, one Ravachol.

'Illustrious dynamiter, furtive and calamitous . . .'[5] Joseph started to sing, but he broke off at the sight of his mother, laden with provisions.

Too late, she had heard, and she went upstairs grumbling, 'There he goes again with his flights of fancy. Those thugs are threatening to blow up the capital. They wouldn't care if we all went up in smoke.'

Joseph let out a weary sigh. 'Maman, I've told you a hundred times. Monsieur Legris would prefer you not to traipse through the bookshop with the groceries. You can easily go through the courtyard – it's not that much of a detour!'

'But the concierge will hold me up! That Madame Ballu, she could talk the hind leg off a donkey. She gets on my nerves!'

'That's not a good enough reason. We're working here and the customers . . .'

'Oh, the customers? I see. Monsieur is ashamed of his

mother; Monsieur would like to see the back of her! Well, don't worry, I'll soon be joining your poor father, and then you'll be happy.'

'I didn't say that! Do you want me to help you?'

'Don't trouble yourself. You obviously have much more important things to see to. Oh the cross I have to bear!' she groaned, climbing the stairs.

Since Christmas Day 1891, when Germaine had solemnly hung up her apron because Mademoiselle Iris balked at eating the turkey, Euphrosine had been preparing meals for Kenji and his daughter, cleaning their apartment and then going each afternoon to Rue Fontaine to cook and dust for Victor and Tasha. For the first few weeks, overjoyed at no longer having to pull her costermonger's cart, she had found her duties light, especially since she went to and fro on the omnibus. But, in spite of these benefits, she had started to complain about her rheumatism, about the demands of Iris's vegetarianism and the weight of her domestic responsibilities, even though she skimped on the housework.

For his part, Joseph, while taking advantage of his mother's absence to meet Iris secretly at their apartment, found it hard to bear being under her eye all morning in the Elzévir bookshop.

He unfolded *La Vie Populaire* and continued to read out loud to himself from Émile Zola's latest novel, *The Debacle*.[6]

'Those white sheets! How he had longed for sheets! Jean could not take his eyes off them. He had not undressed, had not slept in a bed for six weeks . . .'

'Of course, it would be paradise after the butchery of the battlefields,' Joseph murmured.

Tasha woke Victor gently by hugging him tenderly, then bounded out of bed, ran to set the water to boil and snatched up a coffee grinder that she placed between his thighs.

'Get up and start cranking. I could eat a horse! Shall I make you some bread and butter?'

'What time is it?'

'Eleven o'clock. Joseph is going to grumble.'

Barefoot and munching, her slice of bread in hand, she went to study the canvas she was working on, a modern version of Poussin's *Eliezer and Rebecca*. A group of women, seated in a cabaret, were laughingly observing a rather self-conscious young man as he offered one of them some flowers, while a waitress filled an overflowing glass.

In the version of *Moses Saved from the Waters* she had just finished, and in which she had represented a mother bathing her baby in a basin in a wash-house, she had striven to mix realism and symbolism. She had been satisfied with *Moses*, but she could not stop retouching this second composition. In order to be less financially dependant upon Victor, she had undertaken to illustrate an edition of Edgar Alan Poe's *Extraordinary Stories*, and as a result she was suffering from having less time to devote to her painting.

There was a knock at the door. Victor, who was sitting in his underwear, the coffee grinder between his knees, was dismayed to see Maurice Laumier hove into view. That ambitious, daubing charlatan had been hanging around Tasha again for several weeks now. He was trying to persuade her to paint theatre scenery.

'Greetings and prosperity,' he brayed, tossing his top hat on the bed. 'Don't worry about me – I've already had breakfast! Dearest, I just bumped into the young Paul Fort. He has grandiose plans for his Théâtre d'Art. Let's have a go at the *trompe-l'oeils*!'

'You're obsessed,' groaned Victor.

'My dear chap, you are totally incapable of grasping our precept, which can be expressed in ten words: "Scenery is as much created by speech as anything else." Edgar Alan Poe's *The Crow* was performed before a simple backdrop of brown paper.'

Not wanting to hear any more, Victor dressed hastily and was preparing to leave. He would have liked to kiss Tasha, but could not bring himself to under the sarcastic gaze of Laumier.

'What about your coffee?' she cried.

'I'm late for a meeting, then I have to go to Rue des Saints-Pères. I'll be back this afternoon.'

'I'm not sure I'll be here . . .'

'Too bad,' he murmured.

Just as he was about to grasp its handle, the door opened, revealing a small man in bowler hat and pince-nez, smoking a cigar.

'Lautrec! What a coincidence! I went to the Indépendants,' bellowed Laumier. 'It's superbly laid out. I adore your *La Goulue Entering Le Moulin-Rouge*. It's a riot!'

Really, this was too much. Victor strode the short distance to his apartment and went to shut himself in his darkroom. He didn't care that Tasha would reproach him for being surly; he absolutely could not bear to know she was surrounded by those men, each as vulgar as the other. Creative, Tasha called them. And what about his talent, did she not value that?

'Painting, painting, always painting! And what of photography?'

Victor had studied the work of the Scottish photographer John Thomson closely, especially his photographic account *The Illustration of China and its People*. He hoped to do for the people of the streets of Paris what Thomson had done for London, but without falling into pathos and the stereotypical images of misery. He would position his work somewhere between Charles Nègre and Charles Marville.[7]

He looked at his photographs of children at work, taken on Faubourg Saint-Antoine and Rue des Immeubles-Industriels: a girl embroidering cloth with gold, a boy busy sawing wood for veneer, the pupil of a rhinestone cutter, the apprentice of a wallpaper maker. These portraits, taken in apartments converted into studios, had demanded enormous care; he had put as much sensibility as technique into them, seeking to ensure that the subjects stayed natural in front of the camera.

He shrugged on his frock coat, crammed on his felt hat and snatched up his gloves and cane. Since he could not eat with Tasha, he would go and find sustenance on Boulevard des Capucines, at Café Napolitain, and hard luck, Joseph!

Madame Ballu, the concierge of 18 Rue des Saints-Pères, had risen grumbling at dawn, and had been scrubbing the courtyard and staircase of the building ever since. Now she judged that she had earned a little relaxation, and planned to tuck into a plate of cabbage with chopped bacon in her lodge. Then she would allow herself a mouthful of the vintage port with which her late husband, Onésime Ballu, had kept the sideboard stocked. After that she would take advantage of the bright spell to pull up a chair on the pavement and watch the world go by.

This programme was disturbed by the arrival of a woman in a veiled toque and an Orloff overcoat revealing a hobble skirt. The outfit was banded with astrakhan and the woman appeared to be hesitating.

'Who are you looking for?' barked the concierge, eyeing the hatbox the woman was clutching to her chest.

'The people who live on the fourth floor – they're expecting me. I've come for a fitting.'

'The Primolins? Well, make sure you wipe your feet. The mat's not there for decoration, you know.'

The woman had barely entered the hall when she stopped.

'Is the flat on the first floor for rent, by any chance? The shutters are closed . . . I'm just thinking it would be perfect for my elderly aunt, who can't manage more than one flight of stairs. It would be a blessing for her.'

'Sorry to disappoint you, m'dear, you'll have to look elsewhere. The shutters aren't closed because the flat is empty. Monsieur Mori and his companion are abroad. They're coming home tomorrow.'

Madame Ballu, hands on hips, watched the stranger disappear up the stairs.

'It doesn't surprise me that those old skinflints on the fourth floor associate with people who covet other people's homes! Well, am I finally going to be able to tuck in?'

She took the precaution of hanging her *The Concierge is in Town* sign on the door, before closing it firmly.

The visitor, who was standing listening on the third floor landing, heard the door shut. She leant over the banister to make sure she was on her own and then crept downstairs and pressed the bell of the first-floor flat. She counted up to thirty, rang again, waited, then went down to the ground floor and headed for Rue Jacob.

'I'm feeling a little peckish,' hinted Joseph as Euphrosine buzzed around him.

He hoped that would send her off to the kitchen.

'You're a bottomless pit! If you're hungry, chew your fist, or have an apple. And leave me to think about the delicious meal I'm going to prepare for Monsieur and Mademoiselle Mori. Oh, there you are, M'sieur Legris. Just the man I need – what do you think of this? For the entrée, tongue in piquant sauce, followed by lamb croquettes with artichokes, veal pie with fried salsify and braised celery with parmesan. For dessert, a lovely vanilla soufflé. Mademoiselle Iris will have to make do with gratin dauphinois. And what do you think for wine?'

Not bothering to reply, Victor placed a pile of catalogues given to him by a fellow bookseller at the Booksellers' Circle on Kenji's desk.

'Any customers?' he asked Joseph.

'Slim pickings.'

'Well, I'm obviously wasting my breath – I might as well be talking to the sheep on Rue Fontaine. I'll go and put your grub in the bain-marie. Don't bother to thank me.'

As Euphrosine went up, invoking Jesus, Mary and Joseph, two women entered the shop. One was rigged out in a woollen suit and a Tyrolean hat, the other was drowning in a voluminous purple coat and her ridiculous hat was adorned with symmetrical green feathers like the antennae of a giant praying mantis.

'Fräulein Becker, Madame de Flavignol!' exclaimed Victor, strenuously fighting an impulse to laugh.

Joseph had taken refuge behind the counter.

'We've come to see you specially, my dear. Helga has finally found the brochure on the new Papillon cycles, and didn't you say you wanted to buy a bicycle?' simpered Mathilde de Flavignol, who had a secret crush on Victor.

'*Das ist wahr,*' confirmed Mademoiselle Becker. 'Here you are. You can keep it as long as you like. The choice of a velocipede is as fraught as the choice of a domestic animal. One is destined to spend a good many years together.'

'Oh, dear heart, have you seen the dog Raphaëlle de Gouveline has bought to fill the gap left by her Maltese lap dog? It's a hideous black fur ball with no tail. That's too much mourning for my liking, but what can you expect; it's the Prince of Wales who started the fashion for schipperkes . . .'

Just then Euphrosine came into view, descending the stairs with a heavy tread, overburdened with baskets containing her feather dusters and cloths. She was muttering that the lunch was ready and she was going to Rue Fontaine even though her feet were absolutely killing her. 'And of course I don't even have time to apply my Russian corn cream. Ah, now Russia, there's a sympathetic country, not like some I could mention,' she grumbled, jostling Helga Becker.

'Joseph,' murmured Victor, 'please tell your mother that from now on she is not to go to and fro through the shop.'

'Why don't you tell her yourself?' returned Joseph out of the corner of his mouth.

'Do you like animals, Monsieur Legris?' enquired Mathilde de Flavignol. 'You do? In that case, may I suggest you go and see the baby orang-utans adopted by the Botanical Gardens? They come from Borneo – Paul and Virginie are their names, and they are fed exclusively on . . .'

'M'sieur Legris,' Joseph interrupted, 'talking of *Paul and Virginie*, we have a commission from Monsieur Hilaire de Kermarec. He's looking for a copy of the edition published by Curmer in 1838, the illustrations are protected by tissue paper and it has a Simier morocco-leather binding.'

'These gentlemen have started to use jargon, so we should make a move. I'm dying to know the results of the bicycle paper chase[8] that was run on Sunday at La Concorde. Come, my dear,' commanded Helga Becker, in a tone that brooked no refusal.

Mathilde de Flavignol took her leave reluctantly, but not before she had cast a languorous eye over Victor.

As soon as they had gone, the latter turned to Joseph. 'If it hadn't been for your presence of mind, we would still be hearing about the monkeys.'

'Oh, before I forget, some fellow came in to see Monsieur

Mori, and also a woman telephoned. She wanted to sell her collection of seventeenth-century books. She insisted she had to speak to Monsieur Mori, but I told her he was away and that you would be able to do the valuation. If you want to take the business, you'll have to go there early this evening because you won't be the only one interested. I wrote the name and address down for you – 4 Rue des Hortensias, in Neuilly. She's expecting you at seven o'clock.'

'I'd planned to have dinner with Mademoiselle Tasha.'

'Monsieur Mori is complaining that we haven't bought many books since Christmas. Anyway, that's just my opinion . . .' muttered Joseph, his nose already buried in *La Vie Populaire*.

'Now I can get on with it; old Zola knows how to spin a good yarn. Thanks to him, the afternoon is going to fly by.'

It was freezing and Joseph was hastening to shut up shop so that he could get home to Rue Visconti and enjoy the soup he was certain his mother would have prepared. He had the key in the bookshop lock and was about to close the final shutter when a cry drew his attention. A few yards away, a woman had slipped on the deserted pavement. She lay spread-eagled and was trying to get up. He hurried over to help her.

'Are you hurt?'

'More shaken than hurt. I'll be all right, thank you.'

'Would you like me to call you a cab?'

'No need, I can walk.'

Muffled by a veil, her voice was expressionless. Joseph watched the figure moving off in the direction of the Seine and turned back to deal with the shutter. He went to lock the door, and to his surprise saw that his keys were lying on the ground.

'What on earth? My keys are imitating the bells of Rome – they have wings . . . I'm seeing things, which just proves I'm desperately in need of some nosh.'

Saturday morning, 9 April

The emissary turned his head and looked at the wooden cross hanging above the bed. For a moment it was as if the bedroom had disappeared; only the rays of golden dust that fell from the heavens across the slats of the closed shutters existed. Gradually his eyes grew accustomed to the gloom. His hand struck a match and lit the wick of a lamp. The pinkish light quivered above the white page of his notebook.

Lord, I am witness to your glory. I, your emissary, have faithfully followed the mission you have conferred on me. The mark of infamy is hidden. I must prepare to be patient, and to wait for the right moment to annihilate it. No trace of it will remain, and false prophets will be unable to use it to assault your work, and humanity will no longer incur your wrath.

CHAPTER 3

Saturday, 9 April

JOSEPH loved to polish the leather-bound books. Delicately buffing the vellum, morocco-leather and cowhide gave him sensual pleasure. He felt particular joy if he managed to revive the sheen of the gold lettering on the spines and front covers. He was interrupted in this work, which had put him in an excellent mood, by Victor's morning arrival. Joseph greeted him with a smile, a magnificent 'fanfare' binding in his hands. Victor, however, wore a glowering expression.

'I should have realised – it's a ridiculous name!' he burst out.

'What name, Boss?'

'Hortensias. You sent me to Neuilly yesterday evening on a wild goose chase. That street of yours was completely made up!'

Offended, Joseph put the book down on the counter.

'Excuse me, it wasn't *my* street. It was the name the woman gave me on the telephone.'

'You must have misheard, and it wouldn't be the first time!'

'Why don't you say straight out that I'm as deaf as a post or have bats in the belfry? Maybe she's the one who muddled up her flowers. Perhaps it should be dahlias, or zinnias, or magnolias. How should I know?'

Joseph rose suddenly and went out on to the pavement. The boss had succeeded in spoiling his good humour and he felt the need to stretch his legs. A woman, hunched over and wearing a voluminous cape, which made her look like a little barrel, was going into the adjoining building. He recognised his mother and was about to call out to her but held back at the last minute – she was not speaking to him.

Her arms rigidly extended by two baskets overflowing with victuals, Euphrosine ducked under the porch, where she almost stepped on Madame Ballu. The concierge was on her knees, furiously scrubbing the first step of the stairs with a stiff brush.

'Damned floor, it absorbs and absorbs, it eats your soap like a drunkard drinks his spirits and gives you nothing in return! I'll have to scrape that with a knife,' she murmured.

'Madame Ballu, you sound as if you'd like to murder someone!'

'I would, that good-for-nothing on the third floor – a mucky pup who seems to be fatally attracted to coal tar. He's strewn mud everywhere, and one of the tenants stepped in it . . . It's really too much! But, Madame Pignot,' she added silkily, 'don't you use the shop entrance any more?'

'Apparently I don't fit in, and the sight of me offends the customers. They treat me as if I were some kind of slattern,' Euphrosine burst out, choking with indignation. 'How dare they! Me! Having to use the service entrance!'

'But, Madame Pignot, this isn't a service entrance.'

'Oh, you, go on with your scrubbing; you won't be able to console me. The truth is I have reared a serpent. Disowned by my own son!'

'Cheer up, Madame Pignot; would you like to pop in for a

moment? You can have a nice strong juice and tell me all your troubles, eh?'

'No time – I'm paid by the hour. Monsieur Mori and his young madam will be turning up this evening and I have their dinner to prepare. Farewell!' called Euphrosine, with all the majesty of a tragic heroine.

Out of breath, she let her bags drop and inhaled deeply. She put her key in the lock, but the door would not open. It took Euphrosine a moment to understand what had happened: someone had fixed the security chain in place on the inside. She stood there on the landing, assailed by doubt, her mind in turmoil.

'My goodness, I must be losing my marbles. I don't recall . . .'

But suddenly she had a wonderful thought. Overcome with remorse at having hurt his mother's feelings, Joseph had made honourable amends. Not wanting to lose face, he had simply gone to the flat and closed the security chain so that his mother would have no choice but to go through the bookshop to reach the flat. No doubt he could not bear being ostracised any longer, and didn't know how to break the silence.

'That's my pet!'

Buoyed up, she grasped the handle of her baskets and went back down the stairs, much to the annoyance of Madame Ballu, who was busy again burnishing the steps.

Watched balefully by Victor, Euphrosine made a dignified entrance and crossed the bookshop.

When she reached the flat on the first floor, she deposited her load on the kitchen table, hung her cloak on the peg and swapped her clogs for comfortable old slippers. Then she went through to Monsieur Mori's bathroom with its copper bathtub. To Euphrosine it was the height of luxury. She lit the lamp. What joy it would be to open one of the jasmine soaps nestled in the porcelain shell! And perhaps to dry herself with one of those soft towels marked *K. M.* Or even to adjust her chignon in front of the silver-framed mirror. Perhaps the frame was just plate though? One day, when the house was empty, she would fill the bathtub and immerse herself. But would she remove her undergarments? She could not help chuckling at the idea of soaking naked in the warm water.

She had just re-emerged into the dark corridor when her foot met an obstacle. She tripped, grabbed the handle of the half-open door and succeeded in righting herself. Although the light from the bathroom lamp was dim, it was enough for her to make out a jumble of knick-knacks that had no business lying on the dining-room floor. She felt an icy shiver up her spine, and ran towards the stairs, yelling, 'Come quick, help!'

Victor smiled ruefully at his customer who was just paying for Montesquieu's *Dialogue between Sylla and Eucrates,* and took the stairs, four at a time.

'Jesus-Mary-and-Joseph, a burg— A break-in!'

Euphrosine, hands on her cheeks, was blocking the corridor.

'Calm down, Madame Pignot,' Victor begged, shepherding her into the kitchen.

He opened the blinds in the dining room, and stared in stupefaction at the carnage that greeted him. He went into Kenji's part of the flat: the same disorder was to be found there.

'Boss? What is it?' called Joseph.

'Oh, my pet, it's dreadful!'

'Stop wailing, Madame Pignot. You go downstairs. I'll be with you in a moment.'

Victor went through the apartment, careful not to touch anything. Passing in front of the bathroom and the kitchen where the barred windows forbade any intrusion, he reached the end of the corridor. The door to the landing was double-locked, so the intruders could only have come in through one of the windows. But all the shutters were closed. He went back down to the bookshop.

Euphrosine was leaning on the counter and had recovered her poise.

'We've been burgled,' announced Victor. 'But as far as I can see, there hasn't been a break-in.'

Joseph bounded upstairs and returned almost at once. 'Boss, the dining-room window, it's—'

'That was me letting in light. I couldn't see a thing.'

'So how on earth did they get in?'

'There's only way they could have got in – there,' stated Euphrosine with finality, pointing at the door of the shop. 'Do you both have your keys?'

Victor shook his key case, and Joseph replied, 'Of course I have them. I'm the one who opens up.'

'Well, no one could have borrowed mine, because I'm not considered good enough to have keys to the shop!' Euphrosine said pointedly.

'What should we do, Boss?'

'Go and check the basement. I'll telephone the police and then try to establish what has been taken.'

As they went off, Euphrosine grumbled: 'So they're just going to abandon me, instead of giving me some credit! That's what it's like around here!'

Raoul Pérot tore himself away from the mouth-watering window of Debauve & Gallais and let his gaze wander over Rue des Saints-Pères. He made an effort to project respectability, although he was very aware of his shabby suit and worn-out shoes. Under his conformist appearance, emphasised by a superb handlebar moustache, he cherished a secret passion for poetry, especially the work of the aficionados of free verse. He had devoured the works of Jules Laforgue and Marie Krysinska[1] and other decadents who aimed to establish the right of each poet to use their own personal rhythm. Yet he valued his work even though it was badly paid, because it allowed him to confront the terrors of the modern world, and also offered him the opportunity to enrich his imagination.

A squall of wind buffeted him, prompting him to push open the door of the Elzévir bookshop.

A pudgy woman with a wide face stood in the middle of the shop. Raoul Pérot raised his hat and bowed politely.

'Madame, Inspector Pérot at your service. You've been burgled?'

The woman gestured with her chin towards a man who was hurrying down a spiral staircase.

'Victor Legris – I'm the owner. I'm the one who rang you. We—'

'Excuse me,' the inspector interrupted him, touching two

fingers to his hat. 'I have a clandestine passenger in my pocket in need of some air.'

To the astonishment of his audience, he produced a tortoise and set it gently down on the floor.

'That's Nanette, one of our mascots. The poor little creature fell off the back of a lorry with four of her sisters. We're looking after them until we can find them homes. When things aren't too busy we hold a steeplechase in the police station courtyard, urging them on with a lettuce leaf. Nanette's a champion – I've already won a hundred sous in bets thanks to her!'

'It's not surprising that it took such a long time to nail that bomber,' muttered Euphrosine.

'So, you've had an intruder,' continued Raoul Pérot, pretending not to have heard the allusion to Ravachol. 'Has there been a break-in?'

'No, and that's what's so fishy!' cried a blond young man who had just burst through from the back of the shop.

'My assistant, Joseph Pignot. We've checked all the shutters.'

'No break-in . . . No borer, no jemmy,' murmured Inspector Pérot. 'So we're looking at a burglary with false keys. I see, I see.'

'That's what I keep telling them.' Euphrosine was triumphant. 'My pet, when you're alone in the shop with hordes of customers, which you often are, where are your keys?'

'In the pocket of my jacket, hung in the back room, which has not been broken into. How much clearer do I have to be?'

'Don't be cheeky to your mother!'

'Let's not get heated,' advised the inspector, bending down

to stroke the tortoise's shell. 'How many people have these famous keys?'

'My assistant, me and two people who have been away for ten days,' replied Victor.

'Perhaps the burglar took an impression by pressing some wax or putty into the lock,' suggested Joseph.

'Monsieur, don't be taken in by such oft-repeated nonsense. In this type of burglary you can be sure that the burglar had access to the keys. Are you sure that no one could have got hold of them, even for a few minutes?'

'Yes, absolutely, aren't you, Joseph?'

'Yes, yes, I'm sure,' muttered Joseph.

He had suddenly remembered the incident of the night before. The woman who had taken a tumble on the pavement had not seemed hurt by her fall. It was possible that . . . He pushed the thought away and played dumb.

'Why do you ask, Inspector?'

'Because it couldn't be easier or quicker to press a key, first one side, then the other, into some modelling clay without anyone noticing. A skilful locksmith would then be well able, equipped with those impressions, to make a useable copy. If I were you, I would change the locks, Monsieur Legris. Have you drawn up a list of what was stolen?'

'The bookshop has so much stock that it's hard to know if anything of value is missing. At first glance, nothing has been disturbed, unlike in the rooms of my associate and his daughter. They're coming home this evening.'

'So you don't suspect anything's been taken from the bookshop?'

'No.'

'Perfect, perfect. We'll be able to see when you give us the list of valuable items that have disappeared. After all, cat burglars are rarely bibliophiles and if you say there aren't any books missing . . .'

'I would have noticed, Inspector. I'm very observant,' declared Joseph, relieved that his paper kingdom had been spared.

'How I envy you,' murmured Inspector Pérot.

'What? You'd like to be burgled?' barked Euphrosine.

'These books, hundreds of them . . . You see, I myself have modest literary ambitions. I write poetry under a pseudonym, some of which I am delighted to say is published in the literary magazines.'

'You're also a writer!' exclaimed Joseph.

Victor looked resigned and sighed discreetly.

'I cherish the hope that one day I might leave the police force and live by my pen. Alas, I can't rely on the Lord Almighty. As an anonymous writer once observed: "To the little birds He gives pasture, but His bounty doesn't stretch as far as literature . . ." Come on then, Mademoiselle Nanette, back into your shelter, you lucky devil.'

'You're right. The life of a writer is hard,' agreed Joseph.

'The main entrance to the flat is in the adjoining building, is that correct? And that building is under the eye of a concierge?'

'Yes, a widow, Madame Ballu.'

'Let's go and talk to her. Concierges are a mine of information.'

'How very true,' attested Euphrosine, 'and this one, she could write for the newspapers.'

Having finished washing the steps, Madame Ballu was devoting her energy to the handrail, which she was plastering with polish.

She was reflecting on how little time people spent on the stairs, but how much effort they cost her, when she noticed the strange little group coming through the porch.

'There's been a break-in at Monsieur Legris's!' bellowed Euphrosine. 'The inspector here wants to ask you a few questions.'

Delighted at this unexpected diversion, Madame Ballu began by declaring that she had not seen or heard a thing. Then, with an eye on the effect she was creating, she went on, propping herself on her broom:

'Unless . . . That woman with the "Kremlin" look . . .'

'With the what?' asked Raoul Pérot.

'Well, that's what you call it, fashion Russian-style. It's very chic what's more, those Muscovite blouses pulled in with Neva belts, Turkish fabric, striped seersucker . . . Every time I flick through *The World of Fashion* I think I'm in a Persian market . . .'

'You can say that again. Those outfits should only be allowed at Carnival; it's not right,' said Euphrosine.

'So, this woman with the Kremlin look?'

'It was yesterday, the day I had my cabbage with bacon. Anyway, she wanted to know if Monsieur Mori's flat was for rent, as the shutters were closed. She was going to deliver a hat to the Primolins; they're on the fourth floor. She was back down in a blink. I saw her from behind my curtain. And then it struck me — the Primolins are staying with their cousins in Ville-d'Avray. It had gone clean out of my mind otherwise, I can assure you, I would have sent her packing. We concierges have our instructions from the police. Those folk with their dynamite, they don't carry a sign announcing their intentions, so we have to be on our guard; we have to ask questions.'

'What did she look like?'

'You think I can remember anything about her apart from her Russki coat? Wait . . . she was wearing a veil.'

Joseph turned beetroot. That woman who had fallen over on Saturday evening, though he could not have said if her coat had been Russian or Austro-Hungarian, had definitely been wearing a veil.

Inspector Pérot thanked Madame Ballu.

'Make a detailed inventory of anything that's missing, with a description, and bring it to the police station. If you could draw sketches, that would help . . . Um, would any of you like to take in an orphaned tortoise?'

Victor told Joseph distractedly that he was closing the bookshop until the next day.

'You can have time off.'

'Don't you need me to check that nothing has been taken from the bookshop?'

Jojo had been filled with joy at seeing Iris again, and was desolate to see the prospect slipping away as a result of the disaster that had befallen them.

'You know, Boss, although I said I'm very observant, anyone can make a mistake. It would be best to check.'

Victor suppressed a smile – he was not taken in. 'Go on then, I'll be upstairs.'

Joseph pulled the large ladder in front of the shelves. The patron saint of shop assistants was watching over him and he would soon have the bliss of a glimpse of his sweetheart.

'And what about their dinner?'

'It would be better to kill the fatted calf another time, Madame Pignot. They'll make do with a snack.'

'What am I going to do with all this grub? It's deplorable – during the siege of Paris we were desperate for food, now we're squandering it!'

Victor and Kenji were on all fours collecting the books that had been scattered across the study when Iris popped her head round the door.

'This is my first break-in. It's exciting!' she exclaimed looking around at her father's devastated flat.

Kenji was rather less enthusiastic. He started to gather up the sabre hilts, lacquer-work and tea bowls that had been swept from the shelves. An overturned inkwell had saturated the carpet with blue.

'My wardrobe has been emptied, every piece of furniture gone through, the bed pulled out and the mattress turned over. I think the burglar was after something specific,' went on Iris.

'What makes you think that?'

'They didn't bother about my jewellery box, and it was just sitting there. A child looking for sweets would have acted in the same way.'

'Do you think anything of yours is missing?' Victor asked Kenji. 'What about your engravings?'

'I'll have to make sure; it will take me some time,' murmured Kenji, engaged in smoothing the crumpled pages of his books.

Joseph slipped down the ladder to the floor and scratched one ear. He could not understand it. Even if he were not interested in literature, a burglar who took the trouble to make the keys for a bookshop would surely allow himself to be tempted by the three superb octavos of *Roses* by Pierre-Joseph Redouté, displayed in the window, if only for their resale value. And the back room devoted to travel writing and Monsieur Mori's hallowed collection of exotic treasures had been left untouched.

He tried to resolve the conundrum, but the crashes above his head muddled his thoughts. It had been more than an hour since Monsieur Mori and his daughter had gone upstairs, yet Iris had not found a way to escape for five minutes, and he was burning to see her again. So she did not love him. His heart contracted with sadness. But the letter, *her* letter.

'They're keeping an eye on her. That must be it, especially Monsieur Legris. Ever since he's known that she's his sister, he's acted like her chaperone.'

He was about to put the ladder back in place, but stopped dead. That perfume . . .

'My poor Joseph, always doing chores. But you can stop now. I've brought you some souvenirs from London.'

'Iris! Finally!' he cried huskily.

*

'I'm perplexed,' said Kenji. 'They've only stolen two volumes, one very rare one – *The French Pâtissier*, a 1655 Elzévir, valued at between four and five thousand francs, and another of no value at all, which I bought for twenty centimes on the embankment. It's bizarre.'

He slid back the wooden screen door that separated his study from his bedroom. The mat, quilt and wooden pillow kept on the raised platform of the alcove had been moved, but the hiding place that contained his personal papers, built under the slats of the mattress, had not been discovered. But to his displeasure he saw that the iron clasps of the Japanese chest opposite the bed had come out of their hinges.

Victor remained discreetly behind him. The chest held Kenji's most intimate secrets and he hated anyone to see what was inside.

Kenji grimaced and pushed aside a lock of grey hair that had fallen over his forehead. 'I could do with some green tea,' he murmured.

'I'll go and prepare some,' said Victor, slipping away.

Looking over the banister of the interior staircase, he caught sight of Iris and Joseph sitting sedately side by side behind the bookshop's counter. He cleared his throat and signalled to Iris to join him.

'Your stock, Joseph?'

'Untouched, Boss. Every book in its correct place. I just have to pack the deliveries for tomorrow and then I'll close up. Does Monsieur Mori know what has been stolen from him?'

'Not yet. Good evening, Joseph.'

'Good evening, Boss! Good evening, Mademoiselle Iris!'

*

Victor and Iris sat at the kitchen table, a steaming teapot before them. Kenji was silent, his eyes on his cup. Then he said, 'It's certainly a puzzle. Aside from those two volumes, they stole a goblet from my chest, which was only of sentimental value. A few years ago I received a parcel from Scotland along with a letter that I'll read to you:

> *Brougham House, 14 October 1889*
>
> *Dear Monsieur Mori*
>
> *In accordance with the wishes of my brother, who held you in great affection, I am sending you several items he wanted to leave you in memory of your explorations of south-east Asia. He particularly wanted you to have the goblet, which is possessed, according to him, of a mysterious magic power. You are familiar with his sense of humour and his scepticism towards animism, so I do hope you will take this bequest in the spirit in which it was intended. In spite of the ugliness of the chalice, my dear brother was convinced that it would bring you luck all your life. It is in the belief that this will be true that I remain,*
>
> *Your devoted friend,*
>
> *Lady Frances Stone*

'What a shame you never showed me the goblet. I would have loved to have seen it!'

'My dear child, knowing your habit of winkling out my hiding places, I took care to lock my chest,' said Kenji, winking at Victor.

'Are you implying that I'm nosey?'

'Deaf as he is, the old fox is sharp of hearing when the weasel prowls close to his territory. Alas, in spite of the fact that I added a padlock, the tenacity of our thief thwarted my precautions. And the animal had a good nose – that goblet was swaddled in a *furoshiki*.'

'A *furoshiki*?' repeated Victor.

'One of the silk wrappings used for gifts, according to Japanese custom. The one I used came to me from my uncle, Hanunori Watanabe. Fortunately I have an identical one.'

'Decorated with storks with their wings outspread. It's superb! I admired it when I . . .'

Iris turned puce, aware that she had given herself away.

'When you . . . ?' asked her father quietly.

As she did not answer, he continued calmly, 'When you took out the slats of my bed . . . To dust under there, I suppose. Let's not mention it again.'

'Let's go back to the goblet. Can you describe it? I'll ask Tasha to do a sketch,' said Victor.

'It's unique. The skullcap of a monkey – probably a gibbon – attached to a little metal tripod decorated with three jewels and the tiny face of a cat with marbled agates for eyes.'

'It's a paradox,' remarked Victor. 'Someone steals two books and a bizarre goblet from you, but neglects to take your etchings and ignores the bookshop.'

'A real Chinese puzzle,' said Kenji drily. 'I would guess that it was the first outing of an apprentice cat burglar. Come along, Iris, let's tidy up; tomorrow we'll decide what to do.'

*

Joseph was absorbed in trying to translate an article from *The Times*, which he was finding hard. His brow was furrowed; the words refused to yield up their meaning.

'So you're still here, Joseph?'

Joseph raised his head. Victor was looking at him with a mocking expression.

'It's a present from Mademoiselle Iris. Learning by any possible means is all part of the English lessons she . . .'

He bit his tongue – he had been about to let the cat out of the bag. A vacuous smile lit his face.

'Boss, what does *stone* mean in French?'

'Your accent is atrocious – spell it.'

When Joseph had done so, Victor told him.

'And *murder*, Boss?'

Victor gave the meaning. 'That's enough now. You can concoct your murder stories outside working hours.'

'I'm not concocting stories, I'm translating.'

'Well, I approve of that. You should study and persevere. Perhaps Mademoiselle Iris's lessons will bear fruit.'

Exultant at having obtained the tacit approval of his boss, Joseph folded up his paper. However, his exultation was short-lived. As he was leaving, Victor called back to him, 'A word of warning: don't take it too far.'

The studio was empty. Victor looked at the easel before his eyes came to rest on the table. She had left him a note.

Dearest, I'll be home late — I'm up to my eyes in work at the magazine. Don't wait up. Euphrosine has prepared a delicious ragout — you only have to heat it up. I love you and kiss you all over. Tasha

p.s. Your photos of children are wonderful.

Through the skylight he could see slate-grey sky. It was about to rain.

He flopped down on the bed. Opposite him Madame Pignot stood clutching her umbrella to her chest and contemplating the blue outline of the Vosges mountains. Almost complete, the painting resembled some of the compositions of Berthe Morisot.[2]

He awoke with a start in the middle of the night, jerked awake by a thought floating through his dream. It was important, and he was sure it had something to do with the events of the previous evening. But, try as he might, he could not remember what it was.

When Tasha arrived at Rue Fontaine towards three in the morning, Victor was asleep fully clothed, lying across the bed.

CHAPTER 4

Monday, 11 April

'FULL up down below! Upstairs only!' bellowed the conductor, shaking his satchel to collect the three sous fare.

Victor would have done anything to avoid going upstairs in the freezing cold. He regretted having hurried to the Clichy-Odéon omnibus instead of hailing a cab. Wedging himself in beside a young woman, who looked irritated at having to move over for him, he turned up his collar, hoping to keep the draught at bay.

I'll have to buy that bicycle after all, he thought, one buttock hanging off the seat.

He tried to remember his dream from the night before, but it was impossible to pin it down. It kept escaping, drowned out by the conversations that flitted between the seats.

It's like being stuck in someone else's sitting room, he thought in irritation, although he could not help listening to two elderly men, each sporting salt-and-pepper moustaches.

'. . . becoming very alarming. One dare not put one's nose out any more! Any old chemistry student can stock up on chemicals in the university quarter and play at making fireworks, without his neighbours knowing anything about it!'

'I agree. There should be some control over chemicals. But

it's especially important to regulate the use of rounds of dynamite used in mines and quarries. Had Ravachol not been able to steal the dynamite from the depot at Soisy-sous-Étiolles . . .'

'The government promises us measures; it talks of security at every turn! But the expulsion of forty or so foreign anarchists is not going to . . .'

'But, my dear chap, it's a start. And there are too many foreigners now. Ravachol himself is of Dutch descent through his father. He's called Kœnigstein, don't forget.'

The bus lurched, jolting the passengers. A top hat fell on the floor, hooves clattered, horns sounded and coins jangled in a chorus, drowning out the men's conversation. When the bus stopped, the young woman rose and almost fell on top of Victor, whom she gave a filthy look. He caught a glimpse of a scarlet poster exalting the virtues of Tamar Indien Grillon laxative fruit lozenges, and felt a stab of anguish at the thought that Tasha might be hounded from France and he would never see her again.

What drivel! Tasha didn't consort with anarchists.

Just as the vehicle set off again, a pen-pusher in pull-on boots sat down near him, and the two bourgeois men continued their conversation.

'Have you been to Rue de Clichy? It's frightening to see number 39.[1] All the windows exploded, the staircase collapsed, the flats were gutted, only the outside walls are still standing. What's odd is that some of the buildings on either side are intact.'

'According to one of my friends, the furniture has fallen to the bottom in such a bizarre manner that it looks like stones on the edge of a volcanic crater.'

Stone, stone, there were stones in that dream he was trying to remember. *I am fair, O mortals! Like a dream carved in stone*, a rolling stone gathers no moss, carved in stone . . . The flood of words submerged his thoughts.

'. . . fifteen injured, a miracle! But he did manage to kill three people in the Loire. He should get the guillotine for his crimes.'

'I feel certain that he will, dear chap. And in the future Bertillon's methods will surely save us from such plagues. From now on the fact of knowing the murderer's distinctive features will be enough to identify him. It's lucky the Saint-Étienne police who already caught Kœnigstein in '79 for theft used "Bertillonage". They sent the rogue's exact measurements to the police anthropometric department, which sent them to the press. That was how Lhérot, the waiter at the Restaurant Véry, was able to identify Ravachol from the scars on his hand and face, leading to his arrest. Alphonse Bertillon was able to measure and photograph Ravachol and establish that he and Kœnigstein were one and the same. It's simple logic.'

'I would be much less worried if our Minister of Interior[2] could guarantee that Paris does not turn into a barricaded camp; we don't want to end up like Germany or Italy, terrorised by fanatics and everyone running scared . . .'

Victor got off at Carrefour de l'Odéon, glad to see the back of the yellow omnibus as it clattered on its way. He had certainly been shaken by the explosions on Boulevard Saint-Germain and Rue de Clichy, since the first was near the bookshop and the other near his home. But he did not share the general apprehension of the two old fellows. His fear was for those close to him, especially Tasha. What if she were to be caught up in a bombing? Of all the anxieties that had assailed him of late, this new one was the most alarming.

'It always has to rain just as I'm about to do the shopping. I could swear the clouds are spying on me!'

Euphrosine was convinced she was the victim of a conspiracy. She passed the desk without looking at her son, who was busy helping a pretty young woman with a retroussé nose. She had decided that, following the excitement of the previous day, she was perfectly entitled to come and go through the bookshop, and she would complain to Kenji if Victor reproached her for it. She tugged a large purple madapollam parasol from the umbrella stand. A piece of paper fluttered to the ground and she stooped to pick it up, muttering to herself.

'I'm going to do my back in if this goes on. Oh, it's a visiting card. Strange place to leave your address.'

Joseph could see his mother from the corner of his eye, fiddling with the files on the counter. I hope she doesn't mix up the sales slips, he thought to himself. That would be the icing on the cake!

He made a show of turning his back on her as Victor arrived.

Victor immediately spotted the calling card propped against the pencil jar in which Joseph kept his scissors. He quickly read the three lines of neat handwriting:

Dear Monsieur Mori
  I need to see you as soon as possible. Lady Stone gave me

your address and assured me you were the person I should contact.

I do hope you will be able to help me.

Antoine du Houssoye

It took him several minutes to take in the note. Stone . . . Stone . . . When had he heard that name? He flicked the card absentmindedly:

ANTOINE DU HOUSSOYE

Zoologist

Lecturer

The Museum of Natural History

As he leaned on the counter the penny dropped. 'Well, I'll be damned! My dream!' A hail of pebbles raining down in Kenji's apartment, which had turned into a dump with some unfortunate tortoises stranded in the rubble. Everything fell into place. Joseph had asked him the meaning of *stone* in French, and his question had related to an article in a copy of *The Times* brought back by Iris. He remembered that Joseph had also asked what the French for *murder* was. He stood stock still, filled with a feeling of unreality. *The Times*! He would have to look at the paper immediately.

'Joseph, do you have that English newspaper you were struggling to translate?'

Joseph abandoned the young blonde girl and rushed over.

'I wasn't struggling; I was managing very well!'

'May I borrow it?'

Reluctantly, Joseph handed over the paper, which he had rolled into a cylinder and tidied away with his notebook.

'I'll need it back, you know.'

'Don't worry. Tell me, that visiting card – when was it left here?'

'What visiting card? Oh yes! It's from that chap who came in on Friday wanting Monsieur Mori's address.'

'And you gave it to him?'

'Well, obviously, since he lives above the shop.'

'Are you going to be much longer?' added Victor with a nod in the direction of the customer, who was growing impatient.

'She's one of Salomé de Flavignol's friends. She's passionate about Pierre Loti – he's just been received into the Académie Française. We were just exchanging views on *The Icelandic Fisherman*.'

'I didn't know you were keen on cod fishing. Why don't you ask Monsieur Mori to take over? Look, he's just coming down – he'll be delighted to analyse *Madame Chrysanthème* for the benefit of that nice young lady, and you can go to the stockroom and find me La Harpe's *Abridged General History of Travel*.'

'But there are thirty-two volumes and we certainly don't have them all!'

'Just bring up whichever you can dig out. I've promised them to a dealer.'

Joseph obeyed with a lugubrious air. Victor feverishly unrolled *The Times*. It was the edition of 8 April 1892 and it included a macabre item:

LADY FRANCES STONE MURDERED
AT HOME IN BROUGHAM HOUSE

On 5 April at nine o'clock in the evening Miss Olivia Montrose, maid to Lady Frances Stone, discovered her mistress dead. Lady Stone's doctor, Dr Barley was immediately summoned but could do nothing other than confirm the death and state that it had been caused by a gunshot wound. Sergeant John Dumfrie of the local constabulary and officers Dennis Blythe and Peter Starling of Scotland Yard are leading the murder inquiry. According to the witness statements of the Brougham House staff, Lady Stone received a visitor shortly before her death . . .

His mind blank, Victor stared at the words, trying to remember who had first mentioned the name Stone.

'Am I going mad?'

Suddenly he straightened up, struck by an idea.

'Kenji! His letter about the goblet – I'll have to check.'

Salomé de Flavignol's friend, the blonde enamoured of Loti, was still chattering as Kenji listened with a polite smile. Since there seemed to be no end to what she had to say, Victor decided to interrupt.

'Excuse me; may I borrow Monsieur Mori a moment?' Victor asked apologetically. He led Kenji over to the bust of Molière and asked softly, 'Have you noticed whether anything else is missing?'

'No, nothing other than the Elzévir, the Baronne Staffe and that goblet of which I was so fond.'

'Do you know the woman who sent it to you?'

'Lady Stone? I haven't had the pleasure of meeting her; she's John Cavendish's sister.'

'The naturalist murdered three years ago at the Colonial Exhibition?[3] I thought he was American!'

'He was. His sister married a Scottish aristocrat and he was living with them when he died. I would have preferred not to have to think about all this – it stirs up old emotions. Look at this – I found an old letter of his.'

My dear friend,

If you are reading this, it is because I have gone to meet my maker. I shall await you impatiently on the other side of the Acheron.

In 1886, I led an expedition to Krakatoa to study the flora that had grown there after the eruption of the volcano. When I was in Surabaya, I bought this goblet with you in mind. It is the work of a Malayan sculptor from the Trinil region. Although the gems on it are virtually worthless, I am sure it will remind you of the happy days we spent together, in particular that terrible crossing of the China Sea aboard that wretched boat skippered by Captain Finch who was so passionate about scrimshaw. You were very impressed by his collection of engraved whale jaws, especially the ones depicting a whaling expedition. I remember he gave you a walrus tooth decorated inside with a coloured engraving of Commodore Perry's landing on the Japanese coast – did you keep it? Consider this gift a pledge of posthumous loyalty (I have no idea what it's

*meant to be used for. I suppose it's a spittoon or an incense
burner).*

   John Ruskin Cavendish
*p.s. It is said that a jewel loses its burnish when its owner dies.
I am certain that these ones will not fade until well into the
twentieth century.*

'You can understand how painful it is for me to rake this up. I
have never quite accepted my friend's tragic death. That goblet
represented a sign from the hereafter,' said Kenji, carefully
folding the letter.

Victor shook his head sorrowfully, feigning sympathy,
although his mind was racing like an overheated engine. He said
nothing and stared at the bust of Molière.

The abandoned customer left the bookshop at the precise
moment that Joseph reappeared, covered in dust and weighed
down with tomes.

'Here are your shelf-fillers, Boss. All there except for three.'

'Who's that rubbish for?' asked Kenji.

'For Père Maubèche.'

'The bookseller with a stall on Quai Conti?'

'He has some gaps to fill in his display and he only wants
octavos. Joseph, wrap that lot in some canvas. I'll be back in
about an hour.'

'An hour! That's what you always say, but you never are.
Hoy, Boss! My newspaper!' Joseph cried, pointing at Victor's
pocket.

*

The green canvas rested heavily on Victor's shoulder, but he didn't care. He needed to walk to clear his head, and had seized on the excuse which Kenji and Joseph would be most likely to swallow.

It was milder now and the sky, thoroughly washed by the recent rain, spread a veil of blue over the embankment where at this hour of the morning only four or five stall-holders had opened their boxes.

Victor leaned on the parapet of Quai Malaquais and watched the bargemen's children playing a game of 'What's the time, Mr Wolf?' on the river bank. At the head of the pack, one of the kids suddenly turned round and yelled, 'Dinner time!' He ran at his friends, trying to catch them, but they bombarded him with swipes of their handkerchiefs, shrieking and laughing, and he had to retreat, vanquished.

Unperturbed by their noise, Victor thought hard about the two riddles. First, why had Antoine du Houssoye visited the bookshop? The note he had written on the back of his business card left Victor in no doubt that he knew Lady Stone. And, second, was it possible that the burglary was somehow linked to her murder?

The theory was rather enticing. Victor could never resist the lure of a mystery. It was not enough just to live, although life itself could be full of enigma; it was better to dare to venture down shadowy paths, feeling his way along a tunnel, with only the hint of a feeble light at its end, gradually growing brighter until the darkness was no more than a memory, mingled with regret.

From which end should he approach this bizarre tale?

Horace Tenson, also known as the Giant or Little Boots, specialised in the sale of Cazins.[4] He was one of the last stall-holders not to have a box fixed permanently to the parapet, and he was busy taking the compartments that made up his display out of his cart. He gave Victor a gladiatorial salute.

'Hail, Legris. Important news! I've finally succeeded in getting my book published, *The Greedy Octopus*. I strongly urge you to sign my petition calling for the immediate destruction of all the department stores. It's a question of life or death! It's all about saving the livelihood of individual traders. The tentacles of monopoly stretch all around Paris and if we don't take care we will be snuffed out of existence before we know it.'

Inventing an urgent meeting, Victor promised to come back later to sign. Still bowed by the weight of his canvas, he headed back to the bookshop. He had made a decision. He would dash over to the Museum of Natural History that very afternoon and try to find the famous Antoine du Houssoye.

'You didn't drop the books off!' said Joseph, giving up on the parcel he was attempting to tie.

'Père Maubèche wasn't there. I'll have to go back later. I'll just pop these down in the corner.'

'That was well worth botching a sale for then. And she was charming, that lady. The Boss would have been better to go to the police station. Raoul Pérot will be wondering what's going on.'

'Instead of muttering into the beard you don't have, why don't you go and persuade your literary colleague of the merits of Jules Laforgue's prose. I imagine that you will have a lot to say to each other,' Victor retorted.

'Thanks, Boss!'

Victor was not very keen on skeletons and the half-dozen monstrous whales, with their ivory-coloured bones, populating the museum's new gallery were scarcely reassuring. In contrast, the three central displays of stuffed mammals – pachyderms, antelopes and giraffes – looked like household pets. He lost his way among the collections of reptiles, birds and eggs on the upper floors, before finding himself at the display cases of insects which he hurried past, nauseated by the sight of a termitarium next to a giant wasps' nest. He asked a warden where he might find Antoine du Houssoye and was directed to the anthropology gallery where he had already wandered for three quarters of an hour.

It was not at all a pleasure to rediscover a display of the severed Berber heads, decapitated by the Turks with their traditional yagatan sword, and dried under the African sun, next to the squatting Peruvian mummies, their grinning skulls exposed. The plaster cast of the Venus Hottentot, that poor woman wrenched from her native Africa and exhibited in country fairs before suffering a miserable death in Paris, filled him with pity. A second warden, standing watch over a circular glass case displaying a prehistoric human jaw discovered near Abbeville by Jacques Boucher de Perthes, told him that Monsieur du Houssoye was probably in the large amphitheatre where the palaeontologist Albert Gaudry was lecturing.

A crowd of students and lecturers was standing about, deep in discussion, at the entrance to the lecture hall.

After moving from group to group, Victor finally approached a well-built man of about forty whose luxuriant head of hair and horse-shoe beard framed a face that had charm, although the features suggested a certain weakness. His nonchalant voice dominated all the others.

'I'm sorry to interrupt, but I was told you would know . . . I'm looking for Monsieur Antoine du Houssoye.'

The man looked at him curiously. 'He's not here yet. It's not like him. Wait . . . Charles!'

A young man came over. He looked almost out of place in this seat of learning, despite his very smart suit. His tanned complexion, clean-shaven chin, almost transparently blue eyes and long stride that was firm and fluid, but not entirely elegant, made him appear like a country bumpkin come to town.

'Let me introduce Charles Dorsel, my cousin Antoine's assistant. I'm Alexis Wallers, lecturer in geology. To whom do I have the honour?'

'Victor Legris, bookseller, 18 Rue des Saints-Pères. Your cousin came to our shop. He wanted to speak to my associate, Kenji Mori. I thought perhaps it was about a collection for sale . . .'

'I would be astonished if he were proposing to part with his books. What can have got into him? Charles?'

'I don't think he would do that, no. He would have told me.'

'It's strange that Antoine is so late. Although we live in the same house, we don't keep the same hours. Normally Antoine is very punctual. Unless he had a meeting. What is it, Charles?'

'Have you forgotten? He's gone to see Professor Guéret at Meudon. He's writing his memoirs for *All Round the World*,' Charles replied, sounding irritated. 'Here's your chance, Alexis. Monsieur Legris is a bookseller. Didn't you want to haggle over your books and buy some jewels with the proceeds?'

'Haggle over! When will you learn to speak correctly? I was hoping to sell them for a modest sum.'

Charles Dorsel stared at Alexis Wallers insolently, like an accused man certain of his innocence. He had a slight accent, which Victor could not place.

'All right, sell them, but not for a modest sum,' retorted Charles, winking at Victor. 'Oh, look, Monsieur Legris,' he exclaimed pointing out a bent old fellow with a black portfolio under his arm. 'That's Monsieur Lacassagne, a retired warden. He's always on the lookout for J-B Pocquelin's *The Affected Ladies' Jewels* – you wouldn't have that put by, would you?'

'Well, nothing's impossible,' replied Victor, laughing. 'I have a customer who is adamant that the author of *Discourse on Method* is not René Descartes, but someone called Cartesian.'

'It takes all sorts,' Alexis Wallers said. 'Monsieur du Houssoye won't be long. He's taking a class in about an hour.'

'In that case, I'll come back later,' Victor said, taking his leave.

As soon as he reached Rue Cuvier, he changed his mind and went back in. Adopting a stupid expression, he grabbed one of the porters by the sleeve.

'It's such a beautiful watch, I would have kept it, but my neighbour tells me it belongs to Monsieur du Houssoye, so I must give it back to him.'

'You can wait for him here. His lesson starts at three o'clock.'

'Not today, apparently. He had to go home in the middle of Monsieur Gaudry's lecture, because he was suffering from a migraine.'

'Leave it there then,' the usher said grumpily.

'My dear fellow, what do you take me for? Not that I don't trust you, but I feel I have a moral responsibility . . .'

'And how do I know you aren't just going to keep the ticker?'

'I beg your pardon?' cried Victor, raising his voice. 'How dare you doubt the honesty of Guillaume Elzévir, of . . .'

'All right, all right, don't get on your high horse,' grumbled the porter, going to look in a register. 'He lives in Rue Charlot, number 28.'

Victor fled – he had just spotted Alexis Wallers.

Tasha heard the key rattling in the lock and hastily hid the letter. She knew it by heart; the paper was starting to tear along the folds with frequent handling. She stood in front of her easel pretending to be deep in concentration. Her heart was hammering against her ribs. Tomorrow! Tomorrow she would be in his arms, after all these years!

She felt Victor's lips brush her hair and her neck, but dared not turn round in case she revealed her inner turmoil.

'Darling, you'll have to get changed; we're going out for dinner. Are you painting Madame Pignot's portrait? I didn't know you'd asked her to pose for you.'

Victor called this over his shoulder on his way to freshening up at the sink.

He returned moments later with his face buried in a towel, and slipped his arm round her waist.

'How do you fancy a trip to Brittany? The light is beautiful there. You'll be able to paint outside.'

'I don't . . .'

She left her sentence unfinished, feeling rather ashamed.

'Victor, I have to take off for a few days. It's an opportunity for me, an exhibition in Barbizon, and . . .'

'How long have you known this?'

'I've just found out.'

'Can I come? I could take pictures of the countryside.'

'But you have the bookshop.'

He shook his head, tightening his embrace. 'What do you mean? It's not as if Barbizon were the other side of the world.'

'Darling, you have your photography and you go off on your investigations on your own, and you think that's all right . . . I'm the same way. Please don't take it badly; it in no way affects my love for you.'

'I understand,' he said, crestfallen. 'I want you to know how much I respect you, but however hard I try I have nothing in common with the artists with whom you associate.'

'That's why it's best if you don't come.'

He became sullen, like a child who has just been rapped over the knuckles, his face bearing the stubborn expression he wore when he didn't get his own way. He watched Tasha, unable to resist the fascination her every move, each utterance, engendered in him. He could not look at her without experiencing a heart-rending need to possess her completely, as if he would never be whole again if she left him.

Tasha's resolution started to waver. For the first time she was struck by the fear that she might lose him.

'I'll only be away for three days,' she murmured.

They stood facing each other. She was on the point of telling him the truth, but he solved her dilemma by leaning over and kissing her cheek.

'Go and get dressed.'

She smiled at him and he immediately felt reassured; his anxiety melted away.

Monsieur Rivet, feeling relaxed after a good dinner, stopped by the door of the Église Saint-Eustache, crossed himself and whistled for his dog who was loitering around a lamp-post. He relished this hour of the evening when, after dining with his wife in the back room of his haberdashery, he became for a brief interval a free man. Milord and he would roam where their fancy took them. Some evenings they strolled past Les Halles and reached the Bourse du Commerce. Other times they wandered over to the Marais. Tonight, by common accord, they went up Rue de Turbigo. From there, they meandered up Rue de la Grande-Truanderie where it was said that in the reign of Philippe-Auguste, a desperate young woman[5] betrayed in love had flung herself into Ariane's well. Monsieur Rivet was fond of these old tragic stories and as Milord trotted ahead, snout to the wind in search of new scents, he imagined he was a hero of the Arabian nights.

He found Milord sniffing the air vent of a cellar, and was about to cross the road when the dog burst into frantic barking. Intrigued, Monsieur Rivet turned back.

Milord was half-hidden in the dusk, but his tail wagged feverishly as he barked.

'What is it, dog? Have you found a cache of sausages?'

Milord leapt in the air, turned several circles and let out a howl.

Bending double, Monsieur Rivet tried to see down into the cellar. He made out a heap of crates and a disordered jumble nearby. Could it be? Yes, something was moving. Two rats were trotting around a pile of old rags, probably looking for food. A third rat appeared, then a fourth. Monsieur Rivet could see their sharp teeth glinting in the light of the street-lamp and shivered – they had certainly found something to feast on. He had read in *Nature* that each month rats gave birth to something like ten babies. He recalled how legend had it that the descendants of the young girl drowned in Ariane's well were endowed with four paws and long moustaches, and that over the centuries they had multiplied and taken over the sewers.

'Shut up, Milord. All that racket for some poor old rats!'

It was then that he realised what the rats were tucking into with such relish. It was a leg in tattered black rags, attached to a body, of which only the tails of a frock coat were visible.

CHAPTER 5

Tuesday, 12 April

'Recreate the siege of Sebastopol in your own bedroom. Success guaranteed. A single coat of my miracle varnish applied to your bed frame and the bugs will drop dead before your very eyes! A real bargain at sixpence a bottle, Monsieur!'

Victor dodged the flask of yellowish liquid the peddler in Rue de Bretagne was waving in his face, and walked into Le Marché des Enfants-Rouges, whose entrance was sandwiched between a butcher's and a sausage shop.

The grimy windows of the glass roof resting on broad, dark beams filtered out the gloomy morning light, giving Victor the impression of walking into his darkroom. The six storey workers' blocks towering above made him feel as though he'd plunged into an abyss. The hustle and bustle of the market traders setting up their stalls intensified his discomfort. Wherever he looked, death stared back defiantly, in the form of bloody lamb carcasses, pig's offal and veal lights, which a tripe butcher was busy blowing up with a pair of bellows.

Feeling queasy, he sat on the edge of a crate, balancing his camera equipment on his knee. He had brought a hand-held camera that was solid but easy to carry and equipped with a dozen plates and an automatic action that would allow him to take several clear pictures in rapid succession.

'Is Monsieur the photographer feeling a bit peckish? In need of a pick me up? Go on, have a snifter of absinthe. Only fifteen centimes — it won't break the bank. The doughnut's on the house.'

He shook his head, avoiding the gaze of a large moustachioed lady who was browning sausages over a brazier as she spoke.

'No need to run away, dearie; I'm not going to bite your head off. Lord, will you look at him. He's turned white as a sheet!'

Amid the crude guffaws of the regular customers, Victor made a dash for the exit, where the kindly face of a flower seller restored his faith in humanity. Unaware that the bag containing his film plates had fallen open, he tugged on the strap as he attempted to step over a pile of peelings in the middle of the tiny Rue des Oiseaux. There was an almighty crash, and pieces of wood and glass lay scattered on the cobbles. Victor just managed to stop a small pair of hands from picking them up.

'Careful, you'll cut yourself!' he cried out to a skinny girl in a shapeless, ill-fitting dress. At the same time a man perched on a donkey cart called, 'Vivi! Don't cut your fingers!' as he trundled down the street behind Victor.

'That's seven years' bad luck if it's a mirror!' remarked the man as he jumped down off his cart.

'It is only white glass,' Victor replied with a smile that widened as he watched the little girl run her fingers over his camera obscura.

'What a lovely magic lantern,' she murmured. 'Are you an illusionist, like Monsieur Méliès? I often walk past his theatre. They do matinées for children. I'd love to go!'

'No, no, I only take photographs, Mademoiselle Vivi – my name is Victor Legris.'

'Mine's not Vivi, it's Yvette.'

'There she goes again getting on her high horse because her old Papa uses her nickname in front of strangers. Léonard Diélette, market stallholder.'

Victor looked with interest at Léonard, whose features were almost obscured by his dark hair, moustache and beard.

'Market stallholder?'

'Yes, Monsieur, market stallholder and proud of it. I'm done with traipsing up and down Paris all night with a basket on my back and a hook in my hand. I was a rag-and-bone man for many a year and I know what a hard life it can be! Why, I used to cover twelve miles a day searching for junk to pay for my food and lodgings and the clothes on my back. And there was no time for idling I can tell you, because I wasn't alone – there were more than twenty-five thousand of us out there scrabbling around in the rubbish for a pittance. I was worn out by the time I got home. And then at dawn we had to sort through it all before selling it on. Poor as a church mouse I was, but free. I had no fixed working hours. When Vivi came along, I said to my lady wife we can't carry on doing this. When my poor Loulou died five years ago, I saved up enough to buy Père Gaston's position.'

'How much longer are you going to stand there prattling? You're in my way and I've got goods to deliver!' cried a fish-monger strapped to a hand cart.

Léonard Diélette climbed back up on to his perch and at the click of his tongue the donkey moved on.

'His name's Clampin,' Yvette explained, patting the animal. 'He's lame and has a bit of a limp, but he's very strong and never complains, even when the cart is stuffed full.'

Victor was walking along at the child's pace. Her black hair emphasised the pallor of her little face, and although she was clean and well groomed, she reminded him of the little urchins in the paintings of Murillo.

They walked down Rue de Beauce before turning into Rue Pastourelle.

'Are you going far?' Victor enquired.

'Rue Charlot. Some of the houses there have refuse bins and Papa brings them down and empties them into a bigger bin then cleans them and takes them back. In exchange for doing that, the concierges let him rescue what he wants from the rubbish.'

'I'll be honest with you, M'sieur, it's a good life, and I'm a lucky man! And that's without mentioning my little arrangement with the cooks. If the concierge is God on high then the cooks are the guardian angels of the buildings. These good women keep the leftovers for me and in return I fetch water for them, shake out the carpets and every so often I act as go-between when one of them falls in love with a coachman!'

'Would you allow me to accompany you? I should like to take a few photographs of you and Vi . . . Yvette.'

'Be my guest, but don't expect me to pose for you. I have work to do.'

What a stroke of luck meeting these two, Victor thought. Now he had an excuse for going to Du Houssoye's house. Moreover, he could kill two birds with one stone by adding to his photographic series of children at work.

'And where should I deliver the prints?'

'It's good of you to want to give them to us. Cité Doré, between Rue Jenner, Boulevard de la Gare and Place Pinel – near Cité des Kroumirs, not ten minutes from the Botanical Gardens. There's a fortune teller next door to us called Sibylla – well, her real name's Coralie Blinde.'

'I sell pins every afternoon in Rue Montmartre, across from the bar at number 32 – the one with a machine that sells drinks,' Yvette added.

As her father was knocking at the lodge of one of the houses, she remarked in a serious voice:

'It's not allowed.'

'What is not allowed?'

'Selling pins. The gendarmes treat us just like beggars. Last week they picked up my friend Phonsine. She started crying and refused to go down to the station. They told her she would end up a fallen woman if she kept soliciting passers-by with her rubbish. It's not true. She's no thief. She earns an honest living, same as me. I take after my papa. One day someone left a banknote in an old jacket. A lot of money, it was. Well, he took it back to the concierge who'd given him the jacket.'

'Where do you buy your pins?'

'Les Halles, first thing. Then I join Papa. And at midday I fill my basket and off I go to work – I love going on the omnibus! And if I see any gendarmes coming, I hide behind the barrels in the bar with the drink machine. I only sell my pins to ladies. Sometimes, they give me as much as fifteen sous.'

Léonard Diélette handed his daughter several packages, which she placed in the cart. They included two half-eaten lamb chops, some rice pudding wrapped in a bit of newspaper, a few bottle stoppers and jars and some phials and sponges from a chemist's shop on the ground floor.

'Look at this pair of ankle boots. True, the soles have come away, but the leather's in good nick. I'll take them to a cobbler.'

The next building housed a dressmaker's workshop and turned out to be a veritable mine of flannel ends, strips of fabric, selvedges and sheets. This came in handy, as Léonard Diélette was in cahoots with a man who made coverlets.

When he returned, his flushed face indicated that he had said yes to a few snifters of brandy.

'Dad always has a thirst on him,' Yvette declared. 'The trouble is that the plonk he buys from the liquor merchant will end up rotting his liver.'

A plump blonde woman in a black silk dress rushed past them, looking agitated and muttering to herself.

'Good morning, Madame Bertille!' cried Léonard Diélette.

'Oh! I'm sorry. I'm so upset I didn't even see you.'

'What's the matter?'

'A terrible tragedy, Monsieur Léonard, a terrible tragedy. Who would ever have imagined? But I must hurry back. I had to leave the old man while I did the shopping, and it's nearly his lunchtime.'

'Who is she?' Victor asked, indicating the woman who was hurrying away, her hat half falling off her head.

'Bertille Piot. She cooks for a well-to-do family, the Du Houssoyes, who live at number 28. You won't find many women as hard working as that. Stubborn as a mule she is, but with a heart of gold. Thanks to her, two days ago Vivi and I had the pleasure of eating half a *vol-au-vent* and some boiled beef, which she . . .'

'I'll go on ahead,' Victor interrupted him. 'I'd like to take a look at the Du Houssoye's house.'

He reached number 28 just as Bertille Piot, having crossed a cobbled courtyard, was vanishing inside the main body of an eighteenth-century building. Before he had even raised his hand to the door knocker the concierge emerged from the lodge at the entrance.

'I can tell by the look on your face that you're astonished by my rapidity. The gift of foresight, Monsieur – it helps me spot intruders and spares the owners a good deal of inconvenience.'

Despite the very tall hat the man was wearing, he looked no bigger than a twelve-year-old, but this didn't deter him from sizing up Victor most rudely.

He was about to allude to his acquaintance with Léonard Diélette when the concierge, indicating Victor's camera with his chin, continued:

'Do you think I was born yesterday? You're here about the murder. I know, I can smell a hack at a hundred yards.'

'It's that obvious, is it?' Victor said, grinning, barely able to contain his excitement at the mention of a murder. 'I take my hat off to you! You're absolutely right!' he exclaimed. 'Indeed, I was hoping to be the first to describe the scene to the devoted readers of *Le Passe-partout*.'

'You're the first all right, and if I have anything to do with it you'll be the last,' the man rejoined, folding his arms as if to say: 'Halt, who goes there?'

'I give up,' Victor mumbled, playing his last card. 'It's a shame, though. A picture of you on the front cover with the caption: "The concierge at the victim's place of residence" would have caused a sensation.'

As he turned on his heel a voice barked:

'Crevoux!'

'I beg your pardon?'

'Crevoux, Michel Crevoux, that's my name. I want it spelled out in full.'

'That can be arranged,' Victor said, pleased he'd got the better of the little man.

'Well, start taking notes! I've worked here since '86. Before that I was in the army. Oh, I've knocked about a bit! Cochinchina, Tonkin, Annam, Formosa, Los Pescadores. I fought against the Chinese hordes and was wounded at Lang Son. It took me two years to learn to walk again. I've got a peg leg. Would you like to see it?'

'That won't be necessary. Stand over there at the foot of the steps. Don't smile or move. Remind me of your name again. Is that Crevoux with an *x*? And the victim's name?'

'Du Houssoye, Antoine. Double *s, o, y, e*. And you are?'

Victor's heart missed a beat. Antoine du Houssoye murdered! Another murder investigation!

'Are his relatives at home?' Victor enquired nonchalantly.

'They've been summoned to the morgue. All except Madame's old father — he's not quite right in the head and doesn't realise there's been a tragedy. Poor Madame Gabrielle, she's lucky to have Monsieur's cousin living with her; he'll take care of the funeral arrangements. What a world we live in! Such an educated man, a curator at the Museum of Natural History! The police were here this morning, on their best behaviour they were. I was there; I heard everything. Monsieur left on Friday, to be precise, having told his wife and his secretary that he was going to Meudon. And last night he was found with a bullet in his chest! Madame Gabrielle fainted and I had to help Monsieur Wallers lay her out on the sofa.'

'Where did they find the body?'

'In a cellar near Les Halles. His wallet had been pinched, but luckily there was an old laundry ticket stuck to the hem of his coat or they'd have had the devil of a job identifying him!'

'On which floor do the Du Houssoyes live?'

'The first. The cook, butler and servants live on the mezzanine, and the ground floor is owned by a publisher of sheet music. They call it Bérancourt House, but actually it was converted in 1705 by Monsieur de la Garde, you can put his name next to mine.'

Victor aimed his lens at a window in the limestone façade. He glimpsed the vague outline of a face behind the chiffon curtain.

'Zounds! A spy . . .'

Fortunat de Vigneules stepped back from the window and went and stood in front of a fly-specked cheval glass. He straightened the brown top hat perched on his head, to which a few pale strands of hair still clung, and then pulled open his suit jacket to reveal a threadbare yellow waistcoat patched in several places.

'The brave knight cuts a dashing figure. Zounds, we'll drive the traitors from the kingdom! Your Majesty, I shall tear up the dirt with my teeth if I must, but I swear by the Holy Cross that I will restore the Templars' wealth to your descendants. May your execution be avenged!'

He knelt before a portrait of Louis XVI beneath which a few candle stubs sputtered and a bouquet of roses lay wilting. The walls were bedecked with prints of French kings, and a hand-drawn map of the Marais neighbourhood and a lithograph of the old Enclos du Temple, the fortress of the Knights Templar, adorned a marble dressing table. Aside from these few ornaments, the place looked more like a bear's mountain lair than a Parisian aristocrat's apartment. A sea of objects gave the impression of having been dropped higgledy-piggledy through a crack in the ceiling. There was a pile of rusty old swords beside the bed, heaps of clothes and books everywhere and a veritable deluge of scraps of paper: carefully folded, screwed up into balls or torn into tiny pieces.

The old man stood up straight, massaging his back with both hands. There was a knock on the door.

'Who is it?'

The cook entered without saying a word and placed a tray on the edge of his desk.

'Here's your chocolate. Drink it while it's hot. You should let me clean this place up – it's not proper. It's a pigsty!'

'Silence, slattern! Your broom will never cross the threshold of this sanctuary even if I have to fight to the death to keep it at bay!'

He waved a mottled rapier at her. 'A pox on the English Queen, who declared war on us!'

Bertille Piot was accustomed to these outbursts. She shrugged her shoulders and left. She closed the door behind her and stooped to press her eye to the keyhole. The ensuing spectacle might raise her spirits, which were low after Monsieur's death.

After circling the desk for a few moments, as though assessing the enemy's strength, Fortunat de Vigneules settled back in a chair covered in a grey film of dust. He nonchalantly picked up the pot of hot chocolate from the tray, puckering his lips in disgust as he filled a cup, then poured some whipped cream from a jug on to the steaming liquid. Much to Bertille Piot's delight, the old man began to scold the beverage.

'So it's you again, is it, with your white quiff? I thought I told you never to show up at my table again! It defies the limits of disbelief! What? Is that an objection I hear! Look, my dear fellow, you know full well that I'm not allowed to drink you. My liver and my arteries shrivel at the mere smell of you. Do you wish to sabotage my health? I'll have nothing to do with you.

'What are you insinuating, you scoundrel? That you came to take your leave of me for good? Did you indeed? That's what you said yesterday . . . You continue to insist? Stop blathering and be gone, infernal brew! I won't give you the pleasure of turning me into an invalid. May the devil take you!'

Bertille Piot spluttered with laughter. She watched the old man's hand reach out, pause and then pick up the cup.

'Very well, I shall indulge you, but it's the last time, do you hear? If you have the nerve to show up tomorrow I shall hurl you to the bottom of the latrine!'

Fortunat de Vigneules, drank the hot chocolate with a flourish, licked his lips and sighed.

'Ah! You rascal, you're so devilishly delicious . . .'

The performance was over. Bertille Piot scurried away. Almost at once, the old man opened the door and moved stealthily along the corridor towards a flight of stairs. When he reached the ground floor, he rushed to the lobby from which three separate entrances led down to the cellars. He slipped through the first of these. On a small shelf lay a candelabrum and a box of matches.

At the bottom of the steps, the musty air made him sneeze. He crossed the vaulted room crammed with trunks and bits of broken furniture and, after turning a large key in a lock, entered a narrow chamber in which the stench was so overpowering he was obliged to hold a handkerchief to his nose.

'A small dose of medicine will improve matters.'

He noisily snorted two pinches of snuff.

'Here I am, brave companions. Heel, boys, heel. Nogaret! Artois! Mortimer! Loyal to the last. I'll wager Évreux is out hunting bitches. Tallyho! Fall out!'

He was addressing four stuffed dogs – three spaniels and a setter – that stood frozen in various poses on an altar adorned with candlesticks, sprigs of box tree and religious images. He walked over to a tub. Curled up on some blocks of melting ice lay the corpse of a retriever in an advanced state of decomposition. Droplets of wax had hardened into balls on the surface of the water.

'My poor Enguerrand, take heart, you must hold out for a

few more days. I've secretly searched every purse in the house, but I still don't have enough to pay the taxidermist. Not today, tomorrow perhaps . . .'

He walked back the way he had come.

'And that's not all. I need to replenish my supply of snuff. Come, come, a few pennies won't break the bank!'

Returning to the first room, he walked over to a small linen chest concealed behind a double wardrobe. His hand touched an object wrapped in a piece of material. He began to unwrap it, having first placed the candelabrum on a chair. When he saw what it was, Fortunat de Vigneules let out a horrified gasp. No! Impossible! It must be some sort of joke. What wicked person could . . .

'*Vade retro, Satana!* Curses! It's . . . It's . . .'

Fortunat de Vigneules was unable to articulate the horror he felt at that moment. With a shudder he examined the vile object more closely.

'No!' he shrieked, his face screwed up in disgust.

Without bothering to close the chest, he wrapped the object tightly in the piece of material, grabbed the candelabrum and rushed out of the cellar.

Safely back in his apartment, Fortunat de Vigneules was careful to lock himself in. He was about to wrap the loathsome bundle in a copy of *XIX Century* when he hesitated.

'Well, this might make a nice addition to my wardrobe!'

He unravelled the piece of cloth enveloping the reviled object and tossed it on to his bed.

'The game is up this time, Fortunat. Immediate action is required, or else . . . Sodom and Gomorrah!'

After he had finished making his parcel, he made his way to the kitchen, which thankfully was empty. Quickly he lifted the lid of the rubbish bin and shoved the package under a pile of vegetable peelings and a chicken carcass.

Heart pounding, he heard the floorboards creak under Bertille's step just as he reached his bedroom. By this act of bravery he had saved the household from a fate worse than death. He carefully washed his hands so as to cleanse them of diabolical secretions and went to pour the soapy water into the slop bucket. As he did so he noticed the piece of cloth lying crumpled up on the eiderdown.

'A handsome neckerchief! Never lower your guard, though! A gift from the enemy can be lethal! We must protect ourselves.'

He bowed to the south and then to the east, muttering a ritual incantation:

'*Ada ada ada. Per ada. Perdidi. Festina. Dulco. Ignoto. Felix.*'[1]

He spat into his hands, rubbing them together, before finally tying the printed piece of fabric round his neck. He studied himself in the cheval glass, straightened the knot and, content with his reflection, returned to his lookout post beside the window casement.

Under the prying eyes of the concierge, the spy was taking photographs of the little girl while the market toby loaded his cart with his pickings from the refuse bins.

'*Vade retro,* burn in hell, evil relic,' murmured Fortunat de Vigneules, as he watched the man take away the object wrapped in newspaper.

When he was sure that the market toby, his daughter and their donkey had left the premises, he inched open his door.

Just as he was preparing to go, Victor noticed an eccentric-looking old man hopping towards him.

'Who is that?' he whispered to the concierge.

'The deceased's father-in-law.'

Victor, hand outstretched, hastened towards the man, who was dressed in what appeared to be an old-fashioned riding habit, consisting of a waisted woollen jacket, a canary-yellow waistcoat, white trousers with a beige stripe and ankle boots with spurs.

'My condolences, dear Monsieur.'

'Thank you, you are too kind, but do not pity him. His passing into the realm of darkness was painless. He now awaits the taxidermist in a cool place where fresh ice is brought each morning.'

Victor wondered in astonishment at the morgue's outmoded methods, and was about to go deeper into the matter when he noticed the scarf tied round the old man's neck. Why, it looked like . . . It looked like . . .

He had a distinct feeling of déjà vu, and recalled dimly a conversation with Kenji about a piece of Japanese silk.

'Those birds . . . Are they cranes or . . . storks?'

'Hush! The grand master of the order must not find out that this evil gift comes from Jacques de Molay.[2] There's nothing to fear; I have exorcised it. Do you do portraits?' he whispered, screwing up his eyes at Bertille Piot, who was charging towards them, fuming.

'Monsieur Fortunat, you know you're not allowed out!' she chided.

'By God! I'm being kept a prisoner. My son-in-law and nephew are in league against me! Tell the world, Monsieur, and bring me some nude portraits of women to add to my collection. I possess some marvellous prints by Henry Voland for use by painters. Ah, the sixties! Women then were buxom without being flabby!' he cried, glaring insinuatingly at the cook, who was growing impatient.

'Monsieur Fortunat . . .'

'All right, I'm coming. I used to buy from Alfred Cadart, a dealer in prints, Rue . . . Rue . . . Remember me, Monsieur! Nudes, nudes!'

Bertille Piot was already leading him away.

'At your service, Monsieur. Don't forget, nudes!' he cried out.

Victor gathered up his equipment and joined the concierge, who had been observing the scene.

'Is Monsieur du Houssoye's corpse really going to be embalmed?' he asked on his way out.

'I warned you the old man had a screw loose. He was talking about his dog!'

Victor reached the street just as a carriage was drawing up beside the pavement. He ducked behind a cart bearing a load of gravel and watched as two women, one of them more slender and petite than the other, stepped out. They both wore veils and were dressed in the Russian style. A man in a frock coat followed them, and Victor instantly recognised him as Antoine du Houssoye's cousin, whom he had met the previous evening at the museum.

He waited until they had entered the house before continuing on his way. When he reached Rue de Picardie, near the ruined tower at the corner of L'Enclos du Temple, he took advantage of a lull in the traffic to step out into the road. A speeding cyclist narrowly avoided running him down and bellowed furiously: 'Watch out!' Victor took no notice. He was thinking about the neckerchief stamped with the pattern of long-legged white birds.

Victor hurriedly greeted Joseph, who had been assailed by three customers, and went upstairs. He knocked on Kenji's door, but it was opened by Iris, wearing a man's black silk kimono.

'Father is in town buying some books. I was about to clean the bathtub. What a face! Come in then; I am decent. Would you like some tea?'

He followed her into the kitchen. She filled the tea pot and he hadn't the heart to tell her he preferred coffee. He studied the young girl as she neatly laid out the place mats and cups and saucers and then sat down opposite him. A year earlier he would have staked his life on her being Kenji's mistress and now here she was, transformed into a delightful, impertinent sister, whose character — a mixture of pragmatism and inscrutability — he found disconcerting. He felt a sudden surge of warmth, which he could not translate into a gesture, but which was audible in his voice.

'It is odd to think that we share the same mother and that through you I have ties with Japan.'

'Oh! I don't feel Japanese at all! My ways and customs are ever so English and my principles ever so French. Did you know that Father is toying with the idea of naturalising me? In fact, he has already applied.'

'I think it's an excellent idea. That way we shall all remain united. Life is full of surprises, don't you think? We have distant relations living thousands of miles away, in the Empire of the Rising Sun! Astonishing, isn't it? A country that has remained in stubborn isolation since the seventeenth century.'

'You must take evening classes, brother dear. Your information is quite out of date. Japan is in the process of modernising. In 1889, Emperor Mutsuhito granted his people a constitution based upon the English constitution. However, there is still a long way to go, since the situation of women is far from acceptable. Drink your tea or it'll go cold.'

'Goodness gracious! You astonish me with your erudition! Such an attractive young girl . . .'

'Attractive! Don't tell me that you're just like all the other men who believe that a woman should be content merely to be attractive?'

'No, no, you're taking it the wrong way. I am merely making the point that you are very cultured for someone who so stubbornly resists all attempts to interest her in reading. Have you kept in touch with your great-uncle? The one who gave Kenji that . . . that *fukorishi*.'

'*Furoshiki!* Uncle Hanunori Watanabe passed away at the ripe old age of ninety-nine.'

'I'm so sorry. What about the other one?'

'I wasn't aware I had more than one.'

'You know exactly what I mean, you little minx. I'm referring to the *furoshiki*.'

'Oh, I see. You'd like to examine the pattern on it before you give Tasha an oriental dress.'

Victor frowned then raised his eyebrows.

'How did you guess?'

'Ha! Your wide-eyed innocence doesn't fool me for a minute,' she exclaimed, standing up and poking her brother in the arm rhythmically as she chanted: 'Liar! Liar! Liar!'

Victor began to laugh, delighted to be experiencing for the first time this mock fighting between siblings.

'Help! Stop! Iris, you're impossible. You are attributing motives to me . . .'

'My dear Victor, why do you insist on defending yourself? Are you perhaps not entirely blameless? Whatever the case, I forgive you. Come with me.'

They went into Kenji's room. As Iris busied herself moving the cotton mattress and the slats of the bed base, Victor contemplated Tasha's painting of the Parisian rooftops at dawn. He was grateful to Kenji for having hung it above his bed. Iris handed him a package.

'This contains the papers relating to my birth as well as my mother's – our mother's letters.'

Deeply moved, Victor stared at the *furoshiki*. There was no need for him to examine it more closely; he was certain: the white storks on a turquoise background were identical to those on Fortunat de Vigneules's neckerchief. Without saying a word, he handed the package to Iris who put it back where it belonged.

'Thank you for your . . . help.'

'You mean for my transgression, which has allowed you to scrutinise the piece of material identical to the one wrapped around the goblet stolen from my father. You won't succeed in pulling the wool over my eyes, dear brother!'

'What are you talking about?' he asked, ingenuously.

Iris sighed.

'Poor Tasha! She won't be very pleased to find out that you are about to take on another case.'

'You wouldn't snitch on me!' he cried out in alarm.

'Hm. That depends. Mum's the word, but only if . . .'

'Is this blackmail?'

'Only if you give us – that is to say Joseph and me – your blessing.'

'So that romantic idyll is still going on, is it? Look, Iris, you're being foolish. Joseph is our assistant.'

'I love him. An assistant is no worse than a woman painter!'

'But there's no comparison! We are . . .'

'You are in love and so are we. The verb has existed in all its conjugations in every language for all time.'

She mussed up his hair.

'You and I are united by a secret. I hope you don't mind me being so informal; the Englishwoman in me has difficulty getting used to your French formality. I promise I'll say nothing because you're my big brother and I love you,' she whispered.

He felt his initial reluctance give way. Iris seemed so frail and yet she was so strong, and certainly more determined than he. But they had one trait in common and it united them: the appeal of what was out of bounds would prompt them to overcome any obstacle.

'I give you my blessing,' he conceded. 'In any case, Joseph will one day make an excellent bookseller.'

'And a talented writer.'

He pulled a wry face and went to join his assistant, who was rubbing his hands together gleefully at having completed a sale of the unfinished works of Delille.

'Jojo, I am curious about the man who left his visiting card, which you forgot to give me. What did he look like?'

'Oh, Boss, I wasn't looking at him that closely. You're the photographer, not me.'

'If you wish to become a writer, you will need to hone your powers of observation.'

'I'm interested in fiction, not in real life. Now, let me think. He looked completely normal. I seem to remember that he was wearing a bowler hat and glasses. He looked well-to-do, or like a policeman out of uniform – and not a very friendly one.'

'That doesns't help much. Did he mention anything to you about his research?'

'He asked to see Monsieur Mori. What kind of research?'

'Zoology.'

'That queer fellow runs a zoo? What's his name?'

'Antoine du Houssoye,' Victor muttered, sitting down at the desk and pretending to study the sales catalogues.

How did Fortunat de Vigneules manage to be in possession of the *furoshiki*? He couldn't possibly have burgled Kenji's apartment and stolen the goblet! Then who had? One of his relatives? But why? Victor sensed that he had ignited a tiny flame that would soon shed light on all these strange coincidences. He was longing to go back to Rue Charlot and look into the matter further.

Not so fast. You could bump into the police or be recognised by that concierge with the wooden leg, not to mention the cousin from the museum, who would be most surprised if you showed up, he told himself.

Unable to decide on a course of action, he picked up a pencil and on a blotter began sketching a picture of a skinny bird with spindly legs.

You're as bad at drawing as you are at deduction. It looks no more like a stork than you do a . . . an altar boy.

Fortunat de Vigneules, with his top hat at an angle and his neckerchief unknotted and draped over his shoulders, was engaged in swinging a censer and muttering incomprehensible incantations, when he heard a movement outside. Night was falling and clouds were gathering in the sky. He drew back the curtain slightly and was able to make out two police sergeants and a tall man wearing a braided hussar's jacket talking to the concierge in the middle of the courtyard. The man in the jacket straightened his fur hat and hurried up the steps leading to the doorway.

'Holy smoke! A hussar flanked by his two spies!'

Keeping hold of his censer, Fortunat de Vigneules kicked off his shoes, walked across the hallway and crept to the end of the corridor, where he ventured to peek through a crack in the main sitting-room door.

He could see his daughter, Gabrielle, prostrate on the sofa striking the pose of a grieving widow. Lucie, her lady-in-waiting and confidante, sat beside her looking tense and dabbing her eyes with a handkerchief.

'Whore of Babylon!' muttered Fortunat, who was not overly fond of the lady-in-waiting.

Alexis Wallers and Charles Dorsel were standing with their backs to the fireplace facing the man in the jacket, who walked over to Gabrielle.

'My heartfelt condolences, Madame du Houssoye. Allow me to introduce myself: my name is Inspector Lecacheur. I realise how painful this ordeal must be for you, but I am obliged to ask you a few questions out of simple formality. I understand your husband left the house early on Friday morning?'

'Yes, he always leaves early. That day he had to pick up a file from the museum and then he was going to spend four days in Meudon with Professor Guéret. I got up at eight o'clock and we had breakfast.'

'We?'

'Monsieur Wallers, Monsieur Dorsel, Mademoiselle Robin and myself. My father was locked in his bedroom. He is very elderly and not right in the head. He only tolerates the presence of Bertille Piot, our cook. She prepares his meals separately.'

Crouched in the dark, Fortunat spat silently in disgust.

'Oh, the beauty of filial love! Senile, me? The scoundrels! They squander my fortune and force me into a life of thieving! And as for that crank in his hussar's jacket, what's he cooking up?'

The inspector had taken a box of lozenges out of his pocket and was tossing them mechanically from one hand to the other.

'And what did you do then?'

'I had a fitting . . . Oh, this is too much! I am exhausted! Lucie . . .'

'I went out at nine o'clock,' Lucie Robin continued, 'and it was I who posted Monsieur's mail. At eleven o'clock, I joined Madame Gabrielle at Madame Coussinet's on Rue Richer. Madame ordered two floral dresses. We had a snack in town and then went to make a few purchases. We were back home by five o'clock. Monsieur Wallers and Monsieur Dorsel were here working on the draft of a dissertation. Augustine, the chambermaid, served us a light meal, after which I took a short ride in a cab to Madame's jeweller on Place des Victoires, and was back in time for supper. Oh, dear Lord! Poor Monsieur du Houssoye! To think that he braved all those dangers on his travels in foreign lands only to be murdered right here in Paris! It is horrible! Horrible! Could we be excused, Inspector? Madame is tired.'

'Of course,' the inspector replied. 'My respects, ladies.'

Fortunat de Vigneules felt a lump in his throat. 'Antoine! Murdered! Why, it's incredible! Good Lord, the curse is at work!'

'Surely, Inspector, you do not suspect one of the members of this family of having killed my cousin?' asked Alexis Wallers.

'Of course not, my dear Monsieur, but you are no doubt aware that . . . I must make a thorough report. I am a civil servant and officialdom is a serious matter . . . According to the pathologist, Monsieur du Houssoye's death occurred roughly seventy-two hours ago, which takes us back to Friday. It is difficult to calculate the exact moment. Am I to understand that you were here on Friday?'

'Yes. Monsieur Dorsel and I spent the whole day filing Antoine's notes.'

'Forgive me for contradicting you, Alexis, but you went out in the morning, if you recall,' murmured Charles Dorsel.

'Oh yes! So I did. I dropped in on a colleague on Boulevard Saint-Germain. He will confirm it.'

'And you, Monsieur Dorsel?' the inspector demanded.

'I did not leave the house all day. You can ask the servants!'

'Fine, fine,' agreed the inspector, stuffing a handful of lozenges in his mouth, 'I shan't bother you any further. In my opinion, Monsieur du Houssoye was murdered for his money and . . .'

'Excuse me one moment,' Alexis Wallers interrupted him, opening the door.

At first he saw nothing, then he made out a dim shape flattened against the wall.

'What are you playing at, Fortunat?'

Fortunat de Vigneules jumped violently and his neckerchief slipped to the floor. Clasping the censer to his chest, he backed away slowly. Alexis burst out laughing.

'What's that smell? Opium?'

'It's a deadly serious joke, Monsieur Braggart!' retorted Fortunat.

'Really, grandfather, you're getting worse every day! We shall discuss this later. In the meantime go to bed,' Alexis ordered, grabbing him by the elbow.

'*Vade retro*, traitor! It's all the fault of that wicked relic! No one must touch it, ever! Oh, God, protect your humble servant! Help me find a way of saving us from this evil!'

Fortunat was mouthing the words breathlessly. He pulled away suddenly and hobbled as fast as he could back to his chambers.

'Hey! One moment, Fortunat! You dropped . . .'

Fortunat's cry rang out again. 'Warn them never to touch those execrations of Beelzebub! Warn them!'

Alexis stooped to pick up the neckerchief, studied it for a moment then placed it carelessly in his pocket.

'The old man has completely taken leave of his senses,' a woman's voice murmured.

Alexis swung round.

'Have you been here all this time?'

'Yes. The inspector has left.'

'How is Gabrielle?'

'She is lying down. I gave her a sleeping draught.'

Fortunat awoke feeling suffocated. For a moment he thought that his retriever was sitting on his chest; he even imagined he could hear the dog panting. He tried to pat Enguerrand's side and his hand flailed about in the empty air. He realised then that his companion preferred to stay on his blocks of ice in the cellar.

'I am the only one left.'

He felt neglected, weary, at death's door. He was filled with an indescribable sadness.

If only youth were wise and old age vigorous! How charming that little Adeline was whom I met at the Théâtre-Français during the premiere of *Chatterton*![3] And the adorable Mimi Rose from the Opéra-Comique, who sang her love song so well!

> *Combien je regrette*
> *Mon bras si dodu*
> *Ma jambe bien faite*
> *Et le temps perdu . . .*[4]

He hummed.

He lost himself in mental arithmetic as he attempted to enumerate his conquests of the fair sex, only to end in the sad fact of his late marriage to Melaine Le Héron, who had given him a disobedient and ungrateful daughter.

That name, belonging to a wading bird, troubled him. The piece of silk he had exorcised that afternoon before turning it into a neckerchief! Where was it?

He heaved himself off the bed, lit the row of candle stubs underneath Louis XVI and began rummaging through the clothes scattered over the floor. It wasn't there. The scarf with the storks on it had vanished. He heard a creaking noise and stood still.

Somebody was behind the door.

'Who is it?' he whispered.

There was no reply. Everything went quiet again. In a low, husky voice, he said, 'I know it is he. *It is he.*'

The emissary advanced furtively, carrying a bundle over his shoulder. The candle he was holding at arm's length lit up the slippery ground, which was strewn with rubble and refuse. The place gave off a putrid odour. This murder had been more onerous for him than the others. Bending to the will of the Eternal One was no less of an ordeal than self-flagellation and penitence had once been. The emissary had soon learnt to torment his flesh with the helping hand of the one in whose charge heaven had placed him. What tears, what revulsion before finally accepting, enjoying even, the abuse and humiliation! At times the Divine revelation let its rage be felt – a booming reminder of his servitude. Then carrying out the orders became like a moral duty. But not this murder, no, it had not been easy.

The emissary had braced himself, his eyes half-closed, and moved away from the river's edge with its rows of dark trees and rustling leaves. Only the lapping of water against the bridge piers and the creak of a vessel moored to the pontoon of a laundry boat broke the dull murmur of the sleeping city. A passing barge making its way downriver towards L'Hôtel de Ville had masked the sound of the revolver going off, followed by the loud splash.

The relief he had felt at having overcome his aversion would never be surpassed. But it was not over yet. Now he must make the murder look like a disappearance.

He walked for a long time. The rest of the world seemed to recede until he reached the underground passage concealed at the far end of a courtyard overgrown with dandelions.

A grotto. Dank and foul-smelling. It had been rumoured that when the new sewers were being built underneath land that was once inside L'Enclos du Temple, a coffin had been discovered containing the remains of a man wearing the clothes of the order of the Templars. The clasp on his cloak suggested he had been a commander of the order.

The emissary believed that one endlessly deferred crime had yet to be committed. It would constitute the supreme victory. All of a sudden, something brushed against his leg. A rat. It disappeared swiftly between two dressed stones – the perfect hiding place!

The emissary pushed his bundle into the narrow space through which the rat had scurried and, grabbing a handful of mud, filled the gap then walked back out into the fresh air.

Two figures frozen in prayer cast an eerie shadow on the walls of the Église Saint-Germain-l'Auxerrois. The emissary crossed himself, slipped a coin into the collection box, grasped a candle and mumbled a *Pater* and an *Ave* as he knelt on a prie-dieu and addressed the heavens.

'Oh, God, only your Gospel can guide my actions. As man embraces wrong, so will evil be my avenger. Oh, Lord God, arm your emissary! Help me to find the abomination that is a stain on your work of creation!'

Leaning against a pillar, the emissary pulled out of his pocket *Texts and Essays in Holy History*[5] moving his lips as he read.

'From the creation of the world up until the flood: 4963-3308 BC (a total of 1,655 years)

'. . . And so God did take the silt from the earth and with it created the body of the first man to whom he gave an immortal soul, and named him Adam . . .'

CHAPTER 6

Wednesday, 13 April

Attracted by a pile of debris lying in a recess on Quai de Gesvres, a flock of gulls squabbled half-heartedly over a few fish bones. One of them tilted its head towards the river. In the early dawn light it had spied a dark bulky mass buffeted by the leapfrogging current. The gull took flight, circling several times round the curious piece of debris. It hesitated. Should it land on the thing that resembled a biped? Seek out with its beak the soft second skin covering the body? But what if the specimen wasn't really dead? Too risky. The gull decided to content itself with the pile of refuse while the body bobbed slowly towards Le Pont-au-Change.

A pinkish glow made the panelling in the darkened room shimmer. A pair of hands leafed through a notebook filled with a childish scrawl and paused at a page marked with a piece of blotting paper.

You have placed various obstacles in my path, Lord. Are you testing my resolve? I have spent part of the night awake, feeling like a solitary sparrow perched on a rooftop. I will succeed. I have already found a solution to the problem of evil. The avid helper who assisted me is at this very moment floating towards the lake of fire and sulphur. As for the other one, a few coins were sufficient to loosen his tongue and he has shown me the way to the abomination. Henceforth, his lips will be sealed by fear. I march forward wielding my double-edged sword. Look with approval upon your emissary...

Had anyone told Joseph that he would one day lie to Monsieur Mori in order to slip out of the shop for a moment, he would have been mortified.

And yet this model assistant was about to tell an enormous lie and already he felt guilty. Afraid he might let it show, he buried his nose in his handkerchief and blurted out:

'Bonsieur Bori, Bonsieur Bictor basked be to bake sure . . .'

'I can't understand a word. Let go of your nose and breathe properly if you have something to say. Do you have a cold?'

'No,' Joseph replied, turning a deep scarlet as he removed his handkerchief. 'Monsieur Victor asked me to pick up the volumes of La Fontaine he left with the book binder a fortnight ago. Do I have time to stop off at Rue Monsieur-le-Prince?'

'Yes, and while you're about it you can take a copy of my *Travel Literature* catalogue to Monsieur Andrésy. He is a fan of my work. Don't stand there gaping – I have an important meeting to go to at ten o'clock.'

Joseph hurriedly put on his coat and cap. He listened out for the sound of Euphrosine banging her pots and pans upstairs and, reassured, left.

He would have liked to have had time to ensure that the

lodgings he shared with his mother in Rue Visconti were tidy, but no sooner had he arrived than there was a knock at the door of his study. He hurried to let Iris in.

'Did anyone see you?'

'And what if they did? Don't look so conspiratorial. People will think we're plotting an assassination attempt.'

'Let's not stay in here – it's freezing.'

'What a lot of books and magazines! Are they all yours?'

'They were my father's.'

He was about to show her into his bedroom, when he was struck by a sense of impropriety. Taking her into Euphrosine's room would be equally unsuitable. Only the kitchen was neutral terrain.

However, after she had made a tour of it – which didn't take long given its tiny proportions – admiring the stone sink, the stove and the cast-iron casserole, she expressed a desire to explore the bedrooms. Joseph grabbed her by the sleeve.

'Perhaps it would be more seemly if . . . Well, I mean . . . It would be better if . . .'

She glanced at him mischievously, amused by his awkwardness.

'Explain to me, Joseph, why a bedroom is more dangerous than a kitchen?'

She raced into Euphrosine's bedroom.

'How quaint! Your mother must love chintz; she's used it everywhere!'

'It's a very hard-wearing and economical fabric,' he said approvingly, relieved to see that the floor was clean. 'Hold on a minute!' he cried as she headed in the direction of his bedroom.

It was too late. He froze in horror as he envisaged his unmade bed, on which two scrunched up pillows lay next to an apple core and an old comb that had seen better days. 'So this is where you dream of me!' The ghastly image evaporated at the sound of her words. Standing halfway between the wardrobe and the pristine bed, which he now remembered having made and remade three times before sitting down to breakfast, Iris was in raptures over what she referred to as his 'sanctuary in the heart of Paris'.

'There isn't much furniture — not that Maman and I are Spartan, it's just that we don't have much space . . .'

'I like people who can manage with the bare necessities,' she remarked as she plopped herself down on the bed, having noticed that the only chair in the room was creaking under the weight of a pile of laundry.

Mortified, Joseph discreetly opened the window a crack, convinced he had caught a whiff of stale socks.

'Stop moving about. You're making me dizzy.'

'I promised the Boss I'd be back double quick.'

'Are you afraid of him or me? Come here.'

He walked over to her shyly. She took his arm and pulled him down beside her.

Flustered, he tried to create a diversion.

'My English is coming along nicely,' he exclaimed. 'Listen to my irregular verbs: *Arise, arose, arisen. Awake* . . .'

It was too late. Their lips were already touching, their fingers intertwined. His hand moved up instinctively to unbutton Iris's blouse as they fell back on to the bed.

Suddenly, like some deus ex machina, a vision of his mother

appeared before him, glaring, her finger pointing menacingly like the Pharaoh ordering Moses into exile. He leapt to his feet.

'I really must go!' he gasped.

She laughed good-naturedly and replaced her hat, which had rolled on to the floor.

'Darling, you must at all costs convince Kenji that we . . . that you . . .'

'I'll do my best. Are you going back to the bookshop?'

'No. I lied to my father. I am supposed to be in Saint-Mandé gorging myself on Mademoiselle Bontemps's cakes. Instead I'll spend the morning at Le Magasin du Louvre where, notwithstanding the dress and coat sale, I shall be thinking only of you.'

Joseph was walking on air. He bought a copy of *Le Passe-partout* from a little street vendor and marched triumphantly into the bookshop, where Kenji was waiting for him.

'Goodness gracious, Boss, you are dressed up to the nines! What a magnificent yellow cravat! Why, your boots are so shiny I can see my reflection in them! And that eau de cologne . . . Lily of the valley?'

'Lavender, Joseph, lavender.'

Striking a pose, Kenji adjusted his black top hat and pulled on his taupe gloves. He seized his cane with its jade handle in the shape of a horse's head and pulled a face at Molière's bust.

'I'm leaving you now. Don't forget that we're meeting Madame de Brix's new husband, Colonel de Réauville, at three o'clock on Rue Drouot. He wants my opinion on an illuminated manuscript he's interested in acquiring. After that we will accompany him to his villa on Avenue du Bois, stuffed with books on military history, which I shall endeavour to pick up at a good price.'

'You can rely on me, Boss!'

'Incidentally, where are the La Fontaine volumes?'

Joseph suddenly became flustered and, turning bright pink, he stammered:

'The book binder was . . . he was running behind schedule . . . too much work, he's . . . he's very sorry.'

Baffled by Joseph's loss of composure, Kenji decided he'd get to the bottom of it later.

No sooner had the door bell sounded than Joseph took advantage of the empty shop, and flicked through the newspaper. An article signed 'The Virus' caught his attention.

LES HALLES CORPSE

We are now in a position to reveal the identity of the man whose body was discovered by Monsieur Rivet on Monday night at eleven o'clock near Les Halles. He was Antoine du Houssoye, an eminent researcher in zoology at the Museum of Natural History, who had recently returned to France after a long field trip in Java. He was killed by a single bullet fired at close range. We have it from a reliable source that the nation's bloodhound, Inspector Lecacheur, after interrogating the victim's nearest and dearest has eliminated them from his inquiry. It seems we are in the presence of one of those sordid crimes whose increasing numbers can only be lamented . . .

In a fit of nervous excitement Joseph screwed up the newspaper, forgetting to cut out the article.

A zoologist! Du Houssoye! The name and title on the visiting card of the man in the bowler hat! The man Monsieur Legris was casually asking me about yesterday. So, he's been murdered! There's something fishy going on . . . The Boss is on the hunt! If he thinks he can pull the wool over my eyes . . .

He was obliged to interrupt these reflections in favour of making a quick sale of *Essay on the Basic Elements of Conscience* by Bergson to a forlorn lady who looked in need of a book to cheer her up. Just then, Victor walked through the door.

'Do I look like an ass to you, Boss?'

'No, Joseph, nor like a donkey for that matter.'

'In that case why didn't you tell me that your zoologist was a goner?'

He brandished the crumpled newspaper.

'Oh, so you've found out,' Victor muttered, 'and I suppose Sherlock Pignot will now insist on collaborating . . .'

'With Sherlock Legris. Naturally.'

'I had every intention of asking for your help.'

'Did you? Come on then, out with it. Monsieur Victor. I'm all ears.'

'Earlier this month, Lady Stone, an acquaintance of Monsieur Mori, was murdered in Scotland. I found out about it thanks to your translation of *The Times*. It seems this lady gave Kenji the goblet that was stolen during the break-in. And it is more than likely that this seemingly worthless object was responsible for the violent deaths of Antoine du Houssoye and Lady Stone. And, wait for it, Joseph, I think I've located the goblet, which is where you come in. Yesterday, I spoke to an elderly gentleman who might be involved . . .'

'I've just remembered something puzzling, Boss. Last Friday, just as I was locking up the shop a woman tripped and fell on the pavement. I left the keys in the door and rushed to help her and when I came back they were lying on the ground!'

'A set-up do you suppose? If so, then the woman must have had an accomplice . . . Or else it was a simple coincidence.'

'It seems unlikely, Boss. True, I didn't see anyone else, but it would be easy enough to have hidden in a doorway.'

'What did the woman look like?'

Joseph made an apologetic face.

'There's something else bothering me, Boss. The telephone call that sent you off on the wild goose chase to Neuilly – that caller was a woman too. Someone wanted you away from the apartment.'

'We can discuss that later. Right now, I want you to go to 28 Rue Charlot, next to Le Marché des Enfants-Rouges. And take . . .'

'Le Marché des Enfants-Rouges?'

'Do you know where the Conservatoire des Arts et Métiers is? Well, from there you go down Rue Réamur then take Rue de Bretagne and you'll come to it.'

He opened a drawer in Kenji's desk. Lying under a register was a collection of prints. He took one and slipped it into an envelope.

'Give this to Antoine du Houssoye's father-in-law – an elderly gentleman by the name of Fortunat de Vigneules – on behalf of the photographer he bumped into yesterday.'

'But, Boss, what will the Boss say when he notices . . .'

'He won't notice a thing. They're all identical. Do your best to speak to him alone. See if you can get him to tell you the whereabouts of the goblet that was wrapped in the scarf he was using as a neckerchief, and try to find out whether he really is as mad as he seems.'

'Is that all? Do I have to go now?'

'You should already be on your way there.'

'But that's impossible! I have to be at the auction house at three o'clock sharp to meet Monsieur Mori!'

'It's not even eleven o'clock.'

'And when am I supposed to eat?'

'I've made a rough sketch of the goblet: the skullcap of a monkey – probably a gibbon – attached to a little metal tripod decorated with three jewels and the tiny face of a cat with marbled agates for eyes. I know I can rely on your natural curiosity.'

'So I'm nosey, am I?' Joseph muttered angrily as he scoured the street for a cab. 'That's a bit rich.' He leant up against a tree and, turning his back on the passers-by, opened the envelope. The contents made him gasp.

'Oh, moon of my delights!'

'What on earth is going on here?'

A cart piled high with furniture and bundles had stationed itself outside number 28 Rue Charlot. Two stocky men with red faces were straining under the weight of a grand piano they were lugging across the courtyard, while a gang of porters carried crates into the town house.

'Hey! You, what do you think you're doing there?'

The exclamation came from a sour-faced little man stationed at the entrance.

'I'm one of the porters,' Joseph replied on impulse, grabbing a crate filled with tablecloths and napkins.

Clasping it to his chest he marched towards the steps, nervous of being intercepted. He entered unchecked, and found himself in a hall, where he put down his load. Dashing up the stairs, he bumped into a maid on the mezzanine landing, carrying a tray bearing a steaming kettle.

'Excuse me, Mademoiselle; I have an appointment with Monsieur de Vigneules. Where are his apartments?'

'On the first floor. Just follow me.'

'I wanted to offer my condolences to the family.'

'They're not at home. Monsieur Wallers and Monsieur Dorsel are seeing to the transfer of the body. Madame is here, and the doctor. It doesn't help matters having these people moving in on the ground floor. I must hurry. She'll need her tonic before the funeral. Carry on down the corridor and you'll find Monsieur de Vigneules's apartments at the end.'

'Hell's bells and buckets of blood, this place is a veritable labyrinth!'

Joseph wandered for several minutes – the corridor seemed to go on forever. Which room was his? There were five doors – four on the left and one on the right.

He knocked at random. '*Vade retro Satana*,' boomed from within. Joseph pressed his mouth to the door.

'Is that you, Monsieur de Vigneules?' he whispered. 'The photographer from yesterday sent me. He asked me to bring you this print. I'm sure you'll like it.'

'Slide it under the door.'

Joseph bent down and watched the envelope disappear, snatched by unseen fingers.

'Zounds! What opulence!' exclaimed a muffled voice. 'I take my hat off to you, Monsieur. I concede and clear the way forthwith.'

Joseph heard a scraping of furniture followed by the crash of a heavy object. A bolt squeaked and a shrivelled, ferrety face peered out, examining him with keen eyes. 'Come in quick! They're after me, but I can hold out under siege. Have you any more like these?' the old man cried, waving the decidedly provocative print in the air.

'I'll see what I can do,' murmured Joseph.

'Give me the address of the artist – his work is every bit as good as Henry Voland's best.'

'What artist?'

'Why, the photographer of course!'

'18 Rue des Saints-Pères,' Joseph muttered, instantly regretting having imparted the information.

He stepped over a bronze figure of Diana lying face down on the rug and deduced from the dresser pulled away from the wall that the apartment's occupant had barricaded himself in.

'Holy Mother of God! What is the name of this luscious creature whose posterior is so amply and appealingly enhanced by her black stockings, raised veil and charmingly jaunty position?'

'La Goulue. She dances the cancan at Le Moulin Rouge.'

'Oh, the wanton creature! If only this alluring temptress would liven up my solitary nights. I'd rather be the quarry of this huntress than of the deplorable Jacques de Molay.'

'Is he threatening you?' Joseph asked, his eye on the door.

'My poor boy, ever since he discovered that I'm after his treasure he wants me dead, and my soul damned! Why, only the other night I sensed the little runt prowling around, intending to purloin my neckerchief. Had my brave Enguerrand not been here to defend me, suggesting I put up a barricade . . .'

Jacques de Molay, Enguerrand, treasure . . . It's complete gibberish. The old man is clearly off his rocker, thought Joseph, preparing his retreat.

'And where is this Enguerrand?' he enquired, good-naturedly.

'I shall lead you directly to his bedside for he needs cooling down again.'

Oblivious to the look of bewilderment on Joseph's face, Fortunat de Vigneules opened the door a chink.

'Take care. We must be sure the coast is clear. We don't want to run into the slouch who bullies me with her scolding . . . Make haste, but not a sound. Step lightly!'

He moved along the corridor, Joseph following close on his heels.

'The draggletail will be at the market stocking up on game at this hour. We must hurry before she returns to her quarters.'

They went into the kitchen. The old man spied a huge lump of ice on the stone sink.

'Grab it and we'll scarper,' he hissed at Joseph.

Scarcely had Joseph's hands touched the transparent slab than he leapt back.

'It burns!'

'Stand aside, coxcomb! Zounds, I wasn't born in the year of the Battle of Berezina for nothing. My leathery hide has weathered more cold than your popinjay's skin – no offence meant.'

Fortunat removed his waistcoat, wrapped it around the block of ice and led the increasingly nervous Joseph down a narrow staircase to the cellar.

In the dim candlelight the two men bent over the corpse of a dog, which stank enough to decimate a swarm of flies. Joseph felt himself go faint.

'What . . . What is it?' he whispered in a tremulous voice.

'Why, brave knight, it's Enguerrand the sixth.'

'Er . . . Don't you think given the state he's in it might be a good idea to bury him right away?' Joseph said, trying not to breathe.

Fortunat de Vigneules scratched his head, puzzled.

'The thing is . . . I was going to have him stuffed, like the others.'

He pointed to the dogs frozen in various poses on the altar.

'I'm afraid it's too late for that. You'll be lucky if you can make a mat out of him.'

'Very well, but I insist that my faithful friend remains in the company of his brothers. Onward!' Fortunat shouted, grabbing a coal shovel that was propped against a wall and handing it to Joseph.

*

Exhausted and drenched in sweat from digging the beaten earth, Joseph cursed his boss. Fortunat de Vigneules insisted on giving up his yellow waistcoat to line his faithful companion's resting place. Once the animal was in the ground, he knelt down with difficulty.

'Farewell, brave hero. I would have immortalised your remains had the scoundrels who are starving me given me the means. Divine intervention was refused, but I was guided to the accursed chalice with the face of a cat – the demonic symbol of the Templars – and prompted to throw it in the rubbish! *Deo gratias!*

'Who exactly are these Templars?' Joseph asked, assuming that he was referring to people who lived in the area around the Temple Market.

'An order founded at the time of the first Crusades to protect the holy lands. But these rich, powerful soldier-monks failed in their mission. And they practised witchcraft, which is why our good King Philip the Fair had them burnt at the stake.'

God help us, Joseph thought, the man is raving!

'And this treasure, was it theirs?'

'Silence, wretched boy! Once I have unearthed it I shall give it to the heirs of Louis XVIII, to assist them in reinstating the monarchy.'

'And this chalice with a cat's face you threw in the rubbish, it wouldn't happen to be made from a monkey's skull?'

'Abomination! If you hadn't given me the picture of the ample posterior of the Goulue woman and heroically interred the mortal remains of my poor Enguerrand, why, young man, I would suspect you of being a spy in the pay of Molay!'

'Nay, my lord, you would be mistaken, for I, too, wish to make certain that the vile object has been destroyed.'

'I saw the rag-and-bone man take it away with my own eyes.'

'A rag-and-bone man? Where does he live? Miles from anywhere, I suppose?'

'I don't know his name. I'm unfamiliar with the location of his manor. The slattern will tell you that. Fall out! I wish to be alone.'

Who is this 'slattern'? One of the domestic staff, no doubt, Joseph muttered to himself as he climbed the stairs.

When he reached the mezzanine he found himself face to face with the maid who had been carrying the kettle and he asked her if she knew to whom the old man might have been referring. She pulled a face.

'I'm new here. I don't know all the staff. You'll have to ask Bertille Piot; she cooks for the ladies and gentlemen above stairs.'

The plump, fair-haired woman darting between the kitchen and the larder reminded him of Euphrosine, but ten years younger.

'Excuse me, Madame; I am a relative of Monsieur Fortunat . . .'

'I'll wager he's been pinching my ice again!'

'Er . . . He mentioned a slattern, I mean a servant, who might . . .'

'I'll give you slatterns! The old man's getting worse every day. At this rate he'll end up in the asylum. I can assure you there are no slatterns working here, only respectable people who know how to behave.'

'Of course, Madame. Perhaps you can help me then. I'm

conducting a survey of household refuse collection and it would be a great help if I could speak to the rag-and-bone man who comes here. I did ask the concierge, but . . .'

'Oh, him! The less he does the more exhausted he becomes. Well, I'll tell you where to find Monsieur Léonard. He comes here every day, a very meticulous, orderly gentleman. He lives in Cité Doré. Now, if you'll excuse me, I must cook my tripe.'

When Joseph reached the ground floor, the concierge was engaged in vehemently scolding the porters and he slipped out unnoticed. He had three-quarters of an hour to reach the auction house.

Stretched out on the rumpled sheets, Eudoxie Allard studied Kenji's lean, muscular body. He was dressing swiftly but calmly.

'What are you doing today?' she asked him.

'I'm meeting somebody at the auction house. I won't have lunch – you have sated my appetite.'

She laughed even though she felt terribly disappointed. She knew he cared for her. He never treated her like a woman of easy virtue. He was respectful, attentive and showered her with gifts. And yet after they had achieved the peak of pleasure, he became distant and withdrawn.

She propped herself up on one elbow without bothering to cover her nudity.

'Stay,' she murmured.

Her desire for Kenji was intense, and when he had gone the memory of him was powerful enough to make all other men pale into insignificance.

He sighed softly and stared at the flowered wallpaper as though searching deep inside himself to dredge up a reply.

'I already explained to you, Eudoxie. I've been a bachelor most of my life and at my age it's too late to change. This is who I am.'

He spoke in a gentle voice, hoping to impress upon her that she was in no way responsible for this aspect of his character, that she shouldn't feel hurt or disappointed.

'Are all your compatriots as cold as you?'

'I'm not cold. And as for the Japanese, I cannot vouch for their feelings. I left my country a very long time ago!'

'And yet you abide by their superstitions. You don't like the number four and you made me turn my bed round because it was pointing north.'

'One should never sit a woman opposite a doorway.'

'Oh, you and your pretend sayings!' she cried, throwing a pillow at him.

He dodged it, laughing.

'That one's true.'

He drew her towards him.

'Try to enjoy the moment, my dear. Let's be silent. There's never a problem when we're silent.'

She pressed herself to his chest. She was prepared to accept this puzzling side to Kenji, which seemed to insist upon uncertainty. What he did and how he lived his life should not matter, since he always came back to her. She knew him well enough now to know that he needed to feel he was in charge.

'Have you ever been in love, Kenji?'

He looked at her. She wanted him to love her, but since the death of Daphné, love was a language he no longer spoke.

She moved away and studied him through half-closed eyes.

'Our relationship is very pleasurable, Eudoxie. Don't let's spoil it.'

'Forgive me for prying.'

'You weren't to know. I don't want to stir up the past, so let's avoid the subject. I'll see you soon, my darling.'

Colonel de Réauville twirled his whiskers in a gesture of profound satisfaction. Although he only ever read the financial columns of the newspaper and the odd article in *La Revue Illustrée*, the fifteenth-century manuscript he had just acquired would be the pride and joy of his library. He would be able to show it off to the guests who came for coffee, for his new wife had taken it into her head to host an artists' salon at their town house on Rue Barbet-de-Jouy. Paul Déroulède, the founder of the League of Patriots, was one of their guests, as was Édouard Drumont, and the Comtesse de Martel, who wrote charming society novels, along with a group of well-known painters and caricaturists. He thanked Kenji Mori warmly for having snapped up the manuscript from under the noses of the other booksellers and collectors.

I could set up shop with the money he paid for that trifle, Joseph thought as he watched the collectors clustered round the entrance. He recognised the chubby pouting face of the dandy, Boni de Pont-Joubert, and just behind him a heavily built young woman with a pointed nose.

'Goodness me! It's Valentine!'

He felt a sudden stirring of the erotic feelings that the Countess de Salignac's niece had once aroused in him, but to his relief they subsided almost as quickly. Valentine's marriage to that rakish member of the aristocracy had allowed Joseph to fall for a woman who attracted him in other ways. In any event, he felt liberated by the knowledge that Madame de Pont-Joubert was already pregnant.

Joseph followed Kenji and the colonel past sale room number 16, which was reserved for the auction of books that had failed to sell in bookshops. He decided to come back one Friday and study the means by which certain auctioneers managed to raise the reserve on second-rate lots, a practice known as *re-evaluation*, which would be useful to him in his future career as an author-bookseller.

A heavy shower of rain lashed the pavement. A queue of hansom cabs and carriages was blocking Rue Drouot. They climbed into the one belonging to the colonel.

'This problem of traffic jams has to be solved. I don't see why we can't travel by pneumatic tube here in Paris while we're waiting for the underground they've been promising us for the last twenty years,' Kenji remarked.

'Surely, my dear man, you don't mean the ones used to send telegrams!'

'Indeed I do. I'm a man of the future. I read somewhere recently that a company in Hamburg plans to link up with Richen by using the system to ferry passengers at a rate of two kilometres per minute – and why not?'

'Well, you'll forgive me if I stick to my horses,' the Colonel replied brusquely.

He set the manuscript down beside him and began wiping his hands carefully. 'Progress or no, these auction rooms full of filthy clutter are a haven for germs. The best thing would be to disinfect the places and everything in them. The same goes for the whole city, which is becoming like a barnyard with the influx of all these foreigners. Look, there's even one here!' he bawled, his face twisted with hatred.

Out on the pavement, a child of Italian origin, about eight years old, wearing a battered felt hat embroidered with a bouquet of woollen flowers was running in the rain from one passer-by to another.

'Twenty sous for this lovely figurine, Monsieur . . . Cheap at the price, Monsieur . . . Go on; you can have it for fifteen.'

Joseph turned a deep scarlet, and shot a glance at Kenji, who appeared unruffled. The gesture did not escape the colonel's notice.

'Naturally, I was not referring to you, my dear Monsieur Mori. You have nothing in common with these people, who come here to rob us of our daily bread.'

'We must put ourselves in their position,' Kenji replied calmly. 'Man cannot live on caviar alone.'

The carriage wheels ran into the gutter, splashing the legs of the young child, who continued to cry out.

'Please, Monsieur, twenty sous for this lovely figurine. I've got Madonnas and Napoleons too. Look, Monsieur, it's a work of art. Buy it, Monsieur, two for thirty sous . . . Please!'

CHAPTER 7

THE emissary had been waiting for an age at the end of the deserted street, a few yards from a café. Through the steamed up windows he made out the forms of the people leaning against the bar and when a woman opened the door, a blast of animated conversation could be heard, immediately muffled as the door closed. The emissary flattened himself against the wall as the woman muttered, gesticulating wildly. She stood in the middle of the road as if trying to spot him, then burst into raucous laughter and headed in the direction of Gare des Marchandises. The regular passage of the puffing trains stained the pale sky. The emissary resumed his surveillance until a man staggered out on to the pavement and took the same route as the woman. The emissary fell in behind him. The sombre mass of a gasworks loomed up in front of them like the drawing of a fortress by Victor Hugo. The emissary took a gulping breath, managed to steady his breathing and approached the man.

'Léonard Diélette?'

'Yup.'

'Yesterday you took something from Rue Charlot that had been thrown away by mistake.'

'I know that. This morning I told Yvette to go and give back to Caesar what belongs to Caesar.'

'Are you sure?'

'Yes, I'm sure! Of course I'm sure! Don't make out that I'm a liar! We folks are honest, you know. Just because we pick up the cast-offs of the bourgeoisie doesn't mean we don't have morals! I'm an honest pauper. Why, just last year I received an award from the Society for the Encouragement of Good Deeds for returning a banknote I found in a jacket someone had thrown away. It's true. If you don't believe me, come home with me to the Dumathrat quarter and you'll see my certificate.'

'Who's Yvette?'

'My kid. I said to her, that thing must be worth a few bob. Go and drop it off with the owners before you go to work. Honestly, I ask you! All these questions . . .'

'How old is Yvette?'

'Eleven.'

'And you trust her?'

'With my life. She's a chip off the old block.'

'How did you know who to return the thing to?'

'Because of the newspaper it was bundled in – *Nineteenth Century*. Only the people at 28 Rue Charlot read that paper. And I should know, because for three years now the cook has been wrapping up scraps of grub for me in that rag.'

'The problem is, it wasn't returned.'

'Oh, now that's going too far! We're honest and upright, how many times do I have to tell you? We have our dignity, we poor people. I live by the sweat of my brow, I do! Perhaps you should ask your servants. But don't pick a fight with me over it or I'll get angry.'

By this time they were above the railway tracks.

'Did she come home, your daughter?'

'At this hour she should be in bed asleep.'

'We'll go and see, shall we?' said the emissary, putting his hand in his pocket.

'I'm not sure I want to, you . . .'

'Oh, but you do want to, dear fellow. Come on, let's go, otherwise . . . You see this little toy. All I need to do is pull the trigger and there goes Léonard!'

'You're sick!'

Léonard stared, incredulous and open-mouthed, at the weapon pointed at him. His back struck the railing surrounding the station platforms.

'OK, OK, we can go. No problem.'

The emissary shook his head.

'You are the problem.'

The emissary launched himself forwards and the gun slipped from his grasp. His gloved hands shoved the rag-and-bone man violently in the chest.

Léonard Diélette, panic in his eyes, his hair in disarray, toppled over the railings. Tumbling backwards, he rolled all the way down the hill to the railway line at the bottom.

His piercing cry was drowned by the whistling of a locomotive. The emissary turned, and a spindly shadow disappeared round the corner of the gasworks.

A sooty sky hung over the wasteland dotted with hovels just outside the Barrière des Deux-Moulins.[1] Joseph, exhausted and on edge after his afternoon wasted in the company of that old military buffoon Réauville, stopped for a moment. He had not been able to persuade a cabby to take him to the rag-and-bone man's village, so he had walked from Gare d'Orléans.[2] Faced with the cluster of shacks shrouded in fog, he felt reluctant to venture into what looked like a very rough area.

'Shall I or shan't I? It looks worse than the jungle of Montmartre. I shan't go in.'

As he retraced his route, he remembered Iris's whispered words on his return from Avenue Foch: 'Be careful.' How did she know about his secret mission? Had Monsieur Legris confided in her? Or was she referring to the conversation he was supposed to have with her father, but was avoiding. Still feeling uncertain, he took the bull by the horns and plunged into the Cité Doré.

This pompous appellation did not refer to hidden riches invisible to the naked eye. It was simply the name of a previous occupant of the land, Monsieur Doré, a chemist who had decided to divide his property into little plots furnished with rudimentary buildings, in order to supplement his monthly income.

The houses, initially rented by workmen, had slowly fallen into disrepair, and rag-and-bone men, attracted by the low rent and the little parcels of adjoining land, had moved in. They were soon followed by groups of down-and-outs who had built huts made of planks, tarpaulins and tin plate rusted by the rain. This collection of rickety mansions had five avenues and two squares. It was the kingdom of detritus.

Had he arrived in daylight, Joseph might have enjoyed the bucolic flavour of the little courtyards overrun with convolvulus and clematis. And he would have appreciated the calm of the quarter, where fights were rare. But in the dusk, barely alleviated by the faltering gas lamps, he advanced cautiously.

Through doors left open to let the smoke escape, he made out large families sitting on the ground around cooking pots of scraps. There were not many men. Most of them were already doing their rounds, their baskets on their backs, a lantern in one hand and a gaff in the other. On the packed earth floors, next to piles of rubbish to be sorted, bundles of hay served as mattresses.

Joseph approached a silhouette outlined against the yellow square of a window. A man was puffing on a pipe, removing it regularly from his mouth to spit.

'Good evening, I'm looking for Léonard Diélette.'

'Can't help you; I only arrived yesterday. Hang on, I'll ask my brother.'

The shack was one of the more luxurious dwellings. It was furnished with a table, chairs, a lamp and two sprung mattresses, and housed a couple and four little boys who were enjoying a pot of stew.

'Raymond, does the name Diélette mean anything to you?'

'Yes. Just past the Dumathrat crossroads. You're after him, are you? Have a quick drink with us and I'll take you over there,' said the father. 'Are you a wholesaler?'

'Uh, yes,' replied Joseph.

'Perhaps we can do some business together. I have a pile of old boots from an army depot, only left feet – any use to you?'

'I'd have to see them.'

The man freed up a chair by chasing away one of the brats with a flick of his hand while the mother collected the plates. Much to Joseph's consternation, three glasses were filled with red wine. He had no head for alcohol.

'Your health, M'sieur, and to you Estève. Hey! Not so fast, it kills the bouquet,' scolded Raymond.

'Bah! It still perks me up on its way down.'

The brothers, both with red thatches of hair, tossed back their wine and stared at Joseph, who was reluctant to swallow what to him was paint stripper.

'Come on, lad, drink – it'll warm your cockles.'

Joseph downed the liquid in one, just as he had gulped down the cod-liver oil his mother had forced him to take as a boy. A purple veil descended between him and the two fellows, but when it cleared he felt filled with renewed vigour. He stood up. The room swayed and he had to sit down again.

'You're rag-and-bone men?' he asked, hoping to win himself a reprieve.

'No, lad, you see before you a mason. I can't keep count of the shacks I've built. Estève came to lend a hand. I'm overworked; I have to do everything around here. Not only am I the vulture who collects all the rents, but I'm also notary, lawyer and justice of the peace. When trouble flares, it's me who has to sort it out and it's me who distributes the legacies when someone dies. I divvy up the scrap iron for those that'll sell them on to the founder; the old bones go to those who deal with the makers of glue, manure or buttons; and the lint is coveted by the paper makers so I hand it out accordingly!'

Estève, fired up by the alcohol, began to declaim:

> *'In the kingdom of the gaff*
> *The rag-and-bone man rules alone*
> *In the kingdom of rubbish*
> *The rag and bone man rules supreme*
> *O knight of the lamp*
> *O knight of the gaff'*

'Belt up!' Raymond bellowed. 'Finish your drink. We're going with the man. I'm going to drag the rent out of that gypsy.'

They crossed Cité Doré. Joseph imagined that he was venturing into a village of huts in the depths of the unexplored African bush. Was that an elephant trumpeting in the distance, near the Gare d'Orléans? Perhaps it was just the harrowing cry of the locomotives. At the end of Passage Doré, they stopped before a cabin with one miniscule window.

'Here you go – Père Diélette's palace. We'll be over there.'

Joseph knocked, but in vain; no one opened the door to him. Perhaps the rag-and-bone man was asleep. Shouting broke out behind him. He swung round. The two brothers were preparing to demolish the door of one of the wretched little houses, paying no heed to the tears and imprecations poured out by a woman wrapped in pitiful rags.

'It's so cold. I'll die!'

'I warned you, old witch. If you haven't coughed up by tomorrow, we'll take the roof off and if that doesn't make you pay, we'll set your shack on fire!'

'Vultures!'

Falling to her knees, the woman tried to cling to Raymond's legs. He freed himself vigorously, and she toppled into a puddle. Outraged, Joseph hurried over to help the woman to her feet.

'You should be ashamed!' he cried.

'The world's gone mad! You hear that, Estève? Now it's the debtors who're the victims!'

'How much does this unfortunate woman owe you?'

'Two francs fifty.'

Joseph dug in his pocket, gathered up his change and shoved it furiously at the redhead.

As the brothers were leaving, the woman dissolved into profuse thanks and invited her saviour in for a drink.

She lit an oil lamp, revealing an angular face framed by greying hair. Her hut was six feet square and furnished with crates.

'Have a seat and make yourself at home, M'sieur. Fancy a homemade *ratafia*? Sugar and potato liquor. Chin-chin!'

Against his better judgement, Joseph took a sip of the vinegary alcohol and put his glass down. The woman sighed.

'I like it here so much. I look out on the countryside – in summer it's full of poppies. Yes indeed, it's a haven, so it is . . . This week's been dreadful, not a single client. It would have killed me to have to sleep in the open, especially after today's troubles.'

'Uh . . . What is it you do?' asked Joseph, backing towards his escape route.

'Tarot cards, the lines on your hand, anything to do with the future! I can see things for other people, but when it comes to me, darned if I'm not blind. Stupid, isn't it? I didn't even introduce myself: Coralie Blinde.'

'Do you know Léonard Diélette?'

She threw him a sidelong look.

'He didn't come home. Neither did his kid. I fed Clampin, that's his donkey. I think they went off tearing down posters.'

'Why?'

'There have been elections. After the polls, you're allowed to collect the posters stuck up on the railings and tree trunks. Most of the rag-and-bone men want the radical-socialist-irreconcilable candidate. When you're the lowest of the low, you just want to be a thorn in the side of the bigwigs who govern. But, when it comes to collecting the posters, you don't care what colour they are; in fact the white ones sell better than the red ones.'

Disconcerted, Joseph went to leave, but Coralie grabbed him by the sleeve.

'Sibylla can read your hand like an open book. There's no better gift I can give you than a vision of the future.'

Joseph recoiled. For a while now he had been suspicious of clairvoyants.

'Don't you worry! Give us your left hand, the one nearest your heart. Let's see, first your life line . . . very strong! You'll live to see the first half of the twentieth century! Oh yes, and the head line shows that you're intelligent, skilled, hard-working and stubborn. You will achieve your goals, cos your fate line goes straight up to the mount of Saturn . . . You're blessed by Venus, cos the heart line is good, very good. You'll be lucky in love, no matter that you're a hunchback.'

'You can see that?'

'Engraved on your palm.'

'What about the immediate future?'

A look of fear crossed Coralie Blinde's face so fleetingly that Joseph did not notice.

'I see . . . I see . . . a train. Whistling and bellowing . . . its red eye winking in the gloom . . . I see . . . a man going on a long journey . . . Light, light, light as a feather, he flies over the rails . . . I see . . . I see . . . I can't see any more.'

Gee! I hope she doesn't mean I'm going right now – the Bosses wouldn't be happy; I'm indispensable. But when I'm a famous writer I might take a round-the-world tour with Iris like Phileas Fogg. Why not?

Crouched beyond the grimy window, the emissary waited impatiently for the prophetess to finish uttering her predictions to the gullible fool standing opposite her in the entrance to her hovel. He flushed with anger suddenly. Why was that joker wasting his time hanging about the door to the rag-and-bone man's house? He had not ventured out to this hole to have his future told.

I must know! The emissary clenched his fists. No one would stand in his way, no one!

Finally, he saw the bloke leave and the drunken sot shut the door. The emissary slipped out of Léonard Diélette's shack and followed Joseph. His pale face, bathed in sweat, expressed intense rage.

'Dirty kid, dirty little brat, she'll have to come home

eventually. As for that palm reader, I'm not going to let her out of my sight.'

Yvette had laid her arm on the donkey's neck. Her darned jacket offered little protection from the cold. A hint of weariness was evident in her posture, giving her the appearance of a woman-child gripped by worries beyond her years.

Victor pushed the photo to one side. What should the caption be? *Bewilderment? Distrust?* Finally he wrote on the back of the print: *Little pin-seller with her lame protector. April . . .'*

The telephone rang and he jumped, making an ink blot. He cursed and went to answer the phone, finishing off the caption with the receiver tucked under his ear.

. . . 1892, Yvette was only eleven when . . .

'Yes, Joseph . . . Yes, I heard you . . . Yes, you've rung to tell me the rag-and-bone man lives in Cité Doré. I knew that already . . . I didn't tell you because I had no idea it could have anything to do with . . . Well done. Thanks for ringing . . . Tomorrow morning? . . . Good, that's agreed then.'

He hung up, deep in thought, shrugged on his coat, turned off the lamp and crossed the courtyard.

As he pushed open the door of the studio, Tasha was finishing making up a parcel. He embraced her and gave her a kiss, then stared at her enquiringly.

'What's that?' he asked, indicating the parcel.

'Oh that, just some clothes for a friend.'

'Have you forgotten? We're going out for dinner. I booked a table at . . .'

'Bother, it completely slipped my mind! I'm all over the place at the moment. That exhibition in Barbizon is weighing on me.'

'When are you leaving?'

He was trying to sound nonchalant, but his question burst out abruptly.

'You know when. Tomorrow. I'll be back on Saturday evening. Oh, darling, you look just like a painting by that artist who always paints lowering skies and imminent storms in shades of black and dark green.'

'I don't know anything about painting – who are you talking about?'

'El Greco.'

'Oh, thanks for that – those famous religious scenes of suffering.'

She burst out laughing.

'But that's what you look like: sullen, sulky and suspicious.'

'Oversensitive, too sentimental, madly in love and jealous, you mean! Horrid woman. You know I'm paranoid; I'm always worried I'm not good enough for you.'

'How can you even think that? I would never be able to love another man.'

'Really?'

'Yes, really, because I know that no other man would give me the freedom you do.'

'That's the only reason you love me?'

'Don't be ridiculous – you're the man I want to spend the rest of my life with.'

'Then marry me.'

'I love you far too much to let you make that mistake. Why is marriage so important to you? What would being officially united by a civil servant add to our relationship? If I became Madame Legris, people would pity you. They'd say, "That poor Monsieur Legris. His wife is a loose woman: she paints and hangs out with libertines." You would hate that, I know you would. Being your mistress is much more moral in the eyes of society. It's accepted that a man sleeps with a woman like me, but as for marrying her . . .'

'I don't give a toss what polite society thinks . . .'

'Really? Why don't we stay in tonight? I'll fetch your slippers, we'll read the papers and sit by the fire chatting. What do you say to that foretaste of marriage?'

'I'd say that nothing is certain in this world except what we're about to do now,' he whispered, pulling her over to the bed.

CHAPTER 8

THE fog engulfing Paris was beginning to dissipate; the afternoon would be cold but fine. Victor had decided to walk, hoping it would help him to order his thoughts, which were more confused than ever, now that Joseph had been back to Cité Doré very early that morning and knocked on Léonard Diélette's closed door. Finding he was still not home, Joseph had set off to look for the rag-and-bone man, wandering through a labyrinth of paths bordered by sordid dwellings, and asking the residents if they knew anything. But no one had seen Diélette or his daughter. And as for Coralie Blinde, Joseph was informed by her neighbour, a porcelain mender, that she was taking Clampin for a walk over by the gasworks. Joseph had given up and left.

What had become of the rag-and-bone man? That was one of the things Victor was puzzling over. He hoped nothing had happened to the child . . . As he approached Rue Montmartre, he reflected that the goblet was disastrous for anyone unlucky enough to encounter it.

His satchel containing his photographic equipment was growing heavy, so he stopped near the chevet of Église Saint-Eustache. On the horizon, over the roofs of Les Halles, the Tour Saint-Jacques rose up like a sentry lying in wait for devils to appear from the city's thoroughfares. Victor imagined one of them prowling in his wake and even thought he could make out its evil cackling in the neighing of a horse.

He made his way along the pavements, past the hawkers and loafers. His pulse quickened. There, that little person with her back to him, showing off her wares to the passers-by, wasn't that Yvette? He touched her shoulder and immediately realised his mistake when he saw the shrivelled face of a deformed old woman.

'A ribbon, Monsieur?'

He shook his head, slipping on a lettuce leaf at the entrance of a soup kitchen where a cook, a towel round his neck, was laughing raucously. Like a man shipwrecked, clinging to a lifeline, Victor took refuge inside an automated bar at number 32. The barman, perched on a ladder, was offering customers in a hurry the chance to use the new fountains, which would revolutionise French society. Counters mounted on double rows of stacked casks ran down each side of the room, displaying a choice of French beers, punch and Malaga wine. All you had to do was position your glass under a tap, put a coin in the slot and your drink would be dispensed.

'Just ten centimes for half a pint! And they never overflow, do you hear that, Monsieur? Ne-ver. Our machines function like clockwork; the mechanism in the money box responds immediately to each request! And don't go thinking that there are goblins hidden in the barrels busy working the levers! No, Monsieur, it's scientific. However, your glass will not wash itself; it needs the beautiful white hands of Mademoiselle Prudence. So reflect on that as you reach for your tip! Come on, Monsieur, give it a go – it won't bite!'

This was addressed to Victor, who was caught at the

counter. Ignoring the reddish face of the fast-talking bartender, he accosted Mademoiselle Prudence, who looked at him with as much interest as if he too were a machine.

'Madame . . . Mademoiselle, would you by any chance have noticed a little girl of ten or eleven? She sells pins near your bar?'

'Dunno, maybe.'

Indolently she pocketed Victor's twenty sous.

'When did you see her last? It's really important.'

She looked him up and down, suddenly attentive, and he wondered if the coin had set in motion Broca's Area, said to be the part of the brain controlling speech.

'You wouldn't be one of those bastards who picks up kids from the street and screws them?' the women asked him in a shrill voice.

Victor reddened furiously.

'Now hang on a minute, Mademoiselle . . .'

'Well, you're not exactly her father, are you?'

'What's going on, Prudence?' bellowed the bartender.

'This here bloke's after Yvette.'

'Yvette? She was taken off to the police station yesterday evening.'

'Which police station?'

'Oh, she won't still be there. She'll have been taken to the cells by now.'

'Thanks!'

Victor raised his hat and slipped out.

'He comes in, drinks nothing, picks our brains and then leaves,' grumbled the bartender in disgust.

*

The emissary had leant his bicycle against the wall, near the packaging shop. He was crouching down, pretending to check his chain, his gaze fixed on the Elzévir bookshop. The Japanese man had just left and the chap he'd seen the day before in the Dumathrat quarter was reading the paper behind the counter. That morning he had left his home on Rue Visconti and returned to Cité Doré before going to work.

'Do you need any help?'

The emissary jumped, and, fiddling with his pedal, replied, 'No thanks, I'm fine.'

A pair of black ankle boots topped by plump calves, the hem of a tartan cape and a purple overcoat had stopped a little way from his bicycle.

'Dearest, it's no use – you'll never convince me!' cried a female voice. 'They're nothing but trouble.'

'Yes, but Raphaëlle, times change – sixty years ago it would have been out of the question for our grandparents even to think about sitting astride two wheels. Now, I tell you, it's the only way forward. Soon absolutely everyone will be going about on bicycles. Don't you agree, Mathilde?'

'Helga's right. Walking will go out of fashion. Take it from us: soon humanity will crave speed.'

The emissary shrank down. Would these three bluestockings never move on?

Finally the boots walked away, followed by the cape and the overcoat. The emissary leaned forwards slightly and watched the three ladies enter the bookshop. The assistant greeted them, went over to a bookshelf, pulled out several volumes and handed them to the ladies before hurrying over to a desk with a telephone on it. He picked up the receiver. After a minute he hung up and ran upstairs. When he came down again, he had a young girl with him who went over to the customers. The assistant put on his jacket and cap and ran from the bookshop towards Quai Malaquais. The emissary barely had time to scramble into his saddle.

Victor pushed the telephone away and considered the photo of Yvette. It was imperative that Joseph succeed in getting her released from the police cells!

Once he'd left the automated bar, he had thought about Mademoiselle Prudence's lewd comment, and by the time he reached Les Halles, he'd realised he could not just turn up at Quai de l'Horloge[1] and demand Yvette's release without the necessary papers. What should he do? He had made his way amongst the mountains of potatoes, towers of pumpkins and mounds of carrots, turnips and cabbages and found himself at the spot where servants waited to be hired. There they were, twenty or so humble girls sitting or standing around, patiently waiting for a new master or mistress. Poor little atoms lost in this ocean of food, a stone's throw from the immense Pavillon de la Marée, the fish market, where thousands of aquatic creatures lay piled up, lifeless, on marble slabs. And suddenly he remembered the little tortoise and that brought to mind the lanky silhouette of Raoul Pérot.

It was a brilliant idea! He would send Joseph to enquire after the health of Nanette and the inspector's literary projects, and at the same time obtain a duly signed release document for Yvette.

As soon as he had arrived back at Rue Fontaine, he had

telephoned Joseph and given him his instructions.

He consulted his watch. Joseph and Yvette would not be there until four o'clock at the earliest. Unable to concentrate on anything, he crossed the courtyard to the studio. It was his favourite room, the room that harboured Tasha's universe, where each object, each knick-knack, each piece of furniture was redolent of her. It was the room where they made love, discussed their innermost thoughts and made plans. It was here that they were intimate together and where she belonged only to him. The familiar odour of turpentine mixed with *benjoin* perfume hung in the air. He relived their embrace of the previous evening and smiled. He loved the disarray that pervaded the space. He followed the trail of underwear and frames over to the alcove with its unmade bed. With the flat of his hand he caressed the rumpled sheets he had left regretfully a few hours earlier while she was still deeply asleep. He always desired her more in the morning than in the evening.

He could not help picking up the bodice and drawers balled up on the floor and straightening the pillows. As he was putting them in place a piece of paper fluttered to the floor. It was a letter. Without meaning to, he read a sentence written in a round hand:

> . . . *I can't wait to hold you in my arms. After Berlin, where everything was disciplined, regimented and orderly, I dream of sitting with you at a café table on the terrace of a brasserie* . . .

Mechanically he slipped the missive into the pillowcase. For a moment his body continued to obey his brain's instructions: fold this camisole, throw away that piece of bread and wash those glasses. But in the midst of doing those things, grief hit him. He stood frozen, his hand suspended over the stone sink.

The horse was toiling up the crowded Rue des Pyrenées when it was forced to make way for a herd of cows.

'Quickly, quickly,' Tasha chanted, leaning out of the carriage door.

Her impatience had been building over the hours spent closeted at work with her editor. The horse turned down Rue des Partants, passed Hôpital Tenon and went back up Rue de la Chine. This was where Haussman's remodelling of Paris stopped and they entered the city of Eugène Sue. Among the labyrinth of tortuous streets with exotic names, interspersed with courtyards where bare lilacs sprouted up the grey walls, misery hid its wounds.

The horse pursued its ascent with difficulty and stopped in front of a shady hotel.

HÔTEL DE PÉKIN
Furnished Accommodation
Rooms by the Month or by Day

Tasha jumped nimbly from the cab and paid the sullen driver. As she passed through the hall, she held her breath, just like the last time, against the pungent smell of cabbage. Her cheery 'Bonjour' was not enough to raise a smile from the stout woman with the hairy chin presiding over reception.

'He's up there. He hasn't been out all day,' she snapped before Tasha could ask.

She climbed to the third floor, carrying her package, and had scarcely scratched on the door when it opened, and the arms of the man who had impatiently awaited her arrival also opened. She hugged him, happy to feel fragile under the pressure of his palms. She forgot the difficult times, the philandering, and the doubts. The man swung the door shut with his foot. Down below, the harridan raised her eyes heavenwards.

'What a dump! If this continues, I may as well open a brothel!'

Inspector Joseph Pignot marched through the steel door of the police cells, greeted the man on the desk and found himself in a vast gothic hall with imitation marble columns supporting a free stone arch. Opposite him were the glass-fronted offices of the police sergeants and inspectors. To the right was the office where the prisoners were searched. And beyond some fixed glass partitions he could just make out meshed-in walkways.

Inspector Joseph Pignot went resolutely forward, ready to come face to face with crooks, pickpockets and hussies fresh from the police vehicles. Perhaps the mysterious assassin who was terrorising Paris was among them? But of all the individuals he passed, none bore a resemblance to the description provided by witnesses. An old, surly-looking employee started when he tapped him on the shoulder . . .

At that moment a man's voice rang out.

'Move aside!'

Joseph was obliged to abandon the novel he had promised himself to begin, and, much excited at having penetrated the Great Prison, proffered his letter to the man, who was as dried up and twisted as an old vine branch.

'You're mistaken, young man, I'm only visiting,' he quavered, his hand cupped round his ear.

'Get on with it, old man, over there!' shouted an official in grey uniform.

'No need to yell – I'm not deaf!'

Joseph was relegated to the end of a dingy corridor where he watched the officials and municipal guards as they went through the performance of putting the suspects arrested the previous evening through their anthropometric paces. Their physical characteristics and measurements were noted. Joseph, avid for information with which to embellish his new serial, stationed himself a few yards further up the corridor. He saw a new arrival get down from the police vehicle and disappear into a vast room. The door closed. Frustrated, Joseph went and sat down.

'What's going on in there?' he asked a laundress who had come hoping to see her husband, who'd been picked up dead drunk in the street.

'They're lining them up, like in the army. They're noting their names and taking everything they have on them in exchange for a numbered token. Then they're given a bran loaf, a whole one if it's in the morning.'

'And if it isn't morning?'

'Only half a loaf. But they don't care; they get a place to

sleep and that's as good as dinner. Mind you, even the sleeping's not great. If you can afford it, you pay forty centimes to rent some sheets, otherwise you have to bide your time for four days before you're entitled to any. That doesn't bother my man – we took our sheets to the pawnshop ages ago. Next they give all their details to the clerk: name and surname, place of birth, name of father, mother . . . Luckily they don't have to go back to the time of Methuselah! All those niceties just to end up in the slammer. Talk about justice! Don't look at me like that, Monsieur, it's as I say, and I speak as I find.'

'Go on,' murmured Joseph, who was surreptitiously taking notes.

'OK, so the reception committee is responsible for settling them in.'

'Reception committee?'

'The guards and good sisters of Marie-Joseph. They divide them in groups. Some go into cells, others into the communal area. Oh! My turn now, about time too! I won't say see you soon, Monsieur – that'll bring bad luck.'

The wait was interminable. Joseph, marooned on his bench, thought back to his visit to Raoul Pérot, whose cramped office, with its waxed parquet floor, thick green curtains and glass-fronted bookcase stuffed with books, was more reminiscent of a reading room than a police station. The inspector had been leafing through *Gil Blas*. He dreamt of one day contributing to the magazine. He had shaken Joseph warmly by the hand and asked him about the aftermath of the break-in. After dashing off the letter to the prison, he had hurried to turn the conversation to the only subject that gripped him: literature. Nanette, the tortoise, indifferent to this topic, nibbled her lettuce.

'So, young man, today or tomorrow?'

Joseph almost toppled off the bench. He held the envelope out to the plain-clothes policeman who read the missive through twice before folding it up and remarking drily:

'I'll fetch her for you since she's a capital witness.'

After quarter of an hour, he returned, leading a skinny little girl whom he held firmly by the wrist.

'Here you are; your capital witness. Since she's a minor and you're not family, I have to take your name and address,' said the *flic*, taking out a notebook. 'Here, take your basket, and no more illicit trading!'

As he took hold of Yvette's frozen hand, Joseph had to fight against a flood of pity that threatened to bring tears to his eyes. He took hold of himself. Now he was Jean Valjean snatching Cosette from the jaws of misfortune, and, proud of his responsibility, he led the child to Quai de l'Horloge.

'You're free.'

Disconcerted, Yvette stammered, 'Did . . . did Papa send you?'

She blinked, blinded by the light, nervously clutching the front of her overcoat. Joseph thought of his two visits to Cité Doré. It would be better not to tell the little girl that her father was missing.

'No, it was my boss, Monsieur Legris. You know him – he took your photograph.'

'Oh yes, the gentleman with the beautiful box. He's nice. I was so frightened in there! They treated me like a criminal. I begged them to let me go because Papa would be so worried.

They forced me into a vehicle with wicked-looking men and women . . . like Mère Cloporte who picks up men on the boulevard. I spent the night in the dormitory. I was so cold. A big girl wanted me to sleep with her so that we would be warm, but I didn't want to, so she pulled my hair and said rude words to me. I wanted to die.'

She was racked by a brief sob, but did not break down in tears. Joseph on the other hand, discreetly wiped his eyes and murmured, 'The filthy beasts! Do you go to school?'

'You mustn't think that going to school makes you behave well! You know, the big girl who they took away with me, she stole from her boss. I would never steal; we have our standards.'

'So you don't know how to read or write?'

'I know how to read a little. Papa has books at home. It's stupid, you know, I was caught for a sou. The lady didn't even want the pins she paid me for. A *flic* saw everything and that was that! If I'd known, I would have refused the sou.'

Joseph helped the child into a carriage.

'I'll take you to Monsieur Legris and Mademoiselle Tasha. You'll be able to rest and eat. You'll see. They'll look after you. The law is ridiculous sometimes.'

Breathe deeply and think, above all, think. Victor had finally calmed down. It was not the first time he had suspected Tasha. And his penchant for suspicion had always, until now, led him astray. None of the men she spent time with had turned out to be rivals. Tasha loved him, he was sure of that. So, if a foreign friend had turned up in Paris, what would be more natural than that she should hide his letter to avoid one of Victor's fits of jealousy?

Yes, but had she really wanted to hide the letter she would have chosen a better place than the pillowcase of the bed in which they frolicked.

By the time Joseph knocked, Victor had talked himself round again and he was able to greet Yvette with a smile.

'Delighted to see you again, Mademoiselle. Joseph, can you go back to Rue des Saints-Pères and tell Kenji that I'll soon be there and that I'll need your services? Thank you for all your efforts; you've completed the operation brilliantly.'

'That's what I'm here for! The kid is frozen and exhausted. The law is a very blunt instrument, Boss. A blind tool that sweeps up the homeless, the old, kids, thieves and murderers and muddles them in together! . . . Is Mademoiselle Tasha not here?'

'No, she's in . . . Barbizon.'

Once again a terrible doubt assailed Victor. What if she wasn't in Barbizon? What if she had invented the story about the exhibition so she could rendezvous with another man? How would he know? A name came to mind, a hated name, but he would have to overlook that. Tomorrow he would go and have a chat with Maurice Laumier.

Joseph's departure brought him back to earth.

'Are you hungry?' he asked Yvette.

'Um . . . Yes, Monsieur.'

'The bathroom is on the left; you can wash your face,' he said with forced gaiety.

She did not move.

'And comb your hair as well.'

Amazed by the toiletries laid out on the dressing table, she dared not touch anything. Victor went to heat up the fricassee of rabbit prepared with loving care by Euphrosine. He pulled the pedestal table over to the stove and cleared away a stack of pallets to lay a place setting. Yvette stood at the entrance to the studio.

'It's beautiful! Just like the engraving of the confectionary shop in Rue de Bretagne,' she enthused.

'Take a seat.'

She sat down on the edge of the chair opposite the steaming plate, but did not start to eat. Victor moved away, pretending to sort through some sketches, while observing her. She was chewing with a sort of fervour, exactly like those poor wretches in soup kitchens, who swallow everything in sight because they can't take anything away with them.

'Would you like some more meat?'

'Yes, please!'

He went to fetch the photo he had taken of her and showed it to her.

'That's me . . . How strange to see my face on a piece of paper. Is it difficult to make?'

'I'll explain how you do it.'

'But . . . Papa will be worrying about me.'

Her voice faltered and she gave Victor a frightened look.

What should one say to a girl of her age? He had no idea. She seemed worried.

'He might give me a smack,' she murmured.

'Why? It was the police who . . .'

'Oh, not because of that! No, yesterday while he was looking through his harvest, Papa noticed a sort of bowl that had been foisted on us in Rue Charlot.'

'A bowl? What sort of bowl?'

In reply she gave him a wide-eyed look that only increased his unease. Finally the little girl spoke.

'A bowl with precious stones on it. I didn't do anything bad, I just . . . Papa said, "By gad, that's worth its weight in gold! We can't keep that, it would be dishonest." So he told me to take it back to Mademoiselle Bertille before I went to Rue Montmartre. But I . . . I was desperate to buy some sweets. I wanted those big pink and green caramels they sell in jars near Les Halles. I thought no one would know, since they'd thrown the bowl away, so I . . . I sold it.'

Victor leant over and stared at her intently.

'And you sold it to?'

Yvette's terror appalled him because it awakened in him the memory of his stern father. She bit her lips in consternation.

'Please don't scold me! If anyone finds out what I did, I'll go to prison for good. I don't want to, I don't want to!'

Victor felt his irritation grow. He controlled himself.

'Thank you for telling me the truth. Listen, someone threw that . . . that bowl away by mistake and its owner wants it back. No one knows you sold it. If you tell me who has it, I can sort everything out. Do you understand?'

'And you won't tell, ever? Even Papa?'

'I swear.'

'I gave it to a trader who sometimes buys old things from Papa. He's called Clovis Martel. He lives at 127 Rue

Mouffetard. He only paid me twenty sous, because he said it was just a piece of junk.'

'Right, I'll make a phone call, then we'll go to my place of work and my sister will look after you. She's very kind, but she's also inquisitive, and so is her father. He's a Japanese gentleman and he doesn't say much. We'll tell them your father has had a little accident and that he's in hospital. All right?'

'All right, but that's odd. If this Japanese gentleman is your sister's father, he's also your father and you're not Japanese.'

Victor stood up and cleared his throat. He would not be sorry to see the back of the child.

'Our family is a bit complicated. Just a minute, I'll put my coat on.'

As soon as they were in the courtyard, Victor lit a cigar and inhaled deeply. One should never underestimate the candour of children. They could turn anything you said against you. Admittedly they were easy prey for unscrupulous individuals, but their chatter was enough to upset the most balanced adult. He fleetingly pictured Tasha breastfeeding a bouncing baby.

'Not for a long while yet,' he prayed.

The emissary realised that if he went on criss-crossing Rue Fontaine, people would guess what he was up to. It had been a good hour since the assistant had returned with the kid – with whom had he left her?

He went in under the porch of number 36a and leant his bicycle against a water pump encrusted with bird droppings, pretending again to check his chain.

Footsteps rang out on the cobbles of the courtyard. Turning to the left, the emissary could see the window of a low house with a pitched roof, probably the studio of a painter or sculptor. A man went in. Two figures were silhouetted against the door: a little one and a much larger one. The larger one said, 'Come on, Yvette, let's go.'

The emissary smiled.

The man and the little girl reached Rue Fontaine. The emissary immediately stood up, mounted his bike and went after them.

CHAPTER 9

Iris was sitting back in an armchair, her feet resting on a pouffe, carefully embroidering a table runner with the intention of winning over Euphrosine. After much hesitation, she had plumped for a spray of larger-than-life flowers, which, even if they could not be found in a botanical guide, promised to look very decorative in coral and saffron thread. She heard the apartment door open. Much to her surprise, Victor came in with a small girl whom he introduced as the daughter of a rag-and-bone man who was in hospital.

'The poor child has no one else in the world. I was wondering, as Tasha isn't here, whether you might look after her until her father comes out?'

'I'd be only too happy! Where are her things?'

'I'm afraid she has no other clothes.'

'Yes I do,' Yvette corrected. 'The ones the women from the charity gave me. They're at home.'

'I can take up one of my dresses for you. But first of all you must have a snack. Do you like fruit cake? And what about barley water? Would you like some marzipan? Perhaps you'd like to have a bath?'

Struck dumb by this torrent of questions, Yvette allowed herself to be led away into the kitchen, much to the relief of Victor, who went down to the bookshop.

'Any orders?'

Joseph, red-faced with his hair on end, was battling with a piece of brown paper and a roll of string as he attempted to make up three parcels of books. Victor could tell by the look of irritation on his face and the accompanying heart-rending sighs that it had been a busy day.

'Where is Monsieur Mori?'

'At the tailor's having some alterations done,' Jojo grumbled.

Victor told him about Yvette, and asked whether he would back him up.

'OK, so the story is that her father's in hospital. It's good to know you trust me . . . Damn this string!'

'Give me those scissors. I'll let you off this chore and the deliveries can wait until tomorrow. I need you to go and ask after Léonard Diélette.'

Joseph rushed out before Victor could change his mind.

The cabman was nodding off, filled with a sense of well-being. This fare was a godsend. Two hours paid up front just to sit there in Rue des Saints-Pères doing nothing – the only inconvenience had been fitting the bicycle in the back, but a tip had taken care of that little problem.

The emissary, his face pressed up against the window of the cab door, was wondering how long this game of hunt-the-thimble would continue. The handle bars were digging sharply into his ribs, but he didn't mind. What should he do next? Follow the assistant or lie in wait outside the house containing the link in the chain that would lead him to the abomination? If the associate was sheltering the brat, it was because he was on to something.

If I follow the assistant, I risk losing sight of the associate, he thought to himself. What if it's a trap? What if he knows he's being watched and is creating a diversion? He can't fool me! It'll take more than that to shake me off.

Coralie Blinde was next to her shack, cooking offal in a casserole over a small fire. To complement her feast she was baking a potato in the embers – the height of luxury. Clampin the donkey searched the stony ground dolefully with his muzzle, unable to find the hoped for juicy thistles. A half-naked toddler cried out as he lurched forwards on unsteady legs, and was quickly snatched up by his sister who moistened a corner of her skirt with spittle and wiped the grime from his cheeks. The two of them stood transfixed beside the bubbling stew, sniffing its delicious aroma.

As soon as Joseph arrived, they ran away. Coralie Blinde stood between him and the pot, arms crossed in a gesture of defiance, as though protecting her dinner.

'Oh, it's you again!'

'Those children look starving. Call them back and I'll give them a coin.'

'Don't waste your money on those vultures. They stare at you with those big round eyes as if butter wouldn't melt in their mouths, but they don't take me in – I'm not stupid. Their parents should work for a living, but instead they sit all day and watch the world go by, then gaze at the stars all night.'

'You were glad enough of my help yesterday.'

Coralie Blinde pursed her lips, snapped a few twigs and stoked the fire.

'Don't mind me. I'm in a bad mood today. There I was, strolling down Boulevard de l'Hôpital, minding my own business, when Mère Cloporte, a madam who's as fat as a pig and stinks like one too, called me a bag of bones and said I was scaring away the punters. I'm an honest woman, I am. I sell the future, not my body! Go on, show me your palm, it'll only cost you ten sous.'

'No thank you. Once was enough. Have you seen Léonard Diélette?'

'He's vanished into thin air, same goes for his brat.'

She leant forward and whispered in his ear. 'I noticed this morning that someone's been inside their house, so I padlocked their door just in case . . . I don't want any trouble. I've enough problems of my own.'

'Give me the key and I'll go and have a look.'

'What's more, that padlock's new and I'll want reimbursing.'

'Will twenty sous do?'

'Twenty-five with the key.'

A tornado had swept through the single room. A foul-smelling tide of rotting wood, bones, iron, cardboard, cloth and papers had submerged a rickety table, two seaweed mattresses, a horse blanket and a chest of clothes. Joseph's heart sank as he picked his way through the stinking mess without success: there was not a trace of the jewelled goblet. He mouthed the words to a poem he had recently learnt.

> *A king of Thule of old*
> *Was giv'n by his lover*
> *In true memory of her*
> *A chalice of polish'd gold[1]*

Thule's Golden Chalice! That would be the title of his next novel! Thrilled at this unexpected visit by the muse of inspiration, he forgot all about his agreement with Coralie Blinde and handed the key back to her. She waited until he was some way off before calling after him.

'A long journey, a very long journey, one from which there's no return!'

'It's late Madame la Comtesse. We're closing . . .'

'Monsieur Legris,' announced Olympe de Salignac, 'I have no intention of leaving without a copy of *Mortal Loves* by Maxime Fromont and *The Girls of Écouen* by Mary Summer. Contrary to Monsieur Pierre Loti, who admitted during his reception speech to the Académie Française that owing to mental inertia he never reads, *we* are interested in literature.'

Victor made an evasive gesture.

'I'm afraid we only have biographies and novels by acclaimed authors.'

'But, my dear man, Maxime Fromont and Mary Summer are highly esteemed novelists.'

'In that case I shall order them for you.'

'Nonsense, I no longer believe in your promises!'

The door chime rang. Joseph entered, frowning, and shook a newspaper at Victor, who ignored him as he desperately tried to think of a suitably trashy novel with which to placate the battleaxe. His eye lit upon a gaudy cover on top of a pile that was going to the second-hand booksellers.

'Ah! I think I have the ideal thing for you: *The Crime at*

Virieux-sur-Orques[2] – a bargain at sixty centimes.'

'Surely you wouldn't recommend such reading to a young expectant mother?'

'Who is expecting?' Victor asked, caught off guard.

'My niece Valentine. Any day now. What on earth is the matter with that assistant of yours? Is he suffering from St Vitus's dance?'

'It has to do with my cousin Yvette,' Joseph said pointedly.

'And what about your cousin?' cried the countess, squinting at him through her lorgnette.

'I came to tell my boss that we must find her a place to stay urgently as her father . . .'

Joseph gestured with his chin towards *The Crime at Virieux-sur-Orques*.

'Well, in that case I shall leave you alone to discuss your family matters,' said the countess sniffing contemptuously. 'I shall come back tomorrow,' she added, before slamming the door.

'It's terrible, Boss,' Joseph whispered as soon as she had gone. 'The rag-and-bone man – he's dead!'

'Dead?'

'In the cab on the way back, Boss. I'd already bought the paper. There it is, there.'

'Calm down, let me read.'

MAN MUTILATED BY TRAIN

A train driver inspecting the tracks at the goods depot at Orléans yesterday made a gruesome discovery. At the foot of the gasworks on Rue . . .

'How can you be sure that it's Diélette?'

'That street, Boss, it's right next to Cité Doré. And then there's Coralie Blinde's prediction. "I see the big red eye of a train bearing down . . . I see a man flying above the railway tracks." I thought she was seeing into my future and that I was going on a trip, but when I left her just now she shouted after me: "A long journey, from which there's no return!" She looked scared, Boss. I swear she must have had a premonition. And it's no accident because the rag-and-bone man's place has been turned upside down and there's no sign of the goblet.'

'Don't breathe a word of this to anyone, and hide the newspaper.'

'What will you do about the girl, Boss?'

'She can stay here for a few days, and then we'll have to tell her the truth and make other arrangements . . . How awful!'

'Yes, especially since our case seems to have reached a dead end too.'

'I know where the goblet is.'

'You're not serious!'

'Do I look as if I am joking? The girl sold it.'

'Who to?'

'To a bric-a-brac merchant, whom I shall visit without delay. Have a pleasant evening, Joseph.'

The slick, uneven paving stones of Rue Mouffetard rose steeply, and the drizzle glistened in the shafts of light beneath the street-lamps. Unsure where to find number 127, Victor had entered the street at the level of the Panthéon, and was obliged to walk back down the slippery, dark street lined with ramshackle houses. A girl came out of a doorway and paused next to the open brazier of a vendor selling *frites* in greasy paper cones to the customers emerging from the wine bars. Festooned with washing, the façades of the buildings leaned in towards each other, as if confiding their secrets.

Facing the Église Saint-Médard and nestled behind a tiny public garden stood number 127, a tumbledown building next to the offices of the newspaper *La Révolte*. The first floor was occupied by a boarding house and the ground floor by a café. In the narrow smoky room, students, scantily clad young women, navvies and pimps stood elbow to elbow along a bar bristling with bottles and glasses of beer that glowed amber in the gloom. It was the time of day when the Green Fairy[3] washed away all cares, working her poison in the veins of the faithful. Soon drunkards and lovesick tomcats would be singing their sweet songs.

The landlord stood quietly polishing glasses, and occasionally placing a domino next to the ones already spread out on the counter. When Victor asked after Clovis Martel, he raised an eyebrow without looking up from the game, which he was playing with himself.

'I was told he lodged here,' Victor persisted.

This time he elicited a groan.

'Don't waste your breath,' whispered a woman in a low cut camisole that revealed her waning charms. 'He's scarpered. Fancy a tour of the basement with me? I'll show you the philosopher's stone.'

With her bright red lips and cheeks caked in rouge she looked like a doll that had seen better days. She was tall, a head higher than Victor.

'Where is he?'

'You're a stubborn one, aren't you? I told you, Clovis did a bunk.'

'Hop it, Eiffel Tower, you talk too much,' the landlord muttered.

'You shut your trap, Lulu, I'm doing no harm, and if this gentleman wishes to spend the night in my love nest you'll be in pocket, won't you? You're just upset on account of your Clovis running off without coughing up.'

'He can run all he likes. I know where to find him.'

'And where might that be?' Victor asked.

'Why should I tell you anything? We don't know each other.'

Victor leant on the counter.

'Because I'm asking you nicely. I may look harmless, but you wouldn't like to see me when I'm angry.'

'Steady on! You'll find him at the Marché Saint-Médard on a Saturday morning, near number 10. Come on, have a snifter on me.'

'No thank you, I'm on the wagon.'

'So there's no convincing you, eh? Pity. I was ready to show you all my charms from A to Z – including S and M,' murmured the Eiffel Tower.

'Don't trouble yourself, Madame, I'm perfectly familiar with the alphabet,' Victor retorted, exiting the bar.

The icy drizzle made him shiver. He thrust his hands into his pockets. As he hurried towards the lights on Rue Monge, he glimpsed a cyclist pumping up his back tyre.

The emissary stood up and, pushing his bicycle with one hand, walked into the café.

The steep streets of the Faubourg de Charonne dotted with gloomy cul-de-sacs displayed their dilapidated buildings like rows of rotten teeth along the edge of a piece of wasteland. Behind a picket fence, half a dozen caravans were gathered and a few acrobats practised their routines in the light of a camp fire. At the top of Rue de Nice, a woman pushing a barrel organ entered the courtyard of a tumbledown shack. Before parking her instrument under an awning, she stopped and peered through a darkened window. The bric-a-brac merchant's shop was closed. The old pig must be asleep.

The woman climbed the steep staircase, carefully missing the fifth stair, which creaked, and paused on the tiny landing. She could hear voices. The old pig had a visitor. All the better; he wouldn't hear her go up the stepladder and open the trapdoor to her garret.

Anna Marcelli closed the trapdoor without a sound, and lit an oil lamp. She stood up straight, her back stiff after an exhausting day pushing her barrel organ through the streets where she was always cold, even when the sun was shining. How she missed her native Italy, Naples basking in the sun, lapped by emerald-green waters, ragged children running barefoot through the alleys, laughing and carefree despite their empty bellies. She had been one of them until her father had got it into his head that they would find paradise inside Paris's city walls! He had been tempted by his fellow-countrymen's tales of wealth and luxury in the capital.

See Paris and live!

They had packed their bags and crossed the Apennines.

'We'll be rich, Anna. Paris is the most beautiful city in the world; people have money to burn. Surely they can spare a few coins for an organ grinder and a prima donna. With my music and your voice, we'll find fame and fortune!'

They had found only misfortune in the form of that skinflint, Achille Ménager, their benefactor, as her father used to call him for the simple reason that he rented them a draughty garret.

'*Che freddo!*'[4] Anna muttered.

Six months after their arrival Luigi had died of consumption. He was only thirty-five years old. Achille Ménager had paid for a funeral mass and a cheap burial.

'One good turn deserves another,' he had murmured, stroking little Anna's head.

She had paid him back a hundred-fold, so that now she felt nauseated every time a man looked at her in a certain way. Eight years it had been, eight years chasing dreams of gold that had long ago turned to dust.

She hummed her father's last *ritornello*:

> *For love is stronger*
> *Than time that has flown . . .*[5]

She was just nineteen, and had her whole life ahead of her.

She gazed at her reflection in the cracked mirror that hung

on the wall above her straw mattress. She had hazel eyes, a pretty upturned nose, olive skin and, beneath the headscarf she wore tied under her chin, a mane of thick hair. She noticed that the blue pinafore that she wore for work with a white blouse and red dress needed mending again. She hung her cape over the back of a solitary chair and took a plate of lentils from the dresser, placing it on top of the lamp that was beginning to sputter, then contemplated the freezing garret adorned with portraits of Garibaldi and Verdi purchased from a stamp dealer on Quai Conti. She walked over to the shrine she had created in memory of her father. A necklace made out of shells and three pumice stones picked up on the slopes of Mount Vesuvius lay in a circle around the notebook Luigi had used to jot down the words to his songs. Besides these souvenirs, her possessions amounted to a few items of bed linen, a jug and washing bowl, and some chipped crockery. Was this her home? More like the old pig's sty! She could hear his rasping voice through the floorboards.

She knelt down and pulled out a knot of wood, like a stopper, from one of the planks. With her eye to the floor, she could make out Achille Ménager's bald pate. Opposite him a spindly figure in a battered top hat was clasping a shiny object. Finally, Achille Ménager took two coins from his waistcoat pocket. The man in the top hat shook his head. Achille Ménager offered him a third. This time the exchange was successful and, the deal concluded, the man in the top hat took his leave. Achille Ménager went over to the window to make sure he had gone. Anna stood up and ran to open the trapdoor a crack. She could see Achille Ménager's shadow looming large on the wall. He walked down the flight of stairs and, kneeling at the fifth, lifted the plank and stowed his recent purchase in the hollow. He then returned to his lodgings, only to leave again almost immediately, wrapped in a warm overcoat.

'It's Thursday. You're off to see your Belgian whore at the brothel on Rue Petion, aren't you! *Vigliacco!*[6] You know you can't try it on with me any more, even if you do threaten to denounce me to the police for not having a licence!'

She ran down the ladder, retrieved the object from under the stairs and hid it in her barrel organ.

'I'll rob you first then I'll kill you, *sudicione!*'[7]

Burning with hatred, she went back upstairs to bed.

CHAPTER 10

D AWN was heralded by the sound of pigeons cooing. Anna curled up under her coverlet, wrapping it around her as tightly as she could – it was so cold! Above her head, raindrops pitter-pattered on to the skylight that framed a rectangle of grey.

Anna groaned. Why couldn't she be magically transported back to the Bay of Naples, where she would wake bathed in a pleasant heat! She had to get up, leave the house and trudge through the city streets with her barrel organ in order to scrape a living. There was only one thing for it; she must tear herself from her cocoon and pull on her clothes as quickly as possible. They were cold even though they had been under the mattress all night, and she shivered as she dressed. She lit a handful of wood shavings and threw a couple of pieces of coke into the bottom of the stove – a luxury reserved for breakfast. She cut a slice of stale bread and chewed it slowly to make it last longer. While she waited for the water to boil, she washed her face and brushed her hair energetically, before putting on her head scarf. She was about to pour the hot water into the coffee filter, and was lamenting the fact that this was the last spoonful of precious mocha she had bought at great expense at the roaster's, when a loud noise made her jump. She crouched down, unblocked the spy hole and peeped into the old man's lodgings. She could see a tussle going on between Achille Ménager and another person who was holding on to the lapels of his frock coat.

Achille fell to the floor. The figure stepped out of her field of vision. Then there was silence.

All she could hear was the sound of her heart beating frantically. She held her breath and prayed to the Madonna that it would not give her away. Then there came a quiet, continuous scratching noise. Someone was rummaging in the room, while the bric-a-brac merchant lay slumped in a hideous position. Was he merely unconscious? Or was he dead?

She must leave immediately! She lay flat on her belly and, reaching out her arm, inched open the trapdoor. She pulled herself up, gained a foothold on the top rung of the ladder and closed the trapdoor quietly behind her. She slid down, chafing her hands on the sides of the ladder, and stood motionless on the landing.

She remained there for a few moments before making her way down the stairs. Gripping the banister, she stepped over the creaking fifth stair – for if she could hear what went on in Ménager's lodgings, the reverse must also be true.

Only when she reached the corner of Rue de Nice and Rue de Charonne was she able to breathe easily. Suddenly she was overtaken by a fit of trembling.

The rain had stopped. Beyond the railings of the fence surrounding the wasteland, the chords of a guitar picked out a wild flamenco rhythm.

When he was sleepy, Kenji's eyes became heavy, giving him a feline air. He was leaning back against his seat, his hands resting on his cane, as he watched a company of mounted Republican Guards outside the barracks on Place Monge.

'I can't understand why you didn't tell me about this little expedition sooner?' he murmured, leaning over to the window, which he had opened to rid the cab of the smell of tobacco.

Victor exhaled a long plume of smoke from his cigarette. He had established that Clovis Martel would be at Rue Saint-Médard that morning, and it was clear that Kenji was the only one who could identify the goblet. He had telephoned him at ten o'clock the previous evening and, in order to avoid involving Yvette, had made up some cock-and-bull story about a cook at the Du Houssoye residence having told him about a strange goblet she had found in the refuse and given to a junk dealer.

'I only discovered the man's whereabouts yesterday,' he replied, grateful to be telling the truth at last.

'I must say, your enquiries take place at the oddest hours. If it isn't last thing at night, it's first thing in the morning!'

'You've told me enough times that the owl that stays awake catches the field mouse.'

'Don't use my proverbs against me,' protested Kenji, secretly flattered that his adoptive son remembered his sayings. 'So, you went to the residence of the man who left me his visiting card? You might have told me, since it was me he came to see. How did you find his address? It wasn't on the card.'

'Very simple. As I explained to you over the telephone, I asked at the Museum of Natural History.'

'Did you speak to him?'

'No. He wasn't at home, so I grilled the servants instead,

which is why I didn't say anything to you,' replied Victor, preferring not to mention Antoine de Houssoye's murder.

The cab driver, keen to avoid going over cobblestones, pulled up near the small Église Saint-Médard, which was flanked by a tiny public garden inhabited by vagabonds and plucky sparrows. As they made their way up the bumpy Rue Mouffetard, overlooked by the Panthéon's stout dome, they encountered more and more passers-by. Students from the Jesuit schools flirted tirelessly with young servant girls who were out window shopping.

Kenji looked anxious, although, contrary to what Victor imagined, his mind was not on the investigation. Joseph's suspicious behaviour had set him thinking, and instead of going to his tailor the previous day he had dropped off at Rue Monsieur-le-Prince, where Pierre Andrésy ran his book-binding business.

The modest premises were wedged between a four-storey building and a furniture-storage warehouse, and indicated to customers by a sign suspended above a tiny shop window containing a jumble of leather samples. Upon entering, Kenji was surprised by the size of the shop, which was cluttered with large tables, a percussion press and a backing vice. A lingering smell of tanned leather and glue caught in his throat. There were several shelves full of tools: folders made of boxwood and bone, saws for notching, needles, awls, brushes, dividers – all devoted to the creation of works of art.

The master of the house, a spry man of about sixty with blue eyes and a halo of white hair, reigned over this land of paper, whether Dutch, Japanese, laid or woven, duo-decimo or folio.

He had received Kenji with an amiability which, coupled with his skill, had earned him the loyalty of the best-known booksellers. He had appeared genuinely surprised when asked about the two precious volumes of La Fontaine entrusted to his care by Victor Legris. 'No one delivered them here. I have never seen them.' Faced with his customer's insistence, he had shaken his head forlornly, distressed that his integrity was being called into question. Kenji had apologised – no doubt his assistant had made a mistake.

By the time he left the shop, his suspicions had reached fever pitch, and he immediately telephoned Mademoiselle Bontemps to find out whether Iris had been to see her that Wednesday morning. Her awkward perplexity had put an end to any lingering doubts he might have had. If Joseph and Iris had lied to him about their whereabouts at the same time on the same day, it was because they had been together.

He had spent a restless night alternating between insomnia and bad dreams as he brooded over his discovery. On top of everything else, Victor had asked to meet him first thing the next morning. And now he was yawning and glowering by turns, depending on whether his tiredness or his anger had the upper hand.

They turned into a street lined with squat houses whose medieval courtyards with their exposed beams were invaded each weekend by rag-and-bone men, who considered it their territory. Carriage doors opened over piles of junk as second-hand dealers came to stock up, creaming off according to their means the best of the rag-and-bone men's spoils in order to sell them on to private customers.

'Clothes, rags, scrap for sale!'

Either that or they supplied the master rag-and-bone merchants – the elite of that nocturnal community and the only ones able to turn a profit by selling junk on for reprocessing.

Everything that still had a use was displayed on pieces of cloth spread out on the narrow pavements. It was rare for anything to sell for more than a few sous. Women's hats lay alongside empty scallop shells or curling tongs. Next to a collection of rusty nails, piles of lingerie, dresses and threadbare coats were keenly contested by shabbily dressed housewives, who hurled themselves at the clothes with such fervour that one might think they hadn't a stitch to wear and their modesty depended upon snatching what they could from the hands of their rivals. Kenji reflected that he would rather go naked than tussle with these harpies. A lanky individual wearing a rabbit-fur hat and fur-trimmed coat tried to convince Kenji to buy an array of potions whose properties he claimed were pharma-ceutically tried and tested.

'This one works wonders against toothache. You can say goodbye to suffering! Your gnashers will fairly stand to attention. This one's particularly good after a night on the tiles and this one here unblocks the pipes better than any douche. This one puts the hair back on your chest and this one . . .'

Kenji pulled himself away and went to join Victor, who was rummaging through a pile of unfinished novels, from between whose pages an occasional religious image or cutting from an illustrated newspaper slipped out. The vendor, a Martiniquaise wearing a pointed Madras hat, hawked her tat in a throaty voice.

'First-rate stuff, all of it, from a clearance I did at the palace of a rich man who kicked the bucket. Take it, dear, it's yours for a third of the price. Keep looking, you're bound to find something you like!'

'I'd like to know where Clovis Martel's stall is,' Victor said.

'Over there, next to the two old girls, the twins. You can't miss him on account of his nose, which you'll spot a mile off.'

They elbowed their way through the throng, only to find their passage blocked by a crowd gathered at the stall belonging to the two old ladies to whom the Martiniquaise had referred – cross-eyed twin sisters. A short, loutish-looking man in a bright red neckerchief with a cigarette hanging from the corner of his mouth waved a knife at them and spoke with a lisp.

'They call this a knife! It's certainly antique. It must date back to the Cro-Magnon era. I barely touched it and the handle hit the deck!'

The onlookers guffawed.

'If you don't know how to open a penknife, you should stick to fish knives! We only sell the finest merchandise here,' one of the sisters retorted.

'I'll give you one of my finest if you don't give me my money back!' shouted the grubby little man.

'No chance! Go hang yourself!' shouted the other twin.

'And you, carbon copy, you'd better watch it or I'll knock your block off, you louse!'

Victor and Kenji narrowly avoided the outbreak of hostilities. Once they were out of the fray, the street took on a relaxed air again. Finding Clovis Martel proved easy indeed owing to his protuberant nose, whose purplish hue betrayed a penchant for frequenting taverns.

Tall and thin, with a battered hat on his head and a goatee on his pointed chin, he was following the quarrel with a look of consternation as he chewed on the end of a matchstick. Kenji examined the jumble of objects at his feet: a couple of wood planes, a chamber pot, a narwhal's tooth, some hairpins, a poor copy of the Mona Lisa, a pair of clod-hoppers with cracks in the leather that were filled with pitch.

'If those old bats would stop their catfight, I might be able to get started. They're in a class of their own, those two skinflints. They could suck blood out of a stone, whereas me, I'm honest, I've never had any complaints, and if you can't find anything you want here I've a store of other bargains.'

'Like, for example, the skullcap of a monkey attached to a metal tripod decorated with three jewels and the tiny face of a cat with marbled agates for eyes?' said Victor.

Clovis Martel looked at him, amazed.

'We've got a right one here! And where am I supposed to have come across such an item? At Christofle's?[1]

'You bought it from the daughter of a man called Léonard Diélette. However, this gentleman is its rightful owner,' Victor added, pointing to Kenji.

'Me? I haven't bought a thing. And I don't know any Diélette. And besides, since when was free exchange illegal?'

'Where is the goblet?' Victor demanded.

'I don't know what you're talking about, so how should I know where it is? Somewhere in France!' barked Clovis Martel, affecting an interest in rearranging the items on his stall.

Suddenly, he stood up straight, his beady eyes bulging out of their sockets, his face bright red.

'Go to the devil! Let me get on with my work. I didn't come here to twiddle my thumbs, damn it,' he bawled.

Kenji moved towards him, unfazed.

'Allow me to explain. This goblet was taken from me in a burglary. Dealing in purloined items is otherwise known as receiving stolen goods and is punishable by law,' he informed the man calmly.

'Aha! So that's where this little sermon is going! Well, I've been working here for ten years and no one has ever accused me of receiving stolen goods. Call the *flics* if you like and we'll let them sort it out. Did you hear that, Abel?' he hollered to a wine merchant whose belly was the size of a barrel. 'As God is my judge, I know my memory isn't what it used to be, but it's as sharp as ever where business is concerned. Why, you gentlemen are casting a slur on the whole profession!'

A crowd of people had gathered round and were heartily agreeing with Clovis Martel's pronouncements.

'It's still a free country, after all,' growled a rag-and-bone man as big as a house.

'You're absolutely right. It's a free country, is it not?' Clovis Martel echoed the man's words loudly.

Victor muttered to Kenji under his breath. 'This fellow is giving us the run around.'

Fuming, Clovis Martel continued to yell at the top of his voice.

'You two are a right pair of troublemakers! What must I do to convince you? Cut my throat? Or should I throw myself off the top of the Église Saint-Médard?

A smile flickered across Kenji's face.

'Hey, you, Chinaman, you'll be laughing on the other side of your mug in a minute. Now hop it, both of you. I'm tired of looking at you. I mean to say, they give a fellow a hard time and then they laugh at him!'

'I'd forget it if I were you,' said the Martiniquaise, who had wandered over. 'You could float a battleship on the amount of wine he's put away. We're not all like him, but don't go to the police; it wouldn't be right. What is it you're looking for?'

'A stolen item.'

'You can say what you like about Clovis, but he's no thief.'

'He might have sold it on in good faith,' Victor suggested. 'Do you know who his regular buyers are?'

'Let me think. If it's a valuable object, he could have sold it to his friend.'

'What friend? Is he here?'

'Oh no, he's one of the elite. He has a proper shop on a proper street.'

'Which street?'

'Maman Doudou squeal?' she snorted, eyeing the wallet Kenji had just fished out of his pocket.

'Please, Madame, make an effort.'

'I am getting very forgetful, especially first thing in the morning,' the woman murmured, hurriedly stuffing a banknote down the front of her dress. 'He has a shop, and the same name as that Greek warrior, the bravest of the brave, the one who died on account of his heel being exposed. I read it in one of my books, though it makes no sense to me. Achille Ménager isn't the sort to pick a fight. The shop's in Rue de Nice, near Rue de

Charonne, funny how it suddenly came back to me. I can't remember the number, but there's only one . . .'

'You should eat more fish, Madame; it does wonders for the memory,' Kenji said.

The furore had died down by the time they retraced their steps. The twin sisters were fussing over an antique dealer in search of a real treasure; the man in the fur hat was sitting slumped in a broken armchair, enticing passers-by with phials containing the real, the one and only, elixir of youth.

'No more grey hair or wrinkles, Monsieur. A snip at five sous!'

Kenji stopped to listen. Victor was incredulous.

'You don't mean to say you're taken in by this rot?'

'Why not, I was taken in by yours, wasn't I? Speaking of which, isn't Diélette the surname of the little girl you asked Iris to look after?'

Amused by the look of surprise on Victor's face, he added, 'I'm afraid you'll have to go back to the beginning of the story you told me over the telephone, and try not to leave anything out this time . . . You don't look quite yourself, Victor, I think a dose of red meat might help you regain your composure. There's nothing like a good steak to put the spring back in one's step. I'll treat you to lunch at Foyot's. Let's stop off at Rue des Saints-Pères first and tell Joseph, and then we'll go and have a little chat with Achille Ménager.'

The emissary had lost all notion of time.

'I have failed. I am unworthy of your trust, Lord.'

He had turned Achille Ménager's lodgings and garret upside down, so far without success. One thing worried him: the woman's underwear. To whom did it belong? Wading through that pile of worthless bric-a-brac in the shop would be a Herculean task. How would he ever manage to pick through that heap of filthy junk? Why, an army of porters with tongs would have given up long ago.

Nothing. Still nothing. Had the rag-and-bone man with the big nose at the Marché Saint-Médard been lying? No. A banknote and some lurid threats had been enough to loosen the man's tongue.

'Rue de Nice. Achille Ménager. He gave me money for old rope. That thing's a fake.'

But now Achille Ménager had gone to meet his maker and he would provide no more information. Killing him had been a mistake.

The emissary sent a row of mustard pots flying.

'You fool. You've been duped!'

There was a rap at the door and a man's voice called out. 'Monsieur Ménager, are you there?'

The emissary flattened himself against the wall beside the grimy shop window.

'It's closed,' a second voice said. 'No point hanging about if he's not here. We'll try again later.'

The emissary leant forwards cautiously and peered through one of the panes covered in cobwebs.

He made out two figures.

He stepped back quickly. He thought he recognised them . . . Yes! It was them all right. But who had given them this address? The fellow with the big nose?

'I should have killed him, but there were too many people around . . . These two know more about this than I do.'

The Japanese fellow and his associate walked away.

He would follow them on his bicycle. He mustn't lose sight of them. This was his last chance.

In her panic, Anna Marcelli fled without warm clothes. She walked up and down the streets of the Popincourt quarter, her teeth chattering. The bakeries opened their shutters, soon followed by the dairies and fruiterers. Bare-headed women walked along briskly, baskets on their arms; children arrived to fill their tin-plate pots with milk; and navvies began their working day with a glass of red wine or cheap brandy in the cafés.

Anna wandered aimlessly, still reeling from shock. She felt oddly naked without the reassuring weight of her barrel organ in front of her. She had the impression she was in a foreign land and that everyone knew she was a coward and despised her for it.

The clock struck nine. She entered the Église Sainte-Marguerite, where she and Luigi had prayed. She had been visiting that bleak building each week to commune with herself since her father's death. Inside those forbidding walls was a peaceful sanctuary hung with paintings by Italian artists – most notably Salviati, Luca Giordano and Brunetti. Her favourite place to meditate was at the back of the chapel of the souls in purgatory, which was decorated with monochrome *trompes l'œil*. Behind a Corinthian colonnade stood a group of statues.

One of them reminded her of her father, and she liked to kneel and confide her hopes and fears to him. Today she closed her eyes and described the dreadful scene she had witnessed at breakfast. When she finally had the courage to look up, she thought she saw the statue pointing a hand at her and waving the other one in the air in a familiar gesture. It had been Luigi's way of dismissing the young Anna's anxieties. Feeling reassured, she resolved to go back to Rue de Nice to fetch her barrel organ and a few other things before the bric-a-brac merchant's body was discovered and she was charged with his murder. He had probably only fainted, she convinced herself. He had been knocked out, that was all. He would soon come round.

She found a sou in her pocket and bought herself a croissant in Rue Basfroi. The gloomy courtyards were lined with shops selling stretchers, wheels, second-hand springs and bar tops. The scrap merchants, their caps pulled down over their ears, were setting up their melting pots and cauldrons alongside the gutter. One of them grabbed her arm and asked her brazenly whether she didn't want to go and have a bit of fun with him at one of the café-bars. She pulled her arm free and walked away quickly. In the distance, a black strip stood out against the dull sky: the Colonne de Juillet, crowned by a gilded figure of Liberty vainly stretching out its wings. She doubled back. Underneath a chestnut tree, employees of the carriage hire company in copper-buttoned uniforms held their grubby hands over a glowing brazier. She looked at her reddened fingers. How she would love to warm them over the embers, but she was scared to go near the men. Behind a factory smokestack, hemmed in between two buildings, she recognised the pale green of a public garden. She was overcome by weariness. She needed to rest before she collapsed.

The first raindrops began to fall.

The emissary watched the rainwater wash down Rue Tournon. From his shelter beneath the awning of an antique shop that specialised in ancient string instruments, it was impossible to tell whether the Japanese fellow and his associate were still enjoying the main course or had moved on to dessert. Each time the door to Foyot's opened, the emissary's hopes that his persistence would be rewarded were dashed. However, it was impossible for him to leave now, even though it was very likely that the two accomplices would head back to the bookshop.

His stomach was rumbling. The rain stopped and a handful of people ventured out on to the pavements.

Finally, they emerged and began walking towards Carrefour de l'Odéon. The emissary followed at a distance, pushing his bicycle along and pretending to look in the shop windows.

'Do you think this is a good idea?'

'After what you've told me, I am convinced that it is. After all we're not supposed to know about Antoine du Houssoye's murder,' Kenji replied. 'We haven't been notified, have we?'

'It has been reported in the newspapers.'

'But we're not in the habit of reading news items. No, this gentleman wrote to me asking for my help. It is only natural that I should want to meet him.'

'And how did you discover his address?'

'It was easy, Victor. You told me. Don't worry. I have no intention of interfering with your investigation. Sleuthing is not my forte. I shall limit myself to portraying the image that you westerners – who do not know the difference between China and Japan – have of us Orientals.'

'Oh! And how do you propose to do that?'

'I shall look sly and enigmatic and bow a great deal, and if my hostess offers me anything to eat I shall pepper my speech with exotic vocabulary: *Arigato okamisan*: thank you very much, Madame.'

Victor raised his eyes to heaven. 'I never know when you're joking and when you are serious.'

'I am deadly serious. I want to get a closer look at these people, who appear to be caught up in a very shady affair. Driver! Rue Charlot.'

'I'll go with you,' said Victor.

The emissary let the cab go on ahead before he climbed on to his bicycle. Early the next morning he would go back to Rue de Nice and conduct another search.

CHAPTER 11

Friday afternoon, 15 April

T HE door opened to reveal a large waiting room, its walls covered with Chinese engravings. A plump servant relieved them of their coats, looking furtively all the while at Kenji. They were led through interminable corridors to a second waiting room from where a footman in livery showed them into a drawing room.

The vast space contained two apricot-coloured sofas. The curtains depicted scenes from mythology and the chairs were upholstered in this same material. There was a fireplace, four armchairs, old-fashioned oil lamps (the kind that had to be regularly adjusted with a key), framed photographs on the inevitable piano and an oak table near one of the windows.

A woman in a black silk dress stood by the fireplace. Kenji took in her slender figure and energetic expression with approval. He bowed. Victor saw him flinch when she held his hand in hers while inviting him to sit down. Her ingratiating smile was tempered by melancholy. As Victor removed his hat, he noticed the mahogany bookcase lined with magnificent calf-bound books.

'Please excuse my appearance, Messieurs, I wasn't expecting visitors. But do sit down. You knew my husband?'

'No, Madame, we never met. I was travelling when he left

his card in the care of Monsieur Legris, my associate here,' replied Kenji.

Gabrielle du Houssoye rapidly read the words scribbled on the back of the card.

'I don't know what he was referring to,' she murmured. 'My husband did not always keep me informed of his activities.'

'Excuse me, Madame, you speak in the past tense, is Monsieur du Houssoye . . . ?'

'Alas, Monsieur Mori, the poor man was taken from us suddenly. He's been murdered . . . A bullet straight to the heart.'

'Good heavens, that's appalling! Has the murderer been found?'

'The police are investigating.'

Two men came in. One of them was well into his forties, cynical-looking but elegantly turned out. The other, who was young, clean-shaven and tanned, wore a half-smile like a facetious child.

'May I introduce Alexis Wallers, my deceased husband's cousin, and Charles Dorsel, his secretary? Monsieur Mori, Monsieur Legris.'

Alexis Wallers's look of amusement accentuated his air of weary cynicism. 'Let me guess, Mori, Mori . . . You're undeniably not Italian. And you're not Chinese – the surnames of those opium eaters are unpronounceable! You're . . . Japanese! Oh, how I would have loved to explore Japan, that exquisite archipelago of the yellow seas! The home of flowery hospitality and charming . . .'

'I think you're embellishing somewhat.'

'Monsieur Legris, we've already met. At the museum, if memory serves.'

'Correct.'

'To what do we owe the honour?'

'These gentlemen wanted to see Antoine; they have a friend in common,' said Gabrielle du Houssoye.

'Lady Frances Stone,' explained Kenji, 'the sister of a very dear friend of mine.'

'It's most unfortunate,' said Alexis Wallers. 'Alas, I can't be of any help. My cousin was not in the habit of confiding in me. Can you add anything, Charles?'

'No,' the young man replied.

'What's the matter, Charles? You have a face like a wet weekend.'

'I'm in the middle of classifying Monsieur du Houssoye's travel notes. I can't stop thinking about him. I just can't take in his disappearance. Madame Gabrielle, did Lucie show you the translated extract from the review *All Round the World*?'

'Dear boy, you know perfectly well that she left the house in a hurry to go to a sick aunt. I told you that myself.'

'I thought she might have left the article in your study.'

'Really, Charles, now is not the moment.'

Alexis Wallers looked severely at Charles Dorsel, who stared insolently back.

Victor broke the ensuing silence by indicating the photographs on the piano.

'Did you take these, Madame? They're very beautiful.'

'No, my husband took them in Java, a few weeks before the terrible volcanic eruption.'

'Krakatoa?' asked Kenji.

'Were you there, Monsieur?'

'No. By 1883 I had been in Europe for many years, but I was very upset when I heard. I know the Sunda Islands well. I have friends there.'

'We lived through the terrible event. It is etched in our memories,' murmured Gabrielle du Houssoye.

'Where were you at the time?' asked Victor.

'We were staying not far from the Governor General of the East Indies' residence, at Buitenzorg, a town south of Batavia. Antoine had undertaken a study of orang-utans and we were about to leave for Borneo. Early in the afternoon we heard muffled rumbling, like claps of thunder. We thought a storm was brewing. The air was hot and humid. A little while later we heard loud explosions. At about five in the evening they became very violent and that lasted all night. If you have not lived through the experience, it is very hard to imagine how a mountain erupting eighty miles away could shake the ground so brutally. At seven the next morning there was an explosion so powerful that the house shook. Lamps shattered, pictures fell to the floor, doors and windows slammed, generating incredible panic. Then silence fell and the sky darkened. The unbelievable clouds of steam and cinders expelled by Krakatoa were moving towards us. By nine o'clock, the sky was enveloped in darkness, like a window with the curtains drawn. That night was like the end of the world; there were thirty thousand victims.'

Victor hung on every word, remembering the fantastical stories Kenji used to tell him as a child.

'*The blue mountains are home to flying dragons. When the sun beats down, they flap like bats round the fortresses built on the slopes of the volcanoes . . . Once, a long time ago, one of these monsters snatched up a human between its claws. That's how Princess Surabaja was carried away . . .'*

'Gabrielle, may I go and lie down? I'm worn out,' said Charles Dorsel.

Madame du Houssoye nodded.

'You must excuse him, Messieurs; he was absolutely devoted to my husband. He won't be able to rest until he has finished putting his notes in order.'

'And what about me, Gabrielle? Does my contribution count for nothing?'

Alexis Wallers stood at the window, contemplating the courtyard below. The smoke from his cigar formed a halo round his head. Kenji coughed discreetly and changed seats.

'What happened next?' asked Victor.

'Part of the island of Krakatoa disappeared to the bottom of the ocean. The gigantic wave that followed the eruption was almost thirty-six metres high. When it flung itself on the eastern coast of Java, it swept away dozens of villages. The impact of the surge of waves was not only felt in the Indian Ocean, but also in the Atlantic and the Pacific. The photos you see there were taken before the eruption occurred.'

'Yes,' said Kenji. 'I went there with Lady Stone in 1860. At that time the island was covered with thick forest. The vegetation was luxuriant; it was like the Elysian Fields. For months after the cataclysm, strange luminous phenomena were observed all over the world. Do you remember 1883, Victor? We had just opened the bookshop. In Paris and all over France, shimmering clouds were seen at sunset. People thought they were caused by fires.'

Kenji rose. 'I'm very sorry I never met your husband, Madame, and sorry too not to know what it was he wanted from me.'

'The friend you had in common, Lady Stone. Perhaps she could enlighten you?' suggested Alexis Wallers. 'If you find anything out, do let us know.'

'Of course,' replied Kenji. 'Thank you for seeing us.'

Joseph's feather duster had rarely moved so rapidly over the rows of books. The resulting dust clouds tickled Euphrosine's nose. She was overcome by a fit of sneezing.

'What have those books done to you, my pet? Anyone would think you were trying to bite the dust! Isn't it enough that the child – God knows where they dragged her in from – is coming down with pneumonia? And, while we're on the subject, Mademoiselle Iris was wrong to call Doctor Reynaud; his remedies are about as useful as poultry on a wooden leg.'

'You mean poultice, Maman, "as useful as a poultice on a wooden leg".'

'Well, I know what I mean, that's what matters. And there's only one cure for influenza.'

'I know, syrup of snails.'

'No! It's mulled egg!'

'Oh please, now I feel sick!'

'There's no two ways about it – that thing's shaking worse than if we were on a boat.'

Joseph clenched his jaw to stop himself from yelling. What was his mother playing at? She had been stationed at the counter for a good half hour, like a fat hen jealously guarding her egg.

And I'm the egg, he thought. She's suffocating me.

If only Iris would come down. But no. She was so infatuated with Yvette that she never left her side.

Alone, abandoned by everyone and left in his mother's clutches! Please could a customer appear, in spite of the vile weather. Or could one of the Bosses show up . . .

The feather duster resumed its jig, provoking another storm of sneezing from Euphrosine. She made for the door, her eyes watering, and took up her umbrella, ready for action.

'I'd rather brave the hail than stay here. Oh, the cross I have to bear.'

Joseph was immediately assailed by guilt, and was about to persuade her to stay, when Victor and Kenji burst in, soaked through.

'You look like you need to be put through the wringer,' said Joseph, relieved to have a valid excuse not to go after his mother.

'Where's Iris?' enquired Kenji briskly, shaking his sodden bowler hat.

'Upstairs. She's dealing with Dr Reynaud. Yvette's coughing.'

'Perfect. Lock up and join us in the back room,' ordered Kenji, pouring himself a glass of sake. 'Apparently we can't decide anything without you.'

'What's got into him? Has he swallowed his sword?' whispered Joseph to Victor.

'Shh! We've made progress with the investigation.'

So now we're all three investigating together, Joseph thought, aware that an important new phase had begun. The Bosses were treating him as an equal, even though one of them was regarding him in a rather disagreeable manner.

Victor described their escapade to him.

'Madame du Houssoye didn't exactly appear heartbroken by her husband's brutal death. As for cousin Alexis, although he was affecting weary boredom, he's clearly mad about her,' said Victor, addressing Kenji.

'Are they lovers?' Joseph asked.

'Who knows? Lovers, accomplices, it's possible,' replied Victor. 'And then there's the secretary . . .'

'An insignificant youth,' cut in Kenji.

'I think, Boss, they were putting on an act for you . . . They're all in it together.'

Kenji looked doubtful.

'They would have to be masters of improvisation, since they didn't know we were coming. I was observing them closely. Each time I mentioned Lady Stone, they showed no reaction. Perhaps we're on the wrong track in seeing them as suspects. What do we suspect them of? Stealing my goblet? Murdering Lady Stone and Antoine du Houssoye?'

'You're forgetting Léonard Diélette. Are you saying that there might be an *éminence grise* pulling the strings in the background?'

'I don't know,' murmured Victor. 'If we knew what the motive was . . .'

'It's Monsieur Mori's goblet, Boss, definitely!'

'Let me think a moment. We have three suspects, who've done nothing suspicious.'

'Five, Boss. Don't forget the missing lady's maid and the crazy old man. Perhaps he's just confusing us with his pack of stuffed hounds and his Templars' treasure! He might be the brains behind the operation.'

'All right. So my goblet provides the motive. But why? What's special about it? Whatever angle we approach this riddle from, the solution escapes us. I don't believe for a minute in the enchantment John Cavendish's poor sister referred to in her letter,' said Kenji.

'Java!' cried Joseph. 'The goblet originated in Java! John Cavendish bought it there, six years ago. And Antoine du Houssoye had just returned from a long trip to Java when he was murdered. It would be interesting to know if his wife, cousin or secretary went with him, or the maid or the old lunatic. I bet you hadn't considered that question.'

'Joseph, your brilliant deductive powers are opening new vistas for us,' declared Kenji, his voice laden with sarcasm.

'I won't let it go to my head, Boss, don't worry. I'm trying to think of all the possible criminal combinations. There could have been two murderers, one providing an alibi for the other. Fortunat de Vigneules and his daughter, for example, or Madame du Houssoye and cousin Alexis, or even Alexis and the secretary, you can vary the parings . . . Oh my God! The day that woman tripped over in front of the bookshop, as I was closing up, it must have been to distract my attention to allow the woman with her to make an impression of my keys!'

'What makes you so certain there were two women?' Victor demanded.

'Their Russki clothes. Madame Ballu remarked on the strangely Russian appearance of the mysterious visitor, and Madame Ballu doesn't miss a thing. And it was you, Monsieur Legris, who told me about the two battleaxes in Rue Charlot dressed like Muscovite ladies, so I deduce from that . . .'

'But you told me you couldn't remember what the woman who fell over was wearing,' Victor pointed out.

'It could also have been two men disguised as women,' concluded Kenji in a voice trembling with exasperation. 'If you could kindly stop going off at tangents, I might be able to concentrate.'

He unfolded the letter from John Cavendish, which he kept in his wallet, and was about to read it when Victor pushed his chair back.

'There's a vital point we haven't considered. Lady Stone was killed with a revolver; the same goes for Antoine du Houssoye. Two identical crimes committed within a few days of each other, the first in Scotland, the second in Paris. We have to find out if one or several members of the Rue Charlot clan recently crossed the Channel,' he said.

'What about Léonard Diélette, Boss? Do you think he was murdered before he was pushed on to the railway line?'

'What do you think, Kenji?'

Kenji did not reply. He was reading Cavendish's letter under his breath.

'*Scrimshaw,*' he muttered.

He pictured the objects laid out on the pavement in Rue

Saint-Médard and remembered a narwhal's tooth.

Clovis Martel . . . Achille Ménager . . .

'Joseph!'

'At your service, Boss.'

'I want to study my goblet and figure out its secret and I want you to be responsible for retrieving it. Tomorrow, Achille Ménager will surely be at home first thing. I'll pay whatever he asks. Can I count on you to take care of it?'

'You can count on me as you could your own brother, Monsieur Mori.'

'I'm an only child.'

Kenji folded up the missive carefully.

Anna spent much of the afternoon at the back of one of the three chapels of the Église Saint-Ambrose. She did not dare return to Rue de Nice. She was haunted by the image of Achille Ménager sprawled on the floor like a broken puppet, watched over by a shadow, a spider lying in wait for its prey to return.

She remembered that one of her father's friends used to go to a shelter nearby when he had nowhere to stay. Built twenty years earlier thanks to the initiative of the Hospitalité de Nuit and overseen by Baron de Livois, the institution offered temporary refuge for anyone, whatever their age, nationality or religion. Indigents could present themselves between seven and nine in the evening and be assured of a bed and a meal. Her pride was offended at the very thought of it, but she was so cold and hungry that she put aside her reservations and set off for Boulevard de Charonne.

Both sides of the road were lined with low, monotonous-looking buildings, allowing glimpses of the brick chimneys of the workshops behind. The shelter was at the far end, number 122. The door stood wide open and a stream of people, mainly men, was entering. Their attire indicated that they belonged to the working classes. Out of work, and homeless due to unpaid rent, they had come with their meagre possessions. There were a few women, young ones clutching infants and old ones reduced to destitution.

Anna joined the queue behind a stooped old fellow whose top hat and black coat had known better days. Head down, he approached the reception office, where a jovial fellow of about forty greeted him.

'Good evening, Professor!'

The professor filled out his form and went to the end of the corridor to the five-bedded room reserved for the 'silk hats'.

'They don't let us plebs mingle with the gentle folk,' muttered a mason who had just been assigned to the dormitory.

'What are you complaining about? You're going to find work thanks to us. Move on now; you're not the only one here,' said the employee, who was in fact the manager.

As the mason moved away, mumbling a diatribe against the spongers who were sapping France, the manager greeted Anna in a friendly manner.

'You're new, aren't you? Fill in your name, age and occupation. As it's Friday evening, you're entitled to four nights instead of three. The women sleep upstairs, first on the left. Go and have a bit of a clean up and then come down to the refectory.'

She climbed the stairs and found herself alone in a room

furnished with basins, soap and towels. After she had washed herself a supervisor gave her half a loaf of bread. In spite of the kindly manner of the personnel she felt as if she were in prison.

On the ground floor she sank down on to a bench and began to eat, looking around at the other inmates with circumspection.

Books and paper, pens and ink were available for the residents to use, but they seemed to prefer to share their tales of woe. Anna was bitterly aware of how alone she was. She had nobody to write to, no relative or friend to come and comfort her. And over there in Rue de Nice a shadow was waiting for her. Would she be able to retrieve her barrel organ?

The manager and the supervisor stood on a platform and announced to the women that the next day they would be provided with soup, a hot meal, shoe polish and new clothes, and, if needed, an employment book. They read out the regulations of the shelter, and invited the women to join in a short prayer. Then each woman was allocated a bed number.

When Anna saw the dormitory with its thirty cots and the meagre sheets and blankets, her reaction was to flee. But where to? The sight of one young woman cradling her baby and another darning reassured her. The old woman beside her was racked by hoarse cough. Certain she would not sleep a wink, Anna settled down on the pillow and fell asleep immediately.

Victor sat, fists clenched, on the high-backed chair facing the bed. He regretted not having found the time to go and inter-rogate Maurice Laumier. He kept looking at the clock. He had never noticed that irritating tick-tock, which seemed to grow louder with each passing minute. He turned away, wishing that the letter was no longer in the pillowcase.

But it was still there. It burned his fingers. He unfolded it and read.

> *My Dearest Tasha,*
>
> *I'm going to make the effort to write to you in French, since that is now your language. I'm happy that everything is going well with you. Thank you for your kind letter. Don't worry about the money — I'll manage somehow. I'm arriving in Paris next Wednesday and staying at a cheap hotel that was recommended to me, Hôtel de Pékin. If you can, come and meet me at Gare de l'Est, otherwise I'll see you at the hotel. I can't wait to hold you in my arms and see for myself how much your painting has come on. I have dreamt of this moment for such a long time, but as you know events have conspired to thwart my plans. After Berlin, where everything was disciplined, regimented and orderly, I dream of sitting with you at a café table on the terrace of a brasserie. Oh, Paris! The joy of living . . . Don't they say, 'As happy as God in France?'*[1]
>
> *See you soon, my darling,*
> *Your loving old fool*

It took him a few minutes to take in the contents of the letter. He would not read it again. A feeling of detachment took hold, as if his soul were floating in space outside his body. He didn't move. Then grief spread through him. A lump blocked his throat; his hands trembled. Jealousy, that old enemy that never gave up the assault, gnawed at his insides. He was overwhelmed by the thought that Tasha had been unfaithful to him. He knew that some men did not care about emotions. He had been one of those men, passing from affair to affair without bothering to consider what the other person might be feeling, neither happy nor unhappy, simply satisfying his desire, giving in to habit. But that was before Tasha.

Who was this man who signed himself 'Your loving old fool'? Tasha had sometimes spoken of her previous lover, a sculptor from Berlin. Hans? Yes, it was Hans, a married man. It must be him. She had been waiting for him. He folded the letter and slipped it deep into his pocket. He was annoyed with himself for having read it. His dismay was replaced by an irrational remorse at having given in to curiosity. This last sentiment brought with it the absolute certainty that if he were to lose Tasha it would destroy him.

He began to formulate dozens of theories, all designed to convince himself that she had in fact gone to Barbizon. He stared at the ceiling, working out a plan of action. What reason could he give for visiting Laumier unannounced that would not make him look ridiculous?

CHAPTER 12

Saturday, 16 April

THE night in the shelter had restored Anna. She was rested, and the thick pea soup had been very satisfying. What's more, her boots were now polished and she had been given a cape, a donation from one of the local traders. She was all ready to return home. But once outside, partly because of her nightmare, fear twisted her stomach. She had dreamt that Achille Ménager, his mouth dripping blood, had tried to kiss her, before turning into a tiny crow with a beak that dripped deathly poison. She had woken just as the miserable day cast its grey light over the face of her elderly neighbour, who was still racked by a dry cough.

Uncertain of where to go, she leant against a wall, discouraged and shivering. Her hands, holding the sides of her cape, were like two pale stains on the dark material. A man with large sideburns shambled by, eyeing her. He went past her then thought better of it and turned back.

'Hey there, sweetheart, you look exhausted. The night must have been steamy, but I'm sure you've enough ardour left – let's go upstairs together. Coming?'

Anna reared back in disgust and fled, taking refuge under the awning of a bakery.

'Leave me alone, you pig!'

Furious, the man called out to passers-by, 'I've just been accosted by a cheap prostitute, right here in the street!'

He tried to grab her by the arm just as a tall young man came out of the baker.

'Attila the Hun!' he shouted in a strong southern accent.

Catching the fellow by the collar, he spun him round and shoved him away. The unwelcome visitor left without a fuss. Anna's saviour looked down at her and raised the Rembrandt fedora perched on his long hair.

'Sainte Geneviève!' he exclaimed.

Speechless, Anna dared not make the slightest movement lest this stranger, who was visibly deranged, should also threaten her.

'Don't be alarmed, my love – I'm not bonkers. It's just that you look exactly like the heroine of my play, at least you look like the way I've portrayed her.'

'Your play?' she managed to say.

'A drama in five acts called *The Virgin of Lutetia*. I only have two scenes left to write.'

'Oh! You're a writer?'

'Mathurin Ferrant, aspiring poet,' he announced, bowing so low that she smiled in spite of herself.

'Well, I'll be jiggered! So my comic efforts are rewarded with success! Perhaps I ought to abandon tragedy.'

He pulled a *pain au lait* from his pocket, split it in two and offered her one half.

'And whom do I have the honour of addressing, sweet demoiselle?'

'My name's Anna Marcelli.'

'That surname has a Latin ring, like Dante, Aristotle and Tacitus! May I offer you a cup of French coffee, Madame, or is it Mademoiselle Marcelli?'

'Mademoiselle.'

They sat down at the back of an almost empty café at a little table covered with an oilcloth. The short, plump owner served two bowls of *café crème*, as well as some bread and butter, because, she said, she liked to feed up the artists.

'Thank you, Madame Noblat. I'll invite you to the dress rehearsal of my play at Théâtre-Français,' said Mathurin, pinching her cheek.

He waited until she was back at the counter before saying to Anna, 'She thinks I'm going to become a celebrity and then marry her. She's wrong on the second count!'

He chuckled and gulped down his coffee. Anna felt comforted in the presence of this strapping long-haired lad; she couldn't have said exactly why. So when he asked her what she did, she replied on impulse, 'I'm a musician. I sing and play the barrel organ. I perform Italian or French songs, some of them written by my father. He's dead now. When I sing, even when I'm at rock-bottom, I feel happy and I try to inspire my listeners with the same joy. Often they take up the chorus and join in, and that gives me great pleasure.'

'That's like me, when I write! I escape. Sometimes I'm riding over plains and through forests, singing at the top of my voice! I'm unbelievably ferocious. At other times I'm Geneviève exhorting the inhabitants of Lutetia to resist the barbarian hordes, and I feel imbued with a profound sense of inner peace. You and I are made to get on well together. Shake my hand!'

He almost crushed her fingers; his palm was warm and firm.

'You're frozen . . . Madame Noblat, a cognac please!'

Anna wanted to refuse, but Mathurin was so insistent she resigned herself to taking a gulp of alcohol. Her grimace delighted him.

'I was cold myself yesterday evening in my garret. So I went to stay with one of my colleagues from the Lice Voltaire, where I used to be a supervisor.'

'Supervisor?'

'A monitor. Unfortunately I was sacked a week ago on the false pretext that I had read the pupils an immoral tract. Maupassant, immoral! True, I also sold lottery tickets to the boarders, promising them my hat if they drew the winning number . . . Bah! Life is a succession of miseries we must bear in philosophical silence. Another job will come along. I'm rambling. You must be in a hurry to get singing.'

She blushed.

'I can't. My barrel organ's at home and I dare not go back. I spent the night in a shelter.'

'I see . . . A lover's tiff.' He tugged at his beard with his thumb and forefinger.

'No, you don't see. Yesterday morning I was having breakfast when there was a . . .'

'Not another word! It's your secret and I respect it. As I indicated, I don't have any coal, but I do have a place to stay. It's not the Grand Hôtel, although the view over Place Saint-André-des-Arts is rather agreeable. If you promise to pipe down while I wrestle with my alexandrines, I'll invite you to share my little abode. No strings attached, no dishonourable intentions. And I still have a full crate of potatoes. You take the bed, I'll be fine on the sofa – what do you think?'

'It's the nicest suggestion anyone's ever made me.'

'Let's go then, Mademoiselle Anna.'

The cab journey had allowed Victor time to reflect. Although he was trying very hard not to think about the purpose of his journey, he was as anxious as a patient eagerly awaiting a diagnosis from his doctor. Am I ill? Is it serious? Will I recover?

At the same time, his conscience whispered to him that his jealousy was the spice that ensured his continuing love for Tasha, just as this new investigation livened up a routine that might easily have become dull.

The air rang with the sound of bells and pale sunlight fell on the couples climbing the hill in search of a breath of fresh air and a bite to eat before going dancing. Streams of housekeepers were massing round the costermongers interspersed among the pork butchers, pastry cooks and restaurateurs.

Victor turned right on to Rue Tholozé. He felt a pang as he passed the saloon doors of Bibulus with its sign of the suckling dog. The bar was dear to his heart because he had met Tasha there many times before she had moved to Rue Fontaine. Although he immediately recognised the odour of cheap plonk, he was disconcerted by the décor. The owner, Firmin, had thrown out the stools and barrels in favour of cane chairs and pedestal tables. In the middle of the bar was a large porcelain coffee urn decorated with flowers. On the shelves, standing to attention in serried ranks, were bottles, slender or pot-bellied, glasses and cups, all impeccably polished. Gas lamps had replaced the old petrol ones.

'Ave, Firmin, remember me?'

The fat bartender with a ruddy complexion adjusted his spectacles. 'Monsieur Legris! Amen! You haven't changed.'

'What's happened here? War?'

'I married, M'sieur Legris, that's all you need to know. And the wife is very particular. I preferred it in the good old days, but you can't have your cake and eat it, now can you?'

'I'm looking for Maurice Laumier – is he here?' called Victor, already halfway towards the narrow corridor that led to the studio.

'That's all in the past. Bye-bye "Chapelle de Thélème" – my wife has her eye on a different clientele; now it's a snooker hall. What must be must be! It's sad, but I'm about to become a father and that will liven the atmosphere up a bit.'

'Congratulations, Firmin. Do you by any chance know where Laumier lives?'

'He lives over there on Rue Girardon, number 15, near Allée des Brouillards. But I haven't seen him for an age . . .'

Victor retraced his steps, thinking over a Buddhist adage that Kenji was forever repeating: Remember, nothing is constant except change.

As the end of the century approached, everyday life was changing rapidly. Scarcely a day passed without some innovation appearing, and a fashion or quarter falling out of favour. The twentieth century was beating at the door and Victor felt resistant.

Perhaps, he thought, that was the nature of each individual life: the grains accumulate at the bottom of the hourglass and you sink into nostalgia as you advance in years.

Maurice Laumier's apartment, on the ground floor of a courtyard, had a little front garden filled with rose bushes and cats. Victor had to knock several times before a thick voice mumbled, 'Who is it?'

When he'd given his name, the door half-opened, and then stopped as if reluctant to reveal the tousled, naked man.

'You?? This is a shock! . . . Come in, old chap, sorry, you've interrupted saturnalia fit to make a field of poppies blush.'

They went through into a bedroom. All that could be seen of the occupant of the bed was some black curls. The walls were wet with condensation. Laumier tugged on some trousers and a paint-stained sweater.

'It's freezing in here. We'll be warmer in the studio.'

He turned towards the bed, where the owner of the black curls lay stretched out, and said: 'Mimi, go and draw some water and then run over to Rue Norvins and ask the fruiterer for two bowls of soup . . . Or three?' he added to Victor, who shook his head.

'Suit yourself, but you'll regret it – it's free, you know. That bloke's a godsend to penniless artists, and his vegetable soup with bacon will see you through till evening.'

The adjoining room was filled with canvasses of all dimensions, on the ground or propped on easels, all of a dark-haired woman in her glorious nudity, presumably the woman getting dressed next door. The brushwork was reminiscent of Gauguin, even though the paint was almost translucent, as if it had been watered down.

Over-exposed and blurred, Victor concluded.

Laumier opened the flue of a large wood-burning stove and rubbed himself voluptuously against it. After a few seconds, he opened the door of the stove and poured in half a sack of chestnut coal.

'That's better . . . So what brings you here?'

'I need some information. Tasha told me about an exhibition in Barbizon . . . I'd like to join her there, but I wanted to be certain I hadn't got the location wrong.'

'An exhibition in Barbizon? It's possible. It's been ages since I was privy to Tasha's confidences. Oh, and by the way you win; she refused my offer of collaborating on Paul Fort's scenery.'

'I didn't influence her either way.'

Laumier shrugged. 'You only need to frown for her to bend to your will. I know you don't like me, Legris, but you don't need to worry: I'm not going to take her from you. I admit I did set my cap at her, but that was a while ago, before your time, Magnus Victor. It was a fiasco.'

Victor's spirits rose a notch.

'Admit it, she's dumped you, hasn't she?' asked Laumier, yawning.

'Don't rejoice too soon.'

'My God, you've a one-track mind! Personally, I don't give a rap if she leaves you. But if she has taken that step, perhaps it's a way of telling you she needs some breathing space.'

'You're hiding something from me!' shouted Victor.

Laumier burst out laughing.

'Beware of the dog – he bites! I'm as innocent as the pitiful lamb in the fable, Legris. "I am taking a drink of water", etcetera, etcetera . . . I'm just striving to open your tyrannical, possessive, puritanical eyes. Escape is even more necessary for the survival of a couple than warmth is for the survival of an artist.'

He held his hands over the stove and continued.

'I speak as an attentive observer only, since I have no desire to be part of a couple. But I know Tasha. She's crazy about you, and – ugh! Here's a repulsive word – she's faithful. Unfortunately, like all privileged people, you want more than you can have.'

'Please don't lecture me. You haven't answered my question.'

'What question? Oh yes, Barbizon, and on and on. Listen, if Tasha told you she was exhibiting there, she's exhibiting there. Instead of getting in a spin, why don't you jump on a train, go there and find out? Don't forget your photographic paraphernalia. You'll be able to take pictures if something's amiss: adulterer in flagrante delicto. That's a favourite theme for many painters! On that note, I'm going to leave you. My stomach is protesting loud and strong, so you can bugger off now!'

Victor could not get out of the place fast enough. He was exultant. Laumier's exasperation was a balm to his suspicions.

She's crazy about me! She's crazy about me!

He took a few steps along Allée des Brouillards where the succession of detached houses surrounded by greenery gave him the impression of being in Barbizon. He experienced a brief moment of *joie de vivre* so intense that he seemed to be soaring, intoxicated, outside his body. Then he came down to earth with a jolt.

Why had he demeaned himself by turning to that charlatan? He hadn't really learnt anything, and all he could now do was return to Rue Fontaine and await Tasha's return. Or perhaps he should concentrate on something else entirely? A little trip to *Le Passe-partout* might shed some light on Léonard Diélette's death.

The meowing of a cat made him lift his head. Perched on a low wall, a thin black cat was trying to catch his attention.

From her seat on the bed, Anna Marcelli looked around the bedroom, which was constructed from four partitions. She took in piles of books on the floor, mainly from the *Collection Populaire*, an armchair losing its stuffing, a bow-legged table and a squat unlit stove. The bed was covered with striped canvas rather like the regulation garb of convicts. But what delighted her was the window, only a modest skylight, but with a sill on which you could lean your elbows and gaze out at the comings and goings on Place Saint-André-des-Arts.

Anna savoured this little corner of peace and safety. All her worries flew out of the window, to be swallowed up by the sky. The burden of anguish and fatigue that had weighed on her for eight years melted away in the light of this April Saturday. She was astonished that the narrow little garret, with its sloping ceiling, could have such an effect on her.

Mathurin was installed at the table, scrawling on sheets of paper that were immediately screwed into balls. He chewed his pen, stared into space, then began feverishly writing again, murmuring incoherently.

'*The gold of your eyes* . . . No, that's not right. *Your eyes like rare pearls* . . . Yes, much better. *Your eyes like rare pearls that shine at sunset* . . . No! *Shine in the firmament* . . .'

During their long walk from Popincourt to Saint-Michel, he had told her of his youth in Bordeaux, his desire to come to Paris, the opposition of his scrivener father who would only allow him to go on condition that he studied law. For a year, furnished with a monthly allowance of two hundred francs that allowed him to rent a room for fifty francs and buy forty centime steaks at Chartier, Mathurin had climbed the hill of Sainte-Geneviève each morning to start getting to grips with the intricacies of the law. But one day, encouraged by his poet friends who had dropped out of university and with whom he frequented the arcades of l'Odéon, he had bidden farewell to the civil code and embraced the dramatic arts. After he failed his law exams, his father had cut off his allowance, and he had taken odd jobs – porter at Les Halles, stove lighter at police headquarters, bill-sticker, monitor.

'Who knows if my plays will ever be performed? I don't care; I have no regrets. I'm like the genie imprisoned in the bottle until the cork popped out. I'm free! Finally free! I'm rich in liberty!' he had shouted in the street.

Anna had suppressed a sigh. She knew what that kind of richness entailed. They would have to find food, oil and coal, for Mathurin's raw potatoes were not an enticing prospect.

'Eureka! Mathurin began to declaim.

> '*Your eyes like rare pearls shine in the firmament*
> *Of that great city where I'd known such torment*'

He leant towards her, seeking her approbation.

'That's very beautiful. Listen, I'm used to being busy. I'm going to leave you to your inspiration and go home to fetch my barrel organ. Thanks to you, I have the strength to do it. I'll go and sing and with luck I'll be able to buy us something for dinner.'

'Let it never be said that Mathurin Ferrant allows himself to be supported by a person of the weaker sex!'

'No, no, I assure you, I love my work! See you this evening.'

He stared at the closed door.

'Will I see her again? I've never had much success with women. Shame, she's delightful enough to eat, that little one and . . . *Your eyes like rare pearls . . . Your ivory breasts . . .* What rhymes with breasts?'

On the first floor of the smart building on Rue de la Grange-Batelière, the editorial office of *Le Passe-partout* was, as usual, in turmoil. In the middle of the toings and froings, a small, tubby, placid man, an unlit cigar tucked behind his ear, confronted a tall, robust chap in a braided hussar's jacket who was sucking lozenges.

'My dear inspector, with all due respect, writing about Prussia's celebration of Bismarck's seventy-seventh birthday, or telling our readers there is a dog for every dozen people in France, or that Rosita, the gigantic Austrian woman exhibited at Fernando's Circus, is eight foot tall and weighs thirty-four stone, is hardly likely to boost our circulation! On the other hand a juicy, unsolved crime . . . You understand me?'

'Monsieur Gouvier, I am not taken in. From now on, you will have to make do without your police informer. He has been transferred to the provinces.'

Isidore Gouvier smiled angelically at Inspector Lecacheur.

'I couldn't care less. Police headquarters is swarming with moles. I'll dig out another one. In the meantime, our readers are revelling in tales of police negligence. An emeritus professor from the Museum of Natural History gunned down and found devoured by rats – that's what gives the masses a frisson. And they're already stirred up after the anarchist bombings!'

Inspector Aristide Lecacheur shook his lozenge box angrily, turned on his heel and strode across the editorial office. He had nearly reached the door when he almost knocked down a man in a black frock coat.

'Victor Legris! Good God, is it written somewhere that you must dog me wherever I turn?'

'What a surprise! Hello, Inspector, how goes it? I see you are holding out, congratulations.'

'What do you mean, holding out?'

'Cigarettes,' explained Victor, pointing to the box of lozenges.

'Where there's a will, there's a way,' murmured the

inspector. 'I trust that your relations with any criminal investigations are purely platonic, Monsieur Legris?'

'I'm as chaste as an innocent young girl; my morals are intact. I am confining myself exclusively to the sale of philosophical novels.'

'I don't believe a word of it, Monsieur Legris. You're always ready to jump the barrier to satisfy your curiosity. I bid you a good day.'

Victor raised his hat and made his way towards the editor's office.

Antonin Clusel, alias Beau Brummell, alias The Virus, was gesticulating wildly in the midst of a group of journalists and typesetters.

'M'sieur Clusel, where shall we put the theft from the Cluny Museum, you know, the warden who stole the Gallic coins?' one of them was asking.

'Fit it in wherever there's a gap. On the front page in big letters, I want: M. BERTHELET TELLS ALL. Because, my children, melinite and dynamite are the breasts of current affairs, the only subject that can interest both our exalted politicians and the lowest *frites* seller. They all think about them just before they go to sleep, they dream about them at night, they tremble at the thought of them by day. Eulalie! My angel, what are you up to? Pay attention. And, you reporters, open your ears. I want an interview with Berthelet. Besiege the institute, the senate, his home and bring me the expert opinion of our Minister of War. Ask him what's going to happen tomorrow, the day after tomorrow, in the months to come, since the manufacture of explosives is in private hands. What does he think of *The Perfect Anarchist's Handbook*, which is as readily available as lollipops? Are we all in great danger, as much danger as the Russians with their Nihilists? Right now, off you go, and make it good!'

Antonin Clusel wiped his forehead, poured himself a cognac and suddenly noticed Victor.

'My good fellow! Did you hear that? We're not letting the grass grow. Crime! Yes, crime in all its manifestations, the subject our readers love to read about tucked up at home in their slippers. What brings you here?'

'Oh, a little clarification about . . .'

'Terribly sorry, I'm overwhelmed. The Virus has to write a portrait of Ravachol. He'll probably be tried at Montbrison and condemned to the guillotine. Off with his head! See you around, Legris; maybe Isidore Gouvier can help you. Eulalie, back to work,' he concluded, slamming his office door.

Victor spotted Isidore Gouvier and tapped him on the shoulder.

'M'sieur Legris! Where's your crime novel? I'm dying to read it. I thought you were just putting the finishing touches to it?'

'It's maturing slowly, like the finest malt whisky. I suppose you've heard about that rag-and-bone man from Cité Doré who was found on the railway tracks at Gare d'Orléans?'

'Indeed I have. We'll never know if it was an accident, murder or suicide. Why?'

'I wanted to know if he'd been shot.'

'He was so mangled when they found him the sawbones from the mortuary couldn't tell. You'd have to read the tea leaves to find out if there was a gunshot wound. Why? Are you adding a chapter on the perfect crime to your saga?'

'Thanks, Isidore, I owe you one.'

Joseph was delighted to be able to play a key role in the current investigation, but he was desolate at not having an opportunity to see Iris. He had been tucked away in his study since dawn, avoiding Euphrosine's recriminations, and had spent a long time admiring the fountain pen bought in London by his beloved. It was a little marvel that enabled him to write two thousand words without having to fill up. With a pen like that, he would be able to produce a new serial full of adventure and rich vocabulary. And with the money he earned from it he would buy a typewriter even more sophisticated than Monsieur Mori's Lambert: he would buy a Remington. He ran through in his mind the advert he'd seen in *L'Illustration*: 'Unrivalled in simplicity, solidity and speed.'

He began to write, in a firm hand, in the pages of a brand-new notebook.

Frida von Glockenspiel had been hunting in vain for years for the fabulous hidden treasure of the Knights Templar, when in the middle of one stormy night, striped by flashes of lightning, her mastiff began to scratch feverishly on the floor of the cellar.

'Éleuthère!' she yelled.

By the time he arrived at Rue de Nice, Joseph still didn't know what the Teutonic lady's dog would unearth, but he had a strong suspicion that it would be human remains. He laid his cogitations to one side when he came to the isolated little shop, not far from some wasteland. On the outside, painted in whiting, were the words:

ACHILLE MÉNAGER
ANTIQUES AND SECOND-HAND GOODS

Hanging on a dirty little window, another sign read:

Closed for the Day
If Your Query is Urgent, Please Go To Number 4

Fearing he might be confronted with the same spectacle he'd found in Léonard Diélette's shack, he tried the door. To his surprise, it opened. Although there was a good deal of disorder, the contents of the shop appeared to be intact. He made a quick inspection. Everything was covered in dust and smelt musty. The dirt and mess made Joseph wonder whether the bric-a-brac merchant ever sold anything.

'It would be a wonder if anyone stumbled across the shop, but if they actually bought any of this junk it would be a miracle,' he said to himself.

He looked around at the relics.

'A wicker mannequin, a sailor's chest – empty, a copper spittoon, a soldier's tin trunk, a donkey on wheels – flea-ridden, chamber pots, more chamber pots, oh, and broken old mustard jars, an anvil, a suitcase full of Andalusian fans with engraved names: Concepción, Manuelita, Carmen. Olé!'

Dumped amidst this jumble were walking sticks of ivory, ebony and tortoiseshell, as well as bamboo canes. But of goblets decorated with the face of a cat: not a sign.

Unable to tell whether someone had already searched through the junk, Joseph hunted through all the corners of the shop before giving up. And then, since the owner was still nowhere to be seen, he left the shop, went in under the porch next door and crossed a barren courtyard at the far corner of which was a tumbledown dwelling. After casting an eye over a lean-to under which were a barrel organ and a bicycle, he set off up the steep, dark staircase. When he put his foot on the fifth step, it emitted a sonorous creak.

The emissary jumped. Suddenly on the alert, he froze. Footsteps. Someone was coming up.

He abandoned his search and looked around for somewhere to hide, somewhere he could spring out from and overcome the intruder, if he was alone. Too late! There was only one thing to do – it was risky but would put him in a strong position if attack were the only option. He held his breath; the intruder was approaching.

The door half opened. Joseph paused in the doorway. His eyes swept the bedroom, which had been turned upside down. Even the floorboards had been torn up.

'Monsieur Ménager?'

He stopped at the door of a second room, feebly lit by a narrow window. He saw an overturned cupboard, a table and a bed in disarray.

'Monsieur Ménager? Are you there?'

Flattened against the wall behind the door, the emissary

slipped out on to the landing, climbed the ladder and silently lifted the trap door; child's play for someone who was careful to keep himself in shape.

As Joseph entered the room, he saw him. He lay on his back, one arm folded under him.

No, he pleaded silently. Please not that!

He overcame his repugnance and separated the flaps of the overcoat. There, that dark stain in the middle of the body's vest: blood.

He was bending over the body when he heard a noise, coming from outside, in the courtyard. He listened, but now there was silence. He flinched when the noise began again, then went over to the window.

A dark-haired woman wrapped in a black cape was approaching the stairs.

He fell flat on his stomach and scrambled under the bed as fast as he could. An idiotic thought struck him. There must be bugs under here. Frozen against the floor, he could not avoid looking out at Ménager's body. His teeth were chattering faster than castanets. He must control himself!

He heard the woman coming up the stairs – no creaking; she'd been up them before. Then a pair of ankle boots stopped by the body. Joseph kept his head down. The boots turned round. This time the stairs did creak. Joseph shot out of his hiding place and hurried over to the window. The woman was dragging the barrel organ.

Joseph bounded down the stairs and charged out under the porch. The woman, bent over her organ, was hurrying towards Rue de Charonne.

The emissary stood up. His legs propelled him forwards. He tumbled down the ladder, through the upper floor and out into the courtyard, where he glanced into the lean-to. The barrel organ had disappeared.

He mounted his bicycle and drove it forwards.

There they were, walking up Rue de Charonne in single file: the woman with the barrel organ, followed at a short distance by the bookshop assistant.

CHAPTER 13

Saturday afternoon, 16 April

Dressed in her rabbit-skin coat, Madame Ballu was sitting in her chair beside the entrance to the building, enjoying a well-earned rest in the sun. Euphrosine Pignot appeared, out of breath from carrying a basket filled with apples, which she plonked down on the pavement.

'You'll do your back in, you poor thing!'

'Don't I know it? I was going to ask my son to help me, but Monsieur has vanished into thin air.'

'It's normal at his age. You have to give him his freedom!'

'It's not as if I've been trying to hold him back. He can pack up and leave for all I care,' grumbled Euphrosine as she massaged the small of her back.

'You don't mean that. You know you'd miss him. By the way, when is his next serial coming out? I'm looking forward to it.'

'He's not working on it much at the moment. Too busy canoodling with Monsieur Mori's daughter. They can't fool me – there's something going on between those two.'

'Never!'

'Yes! Just imagine what a fine old mess it would be if they got up to any mischief. Why I'd have a half-Charentais, half-Japanese grandchild!'

'Are you from La Charente? It's a lovely part of the world; lots of oysters there.'

'Just La Charente, not La Charente-Maritime – your geography's hopeless!'

'Well, it's all the same to me. That's a nice lot of fruit you have there – it must have cost a pretty penny. I should know. I've a hearty appetite and I spend fortunes!'

'Please, help yourself. An old acquaintance at Les Halles gave them to me.'

Madame Ballu did not wait to be asked twice. She filled her pinny with apples and sat down again, telling Euphrosine as she picked up her basket, 'I would give you a hand only I'm feeling a little worn out myself. Polishing that brass does my back no good at all.'

'Excuse me, ladies, do you know of a photographer's studio at this address?'

Euphrosine and Madame Ballu regarded the woman in the black wool jacket addressing them and shook their heads.

'Not at this address.'

'But I wrote it down, 18 Rue des Saint-Pères!'

The two women looked at one another.

'Someone has given you false information,' Madame Ballu declared.

'No. I'm positive this is right. I have a letter addressed to the photographer who lives at number 18.'

'Wait a minute! That could be Monsieur Legris. Isn't photography his pastime?' Euphrosine asked Madame Ballu.

'More like his hobby horse,' muttered the concierge.

'Don't you mean his hobby? So I wasn't mistaken. Which floor is he on?'

Euphrosine doubted the bookseller would be there, since he'd moved to the ninth arrondissement to be with the woman she discreetly referred to as his 'flame'. However, if the woman would be good enough to follow her, she'd give her note to his associate, Monsieur Mori. 'My son's future father-in-law,' she mouthed to herself.

Iris left Yvette's bedside for a moment and went to open the door for them. She explained that her father wasn't there but that she'd make sure he received the letter. Euphrosine, who was curious about the visitor for whom she felt an instinctive liking and who reminded her of a younger version of herself, asked permission to offer the woman a cup of coffee. Iris told Euphrosine to consider herself at home and apologised for having to administer to her little patient.

'Have you come far?' Euphrosine asked the woman.

'I walked all the way from Rue Charlot. Today's the day I visit my mother. She's a chair attendant at Les Jardins du Luxembourg. They call her Old Mother Ticket. I said to myself, "Bertille, you can kill two birds with one stone."'

'Bertille. That's a pretty name. Mine's Euphrosine. I used to have a costermonger's cart, now I'm a cook.'

'You don't say! So am I, for the Houssoye household.'

'And how many mouths do you have to feed?'

Bertille counted on her fingers.

'Six, no five, on account of one of them died. And that's not including the servants.'

'And there was I feeling sorry for myself... That must be hell!'

'It's not as bad as it sounds. In fact it's as easy as pie. I have several strings to my bow: beef casserole, beef bourguignon or at a pinch bubble and squeak! It's all in the sauce. You must know the expression "It's the sauce that helps the fish slip down"?'

'Fancy that! And they don't complain?'

'Not a bit. They come back for more and grow fatter by the day. A nice thick onion sauce gets them all guzzling!'

'At least you can give them meat. The young lady you just met eats only vegetables,' Euphrosine confided in a whisper.

'Pour a little marrow fat on them and they'll all be licking their chops,' Bertille advised, pushing back her coffee cup and standing up despite Euphrosine's objections.

You can't appreciate music on an empty stomach, thought Joseph, his head spinning from listening to the love songs sung by the Italian girl. For he was certain she was Italian.

'*Amo . . . e disperato è l'amor mio*'[1]

He had followed her all the way from Faubourg Sainte-Marguerite to the Latin quarter. They had gone as far as Place de la Bastille and stopped next to the station, where her barrel organ had droned out its first old refrain, then at three other places along the banks of the Seine near the main bridges, and then finally in front of Notre-Dame, until the Italian girl had spied two gendarmes and fled.

She had come to a complete halt at number 1, Rue de l'École-de-Médecine, outside a second-hand clothes shop owned by Père Blancard, otherwise known as Père Monaco, who spoke to her for a few moments and then hung a sign on her organ.

First rate second-hand clothes
At Jericho's Trumpet

Joseph assumed that the songstress was allowed to leave her instrument there for as long as she liked in exchange for a percentage of her earnings.

Joseph had been hiding for more than an hour behind a flower stall selling violets for two sous a bunch, alternately hungry and cold. He might have endured these inconveniences with more stoicism had he not been incessantly reliving the scene at Rue de Nice. The idea of death didn't frighten him so long as it was natural, for he believed in God and left it to heaven to look after the souls of the dead. But murder was another kettle of fish altogether! He felt bad about leaving Achille Ménager's body lying there.

'She's taking her time. If I hurry, I might just make it.'

The emissary stood in the shadow of a doorway. Where was that fool of an assistant going off to in such a hurry? A café on the boulevard; a call of nature, no doubt.

The emissary could have kicked himself. How foolish to have searched the bric-a-brac merchant's two rooms and forget the lean-to! The organ; the abomination was hidden inside the barrel organ.

Joseph stood in front of the wooden telephone box fixed to the wall and pressed a button that connected him to the central exchange. He gave the number of the person he wished to call. The connection took a while and in the meantime he examined the machine, which reminded him of a toilet-tissue dispenser. The bell finally rang so loudly it almost burst his eardrums. He picked up the receiver and, pinching his nose between finger and thumb, recited into the mouthpiece the little speech he had prepared for Inspector Pérot.

'Hello? Is this the police station? I want to speak to Inspector Pérot . . . He's not there? I have an urgent message. There's a corpse at number 4 Rue de Nice, in the Popincourt quarter.'

He hung up, paid for the call, slugged back a glass of grenadine and rushed back to Rue de l'École-de-Médecine.

Thank goodness, she's still there. It looks like she's made a tidy little sum. Am I mistaken or is she finally going . . . Hurrah!

His suffering, alas, was not over. He was obliged to follow the Italian girl as far as the dark narrow Rue Saint-Severin, where he watched from a distance while she made several purchases. The smell of food wafted out from a shop with a brown façade. He walked over to it, licking his lips at the sight of the hefty casserole dishes from which the customers were serving themselves. He leant against a lamp-post, keeping his eye on the Italian girl. She stepped back out on to the pavement, set down a package on her barrel organ, bought a penny loaf then went into a café and emerged with a bottle of wine and a bag of coal. Then she crossed Place Saint-Michel, its cafés filled with students out on the town and street girls on the lookout for customers. She darted between the carriages and omnibuses surrounded by crowds of commuters waving their numbered tickets in the air, and paused near the dragon fountain, where she placed the goods she had bought inside her barrel organ and headed towards Place Saint-André-des-Arts.

At the beginning of the street bearing the same name, she darted into the doorway of a ramshackle building.

Joseph hesitated. Should he follow the girl and accost her? Under what pretext? Should he wait or should he return to Rue des Saints-Pères? Given that if he died of starvation it would mean an end to the case, he plumped for the latter option.

Rid at last of the interfering assistant, the emissary slipped into the house. His breath quickened; the organ was at the foot of the stairs. He opened the cover, ready to seize the abomination. Nothing but pipes!

Footsteps . . . Voices upstairs. He must leave without his trophy!

Stirred by the thought that not only had Anna come back, but that she had spent hours singing in the streets in order to bring him food, Mathurin Ferrant unlocked a store cupboard and placed the organ inside it before hurrying upstairs. The potatoes were already cooking on top of the squat red stove and creating an agreeable fug.

'Unwrap the chops, cut some bread and uncork the wine. There's still a little paraffin left. I'll buy some more tomorrow.'

'You are an absolute angel, a princess. Ouch!' Mathurin had forgotten the sloping ceiling and banged his head.

'Sit down and eat,' she ordered, handing him a plate.

For a moment the air was filled only with the sound of the stove and their chewing. After they had finished eating and wiped their plates clean, they looked at each other and burst out laughing.

'Heavens! I hadn't realised how hungry I was. For days now I've been tightening my belt, telling myself that man proposes, God disposes. You're my lucky star, Anna. And a star that's fading fast by the looks of it,' he cried as he saw her eyelids begin to droop. 'Come on, time for bed!'

He turned round for as long as it took her to undress and slide under the blanket. She laid her head on the pillow and was surprised by the sudden unbidden memory of Luigi kissing her forehead before blowing out the candle.

'Goodnight,' said Mathurin softly, his limbs spilling over the sofa he had settled down upon.

Bathed in the moonlight streaming in through the skylight, Achille Ménager's goblet sat in the middle of the table, giving off menacing vibrations. However tightly Anna shut her eyes she could still see its orange glow. She was gripped by a sudden panic.

'Mathurin, are you asleep?'

'Hm . . . Yes.'

'Would you mind coming and lying next to me? I'm cold.'

'Are you . . . sure?'

'Yes.'

He tried his best to avoid touching her, but couldn't help it. Not knowing where to put his arm, he finally raised it above his head.

Reassured, she began to tell him what was weighing on her

mind: the death of her father, her awful life with the pig, his murder, which she had witnessed, the theft of the goblet.

'Warm me up,' she whispered.

Mathurin slowly lowered his arm. She trembled as she felt his hand touch her shoulder. She pressed her body against his and held him in a warm embrace. The bed began to rock.

'We're going to capsize,' he whispered.

She placed her finger on his lips.

There should be a statue raised in memory of the inventor of the *frite*, Joseph thought to himself, overjoyed to be eating something at last.

He dipped merrily into his paper cone as he walked alongside a row of coaches on Boulevard de Clichy.

The lamplighter had just passed along Rue Fontaine. Joseph stopped beneath a gas lamp and, after wiping his greasy fingers, succumbed to the temptation that had been gnawing away at him since Iris had entrusted him with the letter left by some woman, a cook at Rue Charlot.

I have a right to know. We're a team after all.

He opened the envelope.

Monsieur Photographer,

    Come at once, I have some important information to give you. I reckon that it's worth at least five or six comely posteriors like the one you already honoured me with.

    Your servant,

    Baron Fortunat de Vigneules

Joseph whistled.

'He must have been a right old rogue in his youth!'

He stuffed the letter back in the envelope and hurried to Victor's house. He regretted having to go there after such a tiring day, but felt obliged to pass on the message, especially since Monsieur Mori had gone out. He pictured Iris in her beautiful Japanese gown, and the tender kisses they had exchanged. No doubt she would take advantage of her father's absence to type out the prologue to *Thule's Golden Chalice* on his precious Lambert.

Victor had changed into a blue shirt with starched collar and cuffs, and a pair of tapered wool trousers. He was about to don a patterned velvet waistcoat when Joseph knocked at the door.

'You look very dapper, Boss! I haven't seen you in a bow tie for a long time.'

'I don't imagine you came here to admire my outfit. Did you manage to find Ménager? What has become of the goblet?'

'I did, Boss, but I drew a blank: no sign of the goblet anywhere and the bric-a-brac merchant's apartment looked like the hippodrome[2] after a steeplechase. And on top of which . . .'

'What?'

'The fellow's dead – a bullet in the chest. I made an anonymous call to Inspector Pérot – I couldn't leave the blighter lying there.'

'You did the right thing,' Victor muttered. 'Are you all right? Do you feel better now? I'm awfully sorry, Joseph. Would you like a pick-me-up?'

'No thanks, Boss. There's another thing. A girl came while I was at Ménager's. She panicked when she saw the body and ran off with her barrel organ, which she pushed around the whole blooming day. She sings Neapolitan songs, so she has to be Italian. I've got them on the brain. I followed her to where she lives at number 3 Rue Saint-André-des-Arts. There's no way of knowing whether she was involved in the murder.'

'Good work, Joseph, a real Sherlock Holmes. Do you think she might have the goblet?'

'Who knows? One of us has to go there first thing and keep an eye on her. Oh, I almost forgot!'

Joseph handed him Fortunat's letter.

'I should warn you, Boss, I opened it,' he said in a defiant voice.

Victor cast an eye over the missive and scratched his head.

'We must divvy up the tasks. How would you like to pay a little visit to our bawdy old gent?'

'Again? He's got a screw loose, that fellow. He gives me the willies – him and those stuffed pooches!'

'Well, if you're scared, I'll go.'

'Scared, me? After all I've been through!'

'In that case you go. I'll leave his gift at the bookshop for you to pick up and you give it to him in exchange for the information. And while you're there try to find out whether anyone in the family is a crack shot or has been to Great Britain recently. In the meantime I'll go and stand guard on Rue Saint-André-des-Arts and you can take over from me at lunchtime. Agreed?'

'At your service, Boss – that's what I call good organisation. I'd better be off home now or Maman will give me an earful.'

222

Victor had reached a decision, and yet he felt nervous. Tasha would be here soon! Was he going to be able to tell her what was on his mind? And how would she react?

There's no point in speculating. I am too good at analysing things. It's a weakness. I scrutinise, interpret and weigh things up according to my own reasoning, and in doing so lose sight of reality. We'll both lay our cards on the table, he said to himself, and if any questions need answering we'll answer them.

He marched to and fro in his apartment, his waistcoat in his hand. Finally, he crossed the courtyard into the studio, which was filled with shadows cast by the fading light. He lit a tiny lamp that gave off a feeble bluish glow. Standing next to the window he watched the carpenter's children. They were playing off-ground tag, their shrieks of laughter echoing back off the walls. He didn't feel hungry. At nine o'clock he removed his bow tie and lay down on the bed in the alcove. At the sight of the pillow, a lump rose in his throat and he sent it flying. Suddenly he was furious with Tasha for making him so unhappy.

What should I say to her? 'I read it, I know, but don't worry, dear, you are free to go and see your ex-lover. I understand perfectly . . .' What drivel! He forced himself to think about the goblet, the monkey's skullcap decorated with the face of a cat. What made it worth killing for?

Sitting nonchalantly, cross-legged with a book in his hand and a faint smile on his lips, Kenji Mori looked as if he were about to utter one of his pet proverbs. Victor turned away from the portrait Tasha had painted two years before. What a mad idea to have hung it opposite their bed! Exasperated, he stood up, grabbed a smock and covered the painting.

At nine thirty, Tasha opened the door. The lamp was still burning, a tiny flicker in the vastness of the darkened room. She walked over to the bed. Victor lay on his back, asleep, his shoes still on. She stood looking at him lovingly and touched his shoulder. He groaned, opened his eyes and sat up.

'It's you . . . Is it late?'

She shook her head.

'Barbizon, your exhibition?'

She so longed to tell him, but she couldn't – she had promised.

'I didn't sell anything.'

As he watched her undress, he knew he wouldn't ask for an explanation. He loved her too much. He took her in his arms and held her tight.

'I missed you,' he murmured.

'I have to go,' Eudoxie said, straightening a hat adorned with huge bows. 'Fifi Bas-Rhin waits for no man. Take your places for the quadrille!'

She winked fondly at Kenji. 'Until Thursday morning?'

He looked at her blankly and smiled. 'I'll phone you, sweetheart.'

She longed to snuggle up in his arms, but she stopped herself – he wasn't keen on displays of affection. She blew him a kiss and left.

As soon as the door was closed, he leapt off the bed, pulled on a dressing gown and sank into an armchair. Kenji had been brought up in a family that had converted to Christianity, but he had always distanced himself from dogma and ritual. Over the years he had formed his own philosophy, effortlessly combining experience and imagination to the point where at times he could no longer tell the difference between the two states. He enjoyed spending long moments contemplating the mirages of his own imagination, without ever really allowing them to dictate his behaviour. It had become second nature to him, carefully to manipulate his emotions and intuitions, while accepting their capriciousness, and in doing so perceive what lay beyond words.

He dressed unhurriedly, feeling in his pocket for the notebook in which he jotted down his proverbs and aphorisms. The thing that had struck him about John Cavendish's letter when he reread it echoed in his head like a binary measure: *Tri-nil, Tri-nil* . . . His intuition was to stay with that name, to drift back in time to a distant landscape buried deep in his memory.

He closed his eyes and remembered. An expedition in a covered cart during a monsoon; a Chinese burial ground where they had got stuck in the mud; the welcome they received in a *kampong*, where the villagers, after eating *ampo*,[3] had danced the *tandak*; Pati, the beautiful Javanese girl who had initiated him into the art of love. Her slender shoulders and breasts and her curved hips enveloped in a sarong, her long hair garlanded with flowers. The stories she had told him in whispers of the *kriss* — the long Malay dagger that could supposedly tell good from evil and mete out justice itself. The bubbling sound of the mounting waters mixed with the girl's hushed tones.

'The River Solo,' he murmured.

He reread the notes he had written that morning as he leafed through *Unknown Countries and their Peoples* by Victor Tissot.

Trinil is a village situated in central northern Java, at the foot of the Lawu-Kukusan volcano on the banks of the River Solo. Flooding is frequent during the rainy season in the last few months of the year.

He sighed. He had only spent one night with his first lover. And yet he had never been able to forget her face. He had left at dawn, promising to return. He had no idea then that he would soon set off for an island shrouded by the mists of the North Sea.

He caught hold of himself and picked up the receiver of the telephone he'd had Eudoxie install. He asked for a London number then went and sat down again. His thoughts turned to Iris and Joseph. Why did his daughter's fondness for his assistant bother him so? Was it because he was afraid that she was reproducing the situation he had created with Daphné? Did not his irritation prove that he was projecting his own past suffering on to these young people?

The telephone rang. He explained the reason for his call to the English person at the other end and gave him the address of the Elzévir bookshop. He was disappointed – he would have to wait two more days for the answers to his questions.

CHAPTER 14

Sunday, 17 April

JOSEPH whistled as he crossed Le Marché des Enfants-Rouges. Housewives laden with bulging string bags rummaged suspiciously through the merchandise set out on rows of stalls. A vendor cried out the benefits of a lotion for insect bites in a mournful voice. The sun had come out and Joseph's spirits were soaring, for Iris had sworn her undying love for him, and he felt free of all earthly cares. He couldn't resist the desire to buy a couple of cured sausages from an obese, moustachioed woman who insisted on pouring him a snifter of absinthe, which he politely refused. He needed to keep a clear head. Sated from his snack, he fingered the envelope the Boss had entrusted to him.

His sleuthing instinct told him he should open it and he obeyed. It contained a catalogue of photographic studies for painters and sculptors of nude women in varying poses: from the front, the rear, side on, vertical and horizontal.

'They're a sight for sore eyes,' he said to himself.

No point in wasting ammunition. He may as well eke out the rewards if he was going to quiz the old goat: one picture for every correct answer. That seemed fair enough. He tore out half a dozen prints and continued on his way.

'Hey! You! The fellow in the cap!'

Joseph smiled broadly at the ill-tempered little runt in a stove-pipe hat who was standing guard beside the entrance to the town house.

'Maman sent me. "Tell Madame Bertille that the Jerusalem artichokes will be delivered tonight."'

The password did the trick, and Michel Crevoux, ex-colonial infantryman, wounded at the battle of Lang Son in the service of France, allowed him through.

Heavens! Joseph thought. I have to find my way back through that maze of corridors.

He walked up to the first floor and promptly got lost. After turning in circles, he opened a door and found himself in an anteroom, the walls of which were covered in grotesque masks that looked like the Oriental cousins of the ones on the Pont Neuf. Hearing voices in the hall, he looked around for an exit and saw another door hidden by a curtain. He opened it a crack. A man and a woman were standing in the middle of a drawing room.

'My dear Gaby,' said a tall, languorous-looking individual with a jaded expression, 'you must admit it is rather incongruous.'

'What is?' asked the woman as she sat down at a piano.

'The show of devastated grief you put on for the servants' benefit . . . Oh no! Not Chopin's "Funeral March". I can't abide Chopin!'

The woman closed the piano lid and looked at him, amused.

'Where is your sense of humour, Alexis? You are so dreadfully serious!'

'I won't deny it. But I can't say the same for you. You seem to revel in making a chaste man out of me. This sinister farce is starting to get on my nerves.'

'Have you no sense of propriety, my poor dear? Antoine is barely in the ground and all you can think of is . . .'

'Since when have you been such a prude? Why not be open about what everybody suspects we have been doing for so long in secret?'

'I . . . Yes?'

A man walked into the room, his back to Joseph.

'What did you want, my dear Dorsel?' the woman asked.

'I have to go out this afternoon . . .'

Joseph missed the rest of the conversation. He heard footsteps approaching. He moved away from the door and plonked himself in front of a Noh mask. The footsteps died away. Joseph glanced out into the corridor. It was empty. He set off, determined to find Fortunat de Vigneules's chamber. In the end he had no difficulty locating it, guided by the sound of raised voices.

'Monsieur Fortunat, your daughter gave me strict instructions not to let you take snuff or smoke. She'll make you pay a penalty.'

'Silence, sloven! I'll die before I give her a penny!'

'I don't care what you get up to!' Bertille Piot cried, turning on her heel. 'But the day you set this place on fire . . .'

Joseph waited until she had gone before knocking on the door.

'By the Devil! *Vade retro*, slattern! Go and stir your pots! How dare you call me an arsonist!'

'Monsieur de Vigneules, I work for the photographer. I've brought you a small gift.'

'Oh, it's you, the messenger – delighted you could come! Enter, servant boy, and inform me of your knight's reply. I see that the slattern delivered my letter.'

'I confess that my knight could make neither head nor tail of it.'

Joseph handed Fortunat one of the prints from the catalogue. The old man eyed it, his eyes sparkling.

'Oh, curvaceous creatures! Alas, I am feeble with age and can no longer hold my trusty sword aloft! Stay there, servant boy,' Fortunat ordered, 'I need a moment to reflect.'

He knelt at the foot of Louis XVI's portrait, uttered a quick prayer then rose to his feet again, frowning.

'I am extremely busy, servant boy. Do I have your word that you will leave nothing out when you relay to your knight what I am about to tell you?'

'You have my word.'

'Well then, I am penniless and haven't an ounce of tobacco left. I am being fed on scraps and held prisoner. I need rescuing! But there's worse . . .'

Fortunat rummaged through a pile of clothes and pulled out a garment that resembled an instrument of torture.

'Look, servant boy. What do you think this is?'

'Er . . . a corset?'

'Quite right. Pretty, isn't it? And very slimming. Why, I could have joined my hands round the waist of the woman who wore it.'

'What are you getting at?'

'Patience, servant boy – every detail counts. This contraption shows off the hips to great advantage. Feel it. It is rigid, yet it fits the contours of the belly, bringing out its rotundity and at the same time pushes up the breasts, and . . . You're not listening!'

'I am, I assure you.'

'As I said, servant boy, every detail counts. The material, for instance, is mauve silk brocade: *her* colour. Oh! How often I watched her undressing in the evening through a crack in the wall! She knew I was spying on her, the temptress, and snuffed out her candle before taking off her underwear. Then a man would join her, and I plugged my ears to block out the sound of their breathless fornication! Look,' Fortunat cried, thrusting the corset under Joseph's nose.

'I can't see anything remarkable.'

'There! The embroidered ladybird with its seven black spots! She has an identical one tattooed on her shoulder. The corset is hers, I am sure. Moreover, she's from Sète.'

'The town of Sète?'

'Yes, not far from the land of the Cathars, that heretical sect!'

'But who are you talking about?'

'Delilah, the wicked woman who cut off poor Samson's hair. Ah, servant boy, the dance of the veils!'

'A thousand pardons, but . . .'

'I digress. How do you account for this petticoat, this garter, this corset, this Book of Hours initialled *L. R.*, all of which I discovered at the back of a cellar on Rue du Poitou, during one of my underground forays?'

'I've no idea.'

'I am glad to hear you say so, for neither have I. And she disappeared five days ago.'

'Who did?' bellowed Joseph.

'Lucie Robin, my daughter's maid. Ah! It's too much! Tell me, swineherd, by what infernal magic did this garter and these petticoats turn up at the exact spot where the remains of one of the order's masters were discovered?'

Joseph felt like saying that he preferred to be called servant boy. The conversation was taking a worrying turn. Was the old eccentric telling him the truth or simply pulling the wool over his eyes? He remained silent, staring at the pear-shaped face of the late Louis-Philippe hanging over the hearth and thinking, I must get out of here.

'I can find no logical explanation,' he replied. 'This Lucie Robin must be dotty to have left her clothes strewn about in a place like that.'

'Are you suggesting that I'm senile? Oh no, swineherd, I am in possession of all my faculties. I cannot trust a single member of that tribe. I demand to be rescued. Confound you, slave! I'll end up losing my temper with you. How would you like a rump full of buckshot?'

If this goes on much longer, I'll have to make my escape through the window, thought Joseph. No. I must remain steadfast and accomplish my mission!

'Let's not get heated, Monsieur le Baron. Let's make a trade and then we can drink to it,' he suggested.

'What do you want from me?'

'An answer for each of these,' Joseph said, holding up a second print with pictures of naked nymphs on both sides.

'Agreed, servant boy. I am all ears.'

'Which members of your family have been to Java recently?'

'All of them, by Jove! They left me at the mercy of the servants for four months to go off and live with the apes. Gibbons and orang-utans are more important in their view than their own progenitor!'

'I want their names.'

'My daughter Gabrielle; her husband Antoine – the devil take him!; cousin Maxime, a spineless creature; their secretary Charles, a good sort; and the whore of Babylon!'

Joseph handed Fortunat a third print.

'Have any of them ever been to Great Britain?'

'Ah! Bounder! Let us take that drink. We'll drink to the health of the French King. Don't mention the name of perfidious Albion in my presence – my grandfather was cut in two at Trafalgar! A pox on England! . . . Antoine used to go there every so often to give conferences on monkeys. Monkeys, monkeys, that's all he was interested in! Ah, servant boy! Without tobacco I am incapable of stringing two thoughts together. Gabrielle, my daughter, has been bewitched. Commoner that you are, I shall let you into a secret. I am plotting a rebellion, armed with rapiers and pistols!'

'Do you know how to use a gun?'

'What an amusing fellow! Why I was taking pot shots at the insurgents back in 1830. Quack, quack! And I taught my daughter to shoot too. Quick, where's my blunderbuss? . . . Run along now, servant boy, I must join the pack; the mort has sounded. Tallyho!'

'One last thing. Besides your daughter, which of the others in the house knows how to use a gun?'

'I understand that in Java their favourite pastime was sniping at melons on sticks, yes, even the whore of Babylon! They think they're the cat's whiskers, but they're beneath my contempt. Melons . . .'

Joseph fled without waiting for him to finish.

The emissary saw the assistant appear at twelve o'clock on the dot and make a beeline for the butcher's shop, the window of which the emissary was using as a mirror. No doubt the fair-haired youth had come to relieve his associate, who had been standing there since the crack of dawn.

A crowd of passers-by had gathered in front of the butcher's block, where the first apprentice, his sleeves rolled up, was sculpting a piglet out of a block of lard using a scraper. From his observation post, the emissary kept a sharp eye on the two accomplices whose reflection mingled with a row of lambs' legs decked in frilly paper crowns. He was well out of earshot, but judging from his emphatic gestures the fair-haired boy was on to something. What were they talking about? The emissary trembled with rage.

For pity's sake, Lord, put an end to my ordeal! Let those scoundrels lead me to the abomination. *Amen!*

'So, Boss, did you see the Italian girl?'

'No. I've been mooching around here since six o'clock this morning. I've seen several women come out of number 3, but none of them looked remotely like a barrel organ player. I assume she must begin her rounds in the afternoon. And what of your visit to Monsieur de Vigneules, Joseph?'

'Wait for it, Boss. I overheard a conversation that left me in no doubt that Antoine du Houssoye was a cuckold. His wife's lover is a man named Alexis. Why such a long face?'

'That's hardly news! Anything else?'

'No. Only that the old goat drove me half crazy,' Joseph added bitterly. 'You can go and pay your respects in person next time. I've had enough!'

Joseph began to tell him a confused story about every member of the household on Rue Charlot having a skeleton in their cupboard. Victor wondered if the discovery of women's underwear in the cellar of a house on Rue du Poitou was significant.

'And you say they belonged to the maid?'

'That's what the old man claims. Her name's Lucie Robin. He showed me her initials, as well as an embroidered ladybird with seven black spots. I can't help thinking, Boss, that he's leading them all a merry dance by pretending to be soft in the head. He fed me the whole story like you'd feed an angry dog a bone, and the old lecher certainly knows his dogs. And then there's . . .'

Victor tilted his head to one side. An astonishing thought had occurred to him. Despite his wise decision never to trust his intuition, he had just remembered something Madame du Houssoye had said about her maid. '. . . left in a hurry to go and look after . . .' Look after whom? 'Yes, that's right . . . the secretary asked her if . . . But when? When did she leave?' he muttered to himself, stroking his moustache.

Joseph was speechless. He looked at his Boss with a mixture of bewilderment and frustration. Monsieur Legris clearly didn't appreciate his efforts. Victor, sensing the pregnant silence and seeing the indignation on his assistant's face, forced a smile.

'All in all, the only new element is the possibility that the maid is the murderess,' he said in a soothing voice. 'She may have tried to fake her disappearance. Well, I'm off to Rue des Saints-Pères. Keep your eyes skinned, Sherlock Pignot, I shall be back at six o'clock sharp!'

'Hey! Wait, it turns out they've all been to . . . And when am I going to eat?' Joseph protested.

'Follow Monsieur Mori's dictum: when you are hungry, eat,' Victor cried out as he hopped on to the platform of the omnibus.

Joseph watched him disappear into the distance. He derived a sense of mournful pleasure from being the victim of a cruel oppressor. For several minutes he entertained a poignant image of his prone body as he lay gasping on the pavement, surrounded by a crowd of onlookers, and failed to notice Anna leave the building with her barrel organ.

Inspector Raoul Pérot had at last returned to his office. He stretched, kicked off his shoes and massaged the soles of his feet, observing that his socks were little more than two holes surrounded by a few strands of wool. He loosened his tie and settled back in his chair. He wouldn't have minded drinking a cordial. The words of Jules Janin sprang to mind: 'Journalism can get you everywhere, provided you know how to get out of it.' He replaced 'journalism' with 'the police force' and concluded that his career would not be a long one, even if it did bring him eight thousand francs a year, a stipend that afforded him the freedom to devote himself to literature.

He had been seized by a morbid curiosity as soon as he spotted the two gendarmes carrying their sinister load through the entrance to the courtyard. Unable to resist the temptation to lift up the blanket that covered the body, he had immediately felt his legs turn to jelly. It was the first time he had seen death close up, and the sight had dampened any enthusiasm he might have had for a career in the force.

He slipped his feet into his shoes and went to close the window. The police station he oversaw was situated at the end of a gloomy back alley behind a building housing several families. It consisted of a guard's room with a bulbous stove that took up almost a quarter of the floor space, a counter behind which Chavagnac and Gerbecourt played at naval battles, and a cell that mostly stood empty. To use the toilet they went up one flight of stairs and down another to Père Arsène's eating house, where they also ate and drank. Owing to some clerical error a telephone had been installed on the wall of his office – a tiny room, which he had arranged to suit his tastes.

Inspector Pérot had been appointed to his post sixteen months earlier, and was doing his utmost to take his responsibilities seriously, although his sector was inhabited by artisans and small businesses and therefore almost without incident. The only cases of interest he had been involved in were the break-in at the bookshop on Rue des Saint-Pères, and the incarceration of some poor devil who believed he had lost his wife in a sock.

Life went by, killing time in its wake, one long day, the

monotony of which broken only by squabbling neighbours, naval battles, regular checks on three local flea-ridden hotels and tortoise races.

So, on the morning of 17 April, when a group of laundresses and anglers invaded the police station, Raoul Pérot and his four subordinates felt as if their routine had been turned upside down. At dawn, Père Figaro, a dog groomer who frequented the banks of the Seine, had noticed a bundle bumping against one of the piles of the Pont des Arts.

'The law of seriality,' concluded Raoul Pérot. For, the previous evening, an anonymous caller had notified him of a corpse in the eleventh arrondissement. He had been obliged to report this to his immediate superior on Boulevard du Palais, since the constables in the eleventh arrondissement had indeed discovered the body of a bric-a-brac dealer with a bullet hole through him on Rue de Nice. Raoul Pérot and his superior, the big shot Aristide Lecacheur, had been at a loss to understand why anybody would inform a police inspector on the Rive Gauche about a crime that had been committed on the Rive Droite.

There was a knock at the door. Anténor Bucherol walked in looking pale, his kepi askew.

'A nasty business, Boss, the body's gone to the morgue. A woman of twenty-five or thirty years old. Pretty underwear, with the initials *L. R.* embroidered on them. She has a tattoo of a ladybird on her shoulder. The doctor is certain that she was shot through the heart then tossed into the river.'

'Poor creature, she must have been fond of beetles,' Raoul Pérot murmured, and rattled off a rhyme:

Ladybird, ladybird fly away home
Avert your gaze from the decline of Rome

'Very heartfelt, Boss! There's a fellow asking to see you.'

'Show him in.'

Raoul Pérot hurriedly laced up his shoes. His face lit up when he saw Victor.

'Monsieur Légris! Have you brought a list of stolen objects?'

'You can close that case. I wanted to give you this hardback by way of thanking you for releasing the girl.'

'*L'Imitation de Notre-Dame la Lune*, by Jules Laforgue! Well, thank you indeed; it is a wonderful anthology! What a shame we can't sit and have a relaxed conversation. I'm dreadfully busy. There's been a murder.'

'A murder? That explains all those people outside the police station.'

'Somebody threw a corpse into the Seine. Poor woman, her lucky ladybird didn't protect her. I have to go the morgue – though I'd rather not. She was shot. Ah! Our lives are so ephemeral.'

'A ladybird!' exclaimed Victor.

'Yes, tattooed on her shoulder. It may help us to discover who she is.'

Victor, suddenly excited, leant forward. 'May I ask you a favour, Inspector? Could you keep me abreast of the investigation? You see, I'm writing a detective novel. Naturally I won't reveal my sources.'

'What a coincidence, Monsieur Legris! You're a writer too. You can count on me to tell you anything that won't hamper the investigation.'

*

He had at last agreed to leave the Hôtel de Pékin in daylight after Tasha had persuaded him that he was not in danger.

'Thousands of foreigners arrive in this city every day. Who is going to notice you? You have an exaggerated idea of your own importance!'

It was chilly, but sunny enough for them to wander aimlessly as had been their custom in bygone days. They walked along Boulevard de Ménilmontant and crossed the eleventh arrondissement without stopping, absorbed in their conversation. Only when they reached Canal Saint-Martin did they feel the need to rest. They sat on a bench on Quai Jemmapes, near Hôpital Saint-Louis.

In silence, they watched the golden flecks rippling out across the water as the laundresses beat their washing. Further on, mobile cranes were unloading barges, dark patches against a sky bristling with factory chimneys.

'Are you cold?' he asked. 'You have such a hectic lifestyle, my little Tasha.'

'You know nothing about my life,' she retorted, suppressing her irritation.

A barge slid quietly by. Two children were balancing on the edge and chasing each other from the prow end to the stern.

'I am not looking forward to my boat trip. I'd enjoy it a lot more if I was even a little bit like those two scamps,' he said with a chuckle, and then became serious. 'Foolish thoughts, since I'm nowhere near embarking.'

'I'm sorry. I've only been able to raise a quarter of the

money. But I promise you'll have your passage by the end of May. My editor assures me that he'll pay me on receipt of half the illustrations for the Poe, and I have high hopes of selling a painting to the Boussod et Valadon Gallery. Of course if you would only reconsider my suggestion, the problem would be solved.'

'No. I already told you.'

'He's very open-minded. He'll lend you the money.'

'No, I said.'

'He didn't build up his stocks and shares himself. He inherited them from his father! He has already offered to cash them in for me several times.'

'And you really believe he'll do it? Put him to the test: tell him who you want the money for and I guarantee you'll be disappointed.'

'He's more tolerant than you think!' she cried.

'How can you be so naïve? In any case, I won't touch his dirty money. The stock exchange is as decadent as a whorehouse.'

'And you're as white as the driven snow, you who left your wife and daughters in order to fight for a good cause!'

'Don't mix private life with politics.'

'Why not? So long as men fail to apply in the home the revolutionary theories they advocate in the street, the world will never change!'

She stood up abruptly, trembling with rage.

'You look so beautiful when you're angry, *katzele*.'[1]

'Stop treating me like a child.'

She strode off until she reached a row of factories towering above the masts of the barges moored on the canal. Near the Bassin de la Villette a sickly smell mingled with a lingering odour of mud filled her nostrils. He caught up with her, out of breath.

'Rage gives you wings, *feigele*.'[2]

'Forgive me. It's just that . . . You're being unfair. Victor may be a member of the bourgeoisie in a social sense, but he has a heart, and it is thanks to him that I have found my place here in France.'

'Love blinds you, and you idealise him. The situation suits Victor very well. You risk everything and he takes no responsibility.'

'That's not true! He has begged me to marry him. I'm the one who doesn't want to.'

'Why not? Then you could become the wife of a dabbler in stocks and shares.'

'You really are impossible!'

They reached the abattoirs. The sweet smell of the blood of slaughtered animals hung in the air. A troupe of butchers with sides of beef slung over their shoulders came and went in the bleak, dirty alleyways. Tasha tried hard not to cry.

It was nearly eight o'clock when Victor finally spotted a young woman with a barrel organ coming round the square. She walked into number 3 Rue Saint-André-des-Arts. He paused, unsure of what to do. Should he call out to her? No. She was their only chance of finding the goblet. When she emerged again on the arm of a long-haired fellow wearing a fedora, he decided to follow them.

Among the crowds of well-dressed students spilling out of the brasseries was an occasional Bohemian dressed in old-fashioned or eccentric garb. Rebels against formalism, they refused to pursue a career that might compromise their desire for freedom, turning their backs on conventional society to form a parallel world of their own. The Italian girl's companion clearly belonged to this alternative universe. He doffed his hat with a flourish at the gaunt-looking individuals dressed in 1880s garb, with their waisted jackets and tight-fitting trousers, and to the long-haired youths wearing berets and voluminous, faded capes who were cadging money for beer.

The Italian girl clearly controlled the purse strings, as she was the one who shook her head. Victor had no difficulty keeping the couple in his sights on Boulevard Saint-Michel, which was heaving with newspaper sellers, women looking for a dupe to buy their dinner, civil servants and clerks mixing with low society.

On the corner of Rue des Écoles, the love birds ducked into Café Vachette. Victor stood in the doorway, hesitating, jostled by the people going in. Finally he decided to enter.

Most of the tables were taken. He would have sat down at the one just behind the Italian girl and her companion, but was put off by the sickening sight of a drunkard sprawled across the bench snoring, his hat covering his face. He managed to squeeze on to another bench within earshot of the couple and, despite the rowdy gathering, could hear some of their conversation.

A fellow with a thick mop of hair hanging down over his face sat down with them. The man in the fedora introduced him to the Italian girl as Trimouillat, the poet. Trimouillat asked how *The Virgin of Lutetia* was coming along.

'She's about to drive back the invading hordes. During the winter of 451, the Huns were camped at Melun and bivouacked at Argenteuil and Créteil. Attila was tightening his hold. Panic had set in at Lutetia, and everybody was trying to flee, which is when Geneviève uttered these words:

> '"*Friends, I implore you!*
> *You are nowhere safer than here*
> *Fear not, Paris will be saved thanks to your*
> *Fervour!*"

And thanks to my muse, Anna,' Mathurin declared with a catch in his voice.

Trimouillat studied the Italian girl as he twisted a strand of hair round his finger. 'Mademoiselle, you are the spitting image of Victoire de Samothrace before she was decapitated.'

'Are you writing anything at the moment?'

'I have just begun a political work entitled *A Crisis at the Elysée.*

> '*Parliament being restive*
> *Drives a minister to drink*
> *The chief of the executive*
> *Is also on the brink*
> *For . . .*'

Interrupted by the waiter plonking a couple of espressos down on the table, Trimouillat lost his train of thought and continued to inspect his hair. The waiter hovered.

'What'll you have?' Mathurin asked.

'Can you afford a cherry brandy?'

'Of course! Oscar, a cherry brandy! We're flush. Not content with being my inspiration, Anna has shared the fruits of her undeniable musical talent with me. Imagine! She sings like an angel. Moreover, she has brought us a godsend in the form of a piece of old junk that will see us through to the end of the month.'

Victor started. Could this piece of old junk be the goblet? He swivelled in his chair, ready to question the Italian girl. The return of the waiter stopped him short.

'One cherry brandy!' shouted Oscar. 'You're quite right to be celebrating,' he added. 'It'll be 1 May soon.'

'And?'

'And the anarchists will be putting on a fireworks display for us, Monsieur Mathurin — watch out for the bangers!'

Victor swigged back his vermouth. He was in luck. Mathurin chose that moment to begin unwrapping a package he had taken out of his pocket. He shared the contents with Anna and Trimouillat.

'It's not good to drink on an empty stomach.'

'Saveloy! Have you struck gold?' Trimouillat, his mouth full, continued. 'You mean it's not good to drink. You only have to look at Verlaine. He's slowly destroying himself. Drunk as a lord he was this evening and causing quite a hullabaloo in Saint-Séverin, bellowing at the top of his voice that he wanted to confess. He's sleeping it off at the police station.'

As an admirer of *Then and Now*, Victor thought that this might be a good moment to join in their conversation. A loud cheer went up as an imposing figure in a monocle, Inverness cape and topper entered, flanked by a group of loudmouths, and imperiously demanded some dominoes and a lamb chop.

'Who is he?' whispered Anna.

'Jean Moréas. His real name is Papadiamantopoulos, a Greek poet and genius. He looks like a dandy, but he's a real gentleman.'

'He made an amusing remark to some flatterer yesterday: "Stand firmly by your principles and they'll end up caving in!" Excuse me while I go and pay him my respects. I'll be seeing you,' said Trimouillat.

'Why don't you go too, Mathurin?' Anna urged.

'No. Moréas makes me nervous. Also, I thought I saw Huysmans and Barrès with him. And Barrès . . .'

Anna felt out of her depth. Never before had she witnessed such a gathering of scholars: professors, lawyers and doctors sitting, not with their students, clients and patients, but in a smoky room, discussing literature or the latest journals. Nauseated by the smell of pipe smoke and cheap cigars, she turned the other way. A pair of brown eyes caught hers. Who was that man staring at her? Why was he getting up and walking over to them?

Victor sat down in Trimouillat's place.

'Allow me to introduce myself. My name is Inspector Victor Pérot. Mademoiselle, a little bird tells me that you are hiding something from me.'

Anna turned pale. Her hand gripped Mathurin's broad thigh.

'Leave this young lady alone,' Mathurin said.

'I won't trouble her for very long. I know she is innocent of any crime and provided she cooperates, no blame will attach to her.'

'How can we be sure that you're a policeman?' Mathurin said.

'Would you like to accompany me down to the station?'

'What is it you want to know?'

'What you have done with the goblet with the face of a cat.'

Anna and Mathurin exchanged uneasy glances.

'On my advice, this young lady sold it this morning to a man who sculpts figurines out of bone.'

Victor's heart missed a beat.

'Did you take your organ with you when you went out this morning?'

'No, because I was taking the goblet to the sculptor.'

Blockhead! Victor said to himself. You were expecting a girl with an organ. You let her slip through your fingers!

'And the name of this sculptor?' he asked, a tremor in his voice.

'They call him Osso Buco. He's an Italian immigrant. He peddles his figurines outside the bistros and sometimes poses as an artist's model.'

'Where can I find him?'

'I walked a long way before I came across him outside Le Procope,' Anna said.

'Another of his haunts is L'Académie des Tonneaux, on Rue Saint-Jacques,' Mathurin added, 'but you'll only catch him there during the day. He goes to bed at sundown.'

'Where does he live?'

'I don't know. Anna and I were convinced that the goblet was a fake or else we would have returned it to its rightful owner.'

'To a corpse, you mean,' Victor said sarcastically.

'In any case we only made a few francs from it.'

'You have a real talent for avoiding answering questions,' Victor commented, getting up.

He was jubilant.

'Am I free to go, then?' Anna asked.

'Stay at 3 Rue Saint-André-des-Arts until further notice. You'll be safe there,' Victor said as he took his leave.

The emissary, who'd been lying sprawled across the bench, sat bolt upright, pulled his hat down over his face and raced towards the exit, knocking into Victor. The abomination was in the hands of a bone sculptor, how ironic! There may no longer be any need to destroy it if its evil power had been neutralised through the transformation of its repulsive form.

> . . . *The deluge begins*
> *The abyss resounds*
> *He raises his hand up high*
> *The sun and moon remain*
> *In their firmament* . . .

The emissary closed the Book of Habakkuk, turned out the lamp and sat meditating. In the past, when the unimaginable had happened, he had heard the thunderous voice. It was booming now, louder than ever. He must act.

The emissary stretched out on the bed.

CHAPTER 15

Monday, 18 April

As it was Easter Monday, the bookshop was closed. Victor had telephoned Kenji early to relay the fruits of his investigations. He was confident he would be able to buttonhole the bone sculptor that afternoon at one of the two cafés the Italian girl had mentioned. He had come to the conclusion that Lucie Robin, the lady's maid, had also been done away with, and so he was planning to pay another visit to Rue Charlot.

'Be very careful, Victor. Report back to me regularly. I'll be back here in an hour, after I've told Joseph what you're going to do.'

Kenji hung up, feeling anxious, and did not notice the frail little figure coming down the spiral staircase.

'Monsieur . . . can I speak to you?' asked a small voice.

Yvette, very pale and dressed in a nightshirt that was much too big for her, looked like a ghost.

'You must wrap up warmly, or you'll get ill again,' murmured Kenji, uncomfortable in the presence of the child. 'Where is Mademoiselle Iris?'

'She's taking a bath . . . Your photographer friend . . . he said Papa was in hospital, but it's not true.'

'I know,' said Kenji, putting his overcoat over her shoulders.

'I don't care if Papa's cross with me; I want to go home.'

'Are you not happy here?'

'Yes, but . . . Papa must be looking everywhere for me.'

'No, no, he . . . knows . . . a-and . . .' stammered Kenji, reluctant to tell the child that she would never see her father again.

The telephone came to his rescue.

'Go back to bed. I'll answer this and then come and see you. Go on, shoo!'

She hesitated, put the overcoat on a chair and went back upstairs.

'Hello? Oh, it's you. Thank you for calling. I'll make a note.' He reached for the order book.

'Dubois, Dutch. Floods forced him to halt his research that winter. Resumed a short while ago. Huge amount at stake. In October 1891 he discovered a . . .'

As his caller filled in the details, what had begun as a small crease at the corner of his mouth blossomed into a wide smile.

It felt like spring – bracing and fresh. To the left of Le Marché des Enfants-Rouges on Rue Charlot, a street hawker was snoozing, lulled by the brouhaha and the pale sun. During the time Victor had been observing number 28, the vendor's four-wheeled display, spilling over with stockings, socks and gloves, had attracted only an urchin in a Russian sailor suit, his hands sticky with liquorice. Victor had moved away a little; he had no desire to come into contact with the brat. A woman carrying a basket charged out of number 28 and planted herself beside the ship's boy.

'How much are these mittens?'

The street hawker continued to drowse on his camp stool, elbows on knees and cap pulled down over his face. He half-opened his eyes and made an evasive gesture accompanied by, 'Ten sous.'

Victor thought he recognised the cook Joseph had described. She was a determined-looking woman whose curves were moulded into a black silk coat.

'Are you Madame Bertille Piot?' he ventured as she regretfully put down the mittens.

She confirmed that she was and said she remembered seeing Victor in conversation with the old man.

'I was just about to pay Monsieur de Vigneules a visit and . . .'

He grabbed her arm and steered her into the market as he caught sight of an imposing-looking individual pacing up and down on the opposite pavement. He could have sworn it was Inspector Lecacheur!

'Do you mind . . .' began Bertille Piot, freeing herself as soon as she could.

'I'm sorry, it was because of that kid: he was about to stain your coat with his sticky fingers – children today, I don't know.'

Mollified, she went over to a costermonger's stall and felt the weight of a bunch of leeks.

'I'd advise you to keep away from the old madman. He's so confused now he's completely incoherent. He stutters so much he can hardly get the words out. As God is my witness, I'm used to his gibberish, but even I can't make out what he's saying now! I think Monsieur's death tipped him over the edge. And then . . .'

An angry exchange followed as the costermonger became exasperated at Bertille Piot's manhandling of her produce. Bertille gave her a piece of her mind and then took her revenge by transferring her custom to the competition, an old man dressed entirely in grey. Victor waited patiently until she had made her purchase.

'His clothes may not be very clean, but his fruit and veg is the best quality.'

'You hadn't finished what you were saying. What's happened to Monsieur de Vigneules?'

'He was in his cellar as usual at the crack of dawn, saying his meaningless prayers over his stuffed dogs. Suddenly, just as he was bending down to put his candle on the floor, a gunshot rang out above his head. He ran upstairs, howling worse than a banshee. Madame Gabrielle, who is not the most sympathetic of people, shouted at him, and Monsieur Wallers bellowed that the old man was becoming so soft in the head that he was going to lock him in the cellar once and for all. Monsieur Dorsel, who's always been kind to poor old Monsieur Fortunat, made him sit down and describe exactly what had happened. It took a while, I can tell you. They called the doctor who prescribed a double dose of sedative, but it took Monsieur Fortunat ages to fall asleep.'

'Perhaps he was telling the truth?' suggested Victor.

Monsieur Wallers went down to the cellar, and looked through it with a fine-tooth comb, but he found nothing unusual. Right, I'd better get on with the shopping.'

'Just one more thing. Did Lucie Robin get on well with her employers?'

'Why use the past tense?'

'She's left, hasn't she?'

'Well, she's left before, but she always comes back. For all she looks as if butter wouldn't melt in her mouth, underneath she's a terrible flirt. They've all been attracted to her, Monsieur Antoine, Monsieur Wallers and even the old man!'

'What about Monsieur Dorsel?'

'Him? He hankers after Madame Gabrielle, but apparently she only has eyes for her cousin.'

'You don't seem to care for her very much.'

'Apart from Monsieur Dorsel, I don't like any of them very much, and Monsieur Wallers least of all. His hands wander so — one of these days they'll go off on their own!'

He watched her as she looked carefully over the butcher's stall. Bertille Piot was wrong. The lady's maid would never return to Rue Charlot.

In his straight tweed jacket, buttoned all the way up, pinstriped trousers, and checked bowler hat, Kenji looked so like an Englishman that Euphrosine almost did not recognise him. She herself was in her Sunday best. Topping off her golden yellow dress with bouffant sleeves was a little round hat decorated with wide loops of ribbon that produced an effect not unlike a windmill.

'I'm going to mass at Saint-Sulpice. If it's Joseph you're looking for, he's in the study. He prefers to blacken his pages than purify his soul at confession.'

Muttering about 'this generation of miscreants', she drew herself in to squeeze past Kenji and headed off to church.

Kenji found Joseph trying to come up with his next line, staring at his fountain pen as if waiting for it to speak.

'Boss! What a surprise! It's the first time you've been here! Excuse the chaos. I'll free up a seat for you.'

'No need, I'd prefer to stand. I've come to update you on the investigation.'

Without dropping his formal tone, he passed on Victor's information to Joseph. As he was speaking, he was congratulating himself on having postponed the painful task of telling Yvette of her father's sad end by instructing Iris to entertain her. Delighted at the prospect of going to *The Enchanted Spring*, the latest show by the stage magician Georges Méliès at the Théâtre Robert-Houdin, the child had forgotten her anguish. And it also meant that Iris would be out of Joseph's reach for the whole afternoon.

'Blimey, another murder! Anyone would think we were collecting them! Let's hope the Boss catches up quickly with that bone sculptor. Then we might finally be able to see clearly!'

'See clearly? Oh, that's rich. Don't imagine that I don't see clearly,' remarked Kenji tartly.

Joseph rose, astonished.

'Why do you say that, Boss? Have I done anything wrong?'

'I hope not. But it would be regrettable if your brazen flirtation with my daughter went too far.'

Joseph turned scarlet. He thought his heart had stopped.

'It's not just flirtation, Monsieur Mori. It's love.'

'So you admit it!'

'Our only crime has been to succumb to our uncontrollable affection for each other,' protested Joseph, happy to have remembered the final lines of a romantic novel he'd borrowed from his mother.

Kenji sighed, disarmed in spite of himself by his assistant's grandiloquence.

'Well, make sure that your uncontrollable affection remains within the limits of decency. Must I remind you that Iris is not only a minor, but also completely feather-brained?'

'You have a strange view of your daughter, Boss.'

'I have known her longer than you. She is quick to fire up, but her passions are often flashes in the pan, absurd pipe dreams.'

'So it's absurd that she should be drawn to me? Because I'm a hunchback? You might as well come out with it and call me a monster!' cried Joseph bitterly.

'You're twisting my words. I did not mention your physique. You're as romantic as Iris, ready to cast yourself as Quasimodo dreaming of Esmeralda.'

'Now you have said it!'

'What?'

'Quasimodo. Beauty and the Beast. Thanks, Boss, thanks very much. Now I know how you regard me.'

'Come off it, Joseph, stop being childish. You know perfectly well the power you exert over women.'

'So it's because I'm just a miserable sales assistant. '

'Don't ascribe to me that contemptible attitude towards a role that was once mine. I am Iris's father. I must protect her from her impulses wherever they might have harmful consequences. And I am also responsible for your conduct. You are both too young. You don't know . . .'

'Young, me! I was twenty-two on 14 January. And anyway, it's not a crime to be young.'

'But it is sometimes a handicap,' concluded Kenji, who was in a hurry to draw the conversation to a close.

He felt he had played the role of indignant father just right. But he also felt annoyed with himself at having complicated the situation. He was growing old. His greying hair was proof – perhaps he should consider dying it.

'Please come to the shop this afternoon if you can. We will no doubt know a bit more about the goblet by then,' he said as he turned to leave.

Joseph sat down, nursing his resentment. 'I don't care what he thinks!'

He wished that something would happen to deflect his thoughts.

He despises me, he thought. But he'll change his tune when my second serial has made me the man of the moment!

He began to scribble furiously.

Éleuthère scratched furiously at the damp floor of the cellar. His sense of smell rarely let him down. Suddenly his claws met a bone. Frida von Glockenspiel gave a shriek of horror . . .

Clouds filled the sky. A brisk wind swept the Carrefour Buci as the concierges shouted to each other from door to door. Then came the downpour. The customers at the terrace cafés scattered instantly. The emissary took refuge under the awning of a grocery, reproaching himself for having the same idea as the associate. They had been hanging around for more than an hour in the hope of catching the elusive Osso Buco visiting Le Procope. Perhaps he should have gone directly to the L'Académie des Tonneaux; that might have enabled the emissary to lay his hands on the Italian first. But too late now, the prey might appear here at any moment.

The downpour abated and Rue de l'Ancienne-Comédie became animated again. In the evening Le Procope attracted young aspiring authors drawn in by Cazals, the cartoonist and song-writer friend of Verlaine famous for his 1830s attire. Now there was only a handful of beer and kümmel drinkers lounging near the pot-bellied stove, digesting their lunch in peace.

Victor had tired of standing about and questioned the waiter, who shrugged his shoulders, merely saying that the macaroni-eater did not follow a precise timetable and that he also hawked his wares on the terraces of La Source, Le Voltaire and Le Soleil d'Or, as well as at L'Académie in Rue Saint-Jacques, as his fancy took him.

'You can stride up and down as much as you like, but what will that get you? Sore legs is all!' The waiter slapped his thigh.

Victor left him to it and headed for Boulevard Saint-Germain. Without paying any attention to the worm-eaten gables of Rue Dupuytren, he crossed over and hurried along École de Médecine. A procession of students, each with his arms round the waist of the one in front, blocked his path. They were celebrating Easter in their own inimitable way – parading through the quarter in lines that were soon joined by ophicleide and trombone players. Coach drivers and pedestrians took their hats off in tribute. Although Victor was champing at the bit, he did the same, and the emissary on his bicycle followed suit. Then they set off again in a deluge of hail.

At the narrowest point of Rue Saint-Jacques, a modern wine shop was nestled in a pretty Louis XIV façade. Victor searched the area in vain – he saw no one resembling a bone sculptor. Discouraged, he entered.

Inside, tables and wooden stools stood between partitions made of casks piled one on top of the other, and an eager audience sat listening to a fellow in a worn-out frock coat who was declaiming and gesticulating wildly. Victor leant on the bar next to a lanky chap who stood open-mouthed, hands on hips, drinking in the words of the orator. As he ordered himself a glass of Sancerre, Victor asked the owner if Osso Buco had been by.

'I haven't seen him. Go and ask his mate – I'm listening to the speech,' was all the owner said, pointing to a ragged-looking individual with a pug nose, who was gloomily staring at his empty glass.

Taking his white wine with him, Victor sat down between the man and a black-and-brown mongrel dog perched on a seat.

'Excused me interrupting, Monsieur . . .' he began.

'Not Monsieur anything, just Big Mouth, that's how I'm known around here. Do you want to buy a picture? Look, there are all sorts: Big Mouth in front of La Panthéon, Big Mouth beside La Sorbonne and how about this fine one, Big Mouth coming out of Vespers at Saint-Germain-des-Près.'

He fanned out an assortment of ill-executed caricatures before Victor, who chose a charcoal sketch of a brachycephalic human squinting at a distorted church, and handed over a franc. 'Very original. I'd also like to get hold of one of those objects your friend Osso Buco sculpts out of bone.'

'I'm too thirsty to talk.'

'Here, have my drink.'

While Big Mouth slurped the Sancerre, Victor had time to study the artisans, street peddlers, mature ladies and unsuccessful poets that made up the orator's audience. The latter finished his peroration, took a bow and was invited by the crowd to taste one of the liqueurs from the jars and bottles squeezed in besides the casks.

'Bravo, Caubel, very accomplished. "The effect of syphilis on toads", that's worth worrying about!' bawled Big Mouth.

'That's Caubel de la Ville Ingan,[1] very erudite, astronomer, assistant at the museum, wine-taster at La Halle de Bercy, chef. All that in one man! Not surprising that he trumps the forty,' he explained to Victor.

'The forty?'

'The forty bigwigs at the Académie Française!' roared Big Mouth, choking with laughter.

After Victor had banged him on the back, causing him spit out a large amount of wine, he continued.

'You're looking for Osso Buco? That moron is a lucky devil; good fortune seems to follow him around; the daubers all fight over him. What's wrong with my face, I'd like to know? Soon the Musée du Luxembourg will be overflowing with paintings of Joseph or Noah or whoever, all with his ugly Italian mug. And if he hasn't just been hired for a version of Vercingetorix!'[2]

'Who by?'

'A big cheese at the institute, a George something or other, something. The last name sounds like a bird.'

'Sparrow? Lark? Finch? Dove?' Victor suggested.

'No, it's on the tip of my tongue . . . Martin, yes, that's it.'

'George Timon-Martin, a disciple of Fernand Cormon, I believe. Where's his studio?'

'Somewhere chic – in the Muette quarter, I think.'

Victor thanked him with another drink.

The emissary stayed tucked against the Louis XIV façade, and was careful not to get back on his bicycle until the associate had hailed a cab. The bookseller was certainly covering the miles. Where was he off to now? There was nothing for it but to stay hot on his heels.

Victor left the cab at Place de Passy and set off along the road of the same name. He asked the street traders where Timon-Martin the painter lived and eventually discovered that it was in Avenue Raphaël.

The shade provided by the trees on Chausée de la Muette was stippled by cyclists. Walking through this peaceful and opulent quarter, strewn with beautiful residences, Victor had the leisure to consider his fears. Two mysteries had been haunting him for several days. One involved the goblet, which trailed death in its wake, the other Tasha's letter. The two had become fused in his mind in an image as clear as a photograph: Tasha's head smiling enigmatically at him from the top of a tripod. He stopped a moment, closed his eyes to shake the image and succeeded in dislodging it.

He strolled on, deep in thought. A whistling sound brought him back to reality. It was a train puffing its way along the Ceinture[3] railway line. It overtook him, reminding him of Léonard Diélette's untimely end.

He reached George Timon-Martin's pretentious villa, as exhausted as if he had circumnavigated Paris. Luckily he had the ability to recover quickly, and he managed to sound quite brisk as he presented himself to the butler. The Cerberus studied his business card haughtily, and Victor had to insist before he was allowed in. He was led to a small salon where he was told not to move or talk and was informed that in quarter of an hour the models would be entitled to stretch their legs. The master would see him then.

The room to which Victor was confined was more like a military junk shop or an exhibition of 'war through the ages' than a salon. There were bludgeons and swords lined up against a catapult, blunderbusses, halberds, crossbows and every type of sabre and dagger. Mannequins in breastplates and uniforms on pegs fought for the meagre space, and any square inches left were taken up with figures displaying helmets from various epochs. Victor noticed a tapestry moving lightly in a gentle breeze. He lifted it. The door behind it was half open, revealing a studio.

The first thing he saw was a large painting on an easel: the light from campfires in a bivouac showed a group of privates parading under a cloudy sky and dreaming of the triumphal armies of Napoleon. Behind the painting, side on to him, were five men on a podium with a handrail against which some of them were leaning. Should their majestic moustaches and breeches have left any doubt as to their identity, the stuffed cockerel brandished above the head of the oldest of them was conclusive: these were Gauls.

'I've had enough. I'm leaving!' threatened the man with the cockerel.

'Hang on. And stop fidgeting or I'll bite you!' responded a glacial voice from the right.

Victor opened the door wider and saw the painter, a slim man of about forty dressed in a jacket with an officer's collar. Brushes and palette in hand, he was installed at the top of a staircase before an enormous canvas, like a captain at the helm of his ship.

'Cannibal,' muttered Vercingetorix.

The master swept down the stairs to judge the effect of his last brushstrokes, and Victor noted the comfortable snow boots he was wearing below his rather formal attire. Then he took the stairs back up four at a time, corrected a detail and declared in a lugubrious tone that he was according them a fifteen-minute break.

'Be careful of the costumes!' he cried to the models, who were removing their blond wigs.

Victor went back to the hallway and mingled with the Gauls as they headed for a little courtyard. He had no trouble spotting the Italian, whose white hair marked him out as the oldest of the models, and touched him lightly on the shoulder.

'Are you Osso Buco?'

The old man, mortified, stared at him and retorted harshly.

'A bit of respect, you're talking to a hero of the Battle of Gergovia!'[4]

'Shame they don't make the Romans and their enemies pose at the same time, old man. I would have bet on Julius Caesar!' remarked a young man with a sharp face.

'No need to waste your money, since we know our much-esteemed chief will be humiliated at the siege of Alesia,' said a young man with an affected air.

Osso Buco contented himself with belching, and followed Victor away from the others.

'Yesterday one of your compatriots sold you an object stolen from one of my friends. It's a goblet made out of a skull. I'd like to buy it back – you can name your price.'

'What does your friend want with that filthy object?'

'It's a family souvenir.'

'With souvenirs like that I'm happy I'm to be an orphan! It's true that I did have it in my mitts briefly, your goblet. I thought I might be able to make something with it, a cup or an ashtray. But when I discovered what it was made of. I got rid of it.'

Victor slapped his forehead in despair.

'You should have given it back to the girl instead of throwing it away!'

'Who said I threw it away? I didn't keep it, that's for sure. I didn't want to be accused of cannibalism! I'm only a humble inhabitant of Piedmont. I hire myself out at the model market on Place Pigalle where that man-eater Timon-Martin took me on for only three francs a day. The French models get five! *Basta!* Normally I'm painted in the costume of a Breton fisherman or a monk. When I'm not posing like a graven image for painters, I sell my artefacts to whoever wants them. I get all my materials from my cooking pot.'

'Where does cannibalism fit in?'

'I'm coming to that. I have sculpted from everything, tibias, kneecaps, vertebrae or parietals. I make mustard spoons and nail files from the bones, all of which come exclusively from ruminants. I never, repeat never, use human bones! Not only because it's immoral and religion forbids it, but because it's against the law! If I was suspected of devouring my own species, they'd put me in jail and throw away the key!'

'I still don't understand.'

'That goblet, it's a baby's skull. It's revolting!'

'Baby? Nonsense, it's the skullcap of a monkey.'

'My eye! I showed it yesterday evening to a medical student and he was categorical: a human skull. So I handed it over to a neighbour on Rue Houdon who's been selling his pigs at the Easter ham fair.'

'What's his name?'

'Esprit Borrèze. By now he will have passed it on to his cousin who sells knick-knacks at the scrap-metal fair.'

'On Boulevard Richard-Lenoir?'

'Yeah, in the Bastoche quarter.'

Osso Buco hastily pocketed a forty-sou piece.

'Thanks for that contribution to the arts. If I see you on Boul'Mich, I'll favour you with an ear pick or bill file made from finest ox femur!'

Victor left the house, not daring to hope. Even though it appeared once again that John Cavendish's goblet was within reach, the ill-luck that contrived to make it as unattainable as the Holy Grail might strike again. He had to tell Kenji immediately.

They had agreed to meet in front of the Gare Vincennes. Kenji and Joseph were the first to arrive, and stood shelling warm chestnuts while a stream of passengers spilled around them. A dandy in a boater with a carnation in his buttonhole waved a bunch of lilacs, and was immediately joined by a young woman dressed in pastel colours. Joseph looked away from the couple, jealous at their public display of affection. Would he ever be allowed to demonstrate his feelings for Iris? He stared at Kenji who was chewing, impassive, among the tide of dressed-up families. Because of him their love would languish in furtive kisses in the back room, until Iris married some aristocratic drunkard, like Valentine before her!

A cab ground to a halt, hemmed in between a company of Republican Guards and the Bastille-Porte-Rapp omnibus. Victor sprang out and raised his cane to attract their attention. They barely exchanged a word – everything had been said on the telephone. They crossed the busy square and reached the boulevard. The sun had returned and all around them a whitish dust was thrown up by the passers-by.

They soon found themselves among small houses that were squashed one against the other, salivating at the aroma of frying bacon. A land of plenty greeted them, one given over to the glorification of smoking and curing meat. Rosaries of sausages hanging from hooks, tripe like organ pipes and choirs of sausages swaddled in silver paper paid tribute to the joy of the feast. Joseph stopped as if hypnotised before a display of hams nestling on a bed of leaves, and Victor had to take him by the arm.

'Come on, we don't have much time!'

Led away despite himself, Joseph almost knocked over a little boy having a tantrum.

'Want juice!' he was yelling, ignored by his parents, who were leaning over a regiment of black puddings.

'They're the best, my *crépinettes* – they melt in the mouth, not in the pan!'

'Galantines as rich as butter!'

Stallholders in regional costume or white aprons were noisily promoting their produce, brandishing knives ready to cut slices to offer to the passers-by. Victor, still holding on to Joseph, was trying to read the placards bearing the names of the traders.

'Kenji!' he called suddenly, pointing to a broad banner in the middle of a swarm of pigs. Painted green letters announced:

ESPRIT BORRÈZE
King of Touraine Rillons
12 Rue Houdon, Paris XVIII

Joseph was captivated by a pretty young gypsy girl from La Franche-Comté, who was feeding him little pieces of pâté.

'Come on, Monsieur, taste that, delicious enough to make you swoon!'

Victor retraced his footsteps and yanked his assistant away from the outraged trader and dragged him to the stall where

Kenji stood waiting. Borrèze was a large lad with a booming laugh, whom customers could spot from afar by his ruddy complexion.

'A piece of the finest head cheese, Messieurs? Or perhaps you prefer *rillettes?*'

'We'd like to retrieve a goblet that Osso Buco sold you. He told us that you would probably pass it on to your cousin.'

'And he's right, the old villain! I offloaded it on Jean-Louis Digon, whose stall's next door, in the scrap-metal fair.'

'Where exactly?'

'I don't know – we did the deal in a bar. But you can't miss him; he lost an eye and wears a black patch like a pirate.'

Joseph, flanked by his Bosses, regretfully abandoned the gourmand's paradise for the much less enticing world of junk.

A progression of grey huts housing the second-hand dealers stretched out along the alleys, interrupted here and there by fabric shops or second-hand clothes stalls spilling in a torrent on to the pavement. Eager crowds jostled their way along. It was no use Victor being impatient; he had to wait behind these bargain hunters.

'What are all these dawdlers after? I can understand people wanting to buy all that grub back there. But this heap of old rubbish . . . There's nothing to get excited about,' grumbled Joseph.

'I agree,' responded Kenji. 'It only confirms my view of the décor of western homes: incoherent and cluttered. What I find curious is that people come to sell off a porcelain ring or a coal shovel inherited from their great-grandmother then hurry off and buy a bust of Jean-Jacques Rousseau that a dealer has persuaded them is extremely rare. Objects just move round from house to house.'

'Nature abhors a vacuum,' Victor grunted, resisting the urge to inspect some photographic equipment complete with flasks and trays displayed in a spanking new portmanteau.

For his part Kenji regretted that, having poured scorn on the buyers, he could not now, despite his profession, take a good look at the books. He recalled how at last year's fair, a bookselling friend had come across a Molière illustrated by Boucher. Their progress was held up again by a girl in fashionable ankle boots who had decided to scramble up to the top of a pile of crates to sell her wares. She was offering locks, keys, corroded saucepans and pokers which she claimed were all very modern, and all at half the price of shop goods! Joseph was gazing appreciatively at her silk clad calves when the girl broke off. Joseph's glance slid to the girl's left and alighted on a dark shape. His brain made the connection.

'Over there! The man with the eye patch!' he shouted.

Although Jean-Louis Digon's stall displayed a mishmash of disparate goods from ballet pumps to stuffed alligators, he mostly sold used umbrellas.

'Ten francs! Five francs a brolly! Come on now, everything reduced, three francs, Madame. Of course the spokes aren't rusty, no more than the stays of your corset, my love, and they're doing a lovely job in giving you the body of a goddess. Aphrodite in person! And this gentleman will agree with me!' shouted the one-eyed man to Kenji, indicating the buxom matron.

Kenji bent down and, reaching under a battered tricorne,

pulled out an object that neither Victor nor Joseph had spotted.

'How much?'

The man immediately lost interest in the goddess and the umbrella.

'Ah, now that's very valuable, Monsieur. It looks a bit strange, but it's a rare pearl. An exotic chalice I'm told was used by a Patagonian to prepare the poison he soaked the tip of his arrows in to hunt wild boar in the forests of the Amaz—'

'How much?' repeated Kenji with a disdainful sniff.

Cut off in the middle of his improvisation, the one-eyed man blurted out, 'Ten francs,' and closed his mouth.

Kenji paid with two silver coins.

'Aren't . . . aren't you going to bargain with me?'

'No point, didn't you say it was a Patagonian chalice?'

'Wait, I'll wrap it for you.'

'No need,' replied Kenji, who was already pushing his way through the crowd, watched tenderly by Aphrodite.

Joseph almost applauded the stallholder, impressed by his rhetoric. But he didn't have time – his Bosses were leaving. He hurried to catch up with them, cursing their tyranny.

'You paid much too much for your Patagonian chalice! It's trash. You're flinging money away,' he grumbled.

'Really? You think so? Shame you kept that to yourself instead of proffering your advice. Too bad, I'll keep the sum back from your wages,' Kenji retorted, without slowing his pace.

Joseph was so furious that he whisked back through the Easter ham fair seething with curses that he could not utter. When they reached Place de la Bastille with its knot of vehicles, he marched purposefully along the road, savouring in advance the little speech he would make to Kenji when he caught up with him. 'Tomorrow morning, Boss, it will be my turn. I'm going to give you a piece of my mind. For ages I have been burning to get things off my chest, and when I've finished I'm going to run off with your daughter!'

He did not hear Victor saying, 'He's only joking – ignore him,' nor did he notice the bicycle behind him forging its way through the traffic. It was only when he heard a rustling that he realised a bike was brushing past him. He was about to shout at the rider when he saw the machine swoop down on Kenji. An arm shot out and grabbed the goblet; the bike set off again, gathering speed before crashing into the Vincennes-Louvre omnibus. The rider went sprawling across the road just as the bus driver yelled a warning, and the passengers on the upper deck shrieked. The cyclist got to his feet, still clutching the goblet tightly, abandoned his bicycle and ran round the bus. Victor gave chase. Kenji, entangled in the crowd, eventually managed to free himself, and Joseph, bringing up the rear, was filled with exhilaration as he zigzagged between the carriages and coaches, deaf to the imprecations of the coach drivers. Where on earth was the wretched thief headed?

My goodness, he's heading for a dead end! No, he wouldn't be that stupid . . .

But the thief was indeed headed for the Colonne de Juillet. Was he going to climb the monument? A warden was guarding the entrance, arms spread wide. There was a shot. The guard screamed. The thief disappeared, followed at speed by Victor.

A second shot rang out.

The bullet caught Victor on his right side, spinning him round. Kenji ran past, not noticing that Victor had been shot, and up the stairs, hard on the heels of the thief. For several seconds Victor did not move. Then he felt himself falling, just as Joseph appeared.

'Boss, no!'

Victor made an effort to pull himself up on a wall and managed to stagger to his feet. He tried to undo his belt, gave up and stumbled. He collapsed slowly, his hands pressed to his side. His eyes closed.

'Boss, Boss, are you all right?'

'It's not serious . . . just a scratch . . . Kenji . . .'

'But Boss, you're bleeding! You need a doctor!' Joseph wailed.

Victor struggled to open his eyes. He saw Joseph's worried face and whispered, 'Kenji . . . needs you . . .'

'Boss, I . . .'

'Run . . . quick . . . it's urgent . . .'

Voices around him . . . A welcome woozy feeling . . . Strange murmurings like the rustling of trees. Then darkness.

The spiral staircase was wider and lighter than Joseph would have imagined. The sight of Monsieur Legris covered in blood had frightened him. And running up two hundred and forty stairs had the same effect as the wine he had drunk in Cité Doré. By the time he burst out on the viewing platform his thoughts had lost all coherence. He didn't know whether to turn left or right. Blinded by the light, everything appeared deformed, distorted and striped with dazzling flashes. His ears were pounding.

A stifled cry brought him back to earth. An incredible scene was being played out before him. The thief's weapon pointed upwards, his raised arm firmly restrained by Kenji. Joseph's heart was about to explode, and he stood, paralysed. Then the thief made an unexpected move. He stopped resisting and dropped, limp as a rag, before suddenly pulling back and kicking Kenji in the groin. Doubled over with pain, and unable to avoid his assailant, Kenji fell to his knees and was struck on the temple with the butt of the gun. He toppled over, stunned. Joseph heard a click and saw the barrel of the revolver pointed at his employer's neck. As the thief was about to pull the trigger, a murderous rage took hold of Joseph. He launched himself forwards, feverishly removing his jacket. He threw it over the thief's head and pulled backwards. The bullet narrowly missed Kenji; the gun fell to the ground.

The thief struggled fiercely and freed himself. He grabbed Joseph by the throat and kicked his legs out from under him. Joseph found himself spread-eagled on his back with the thief sitting on his chest, making it hard to breathe. When the thief clouted him in the face, Joseph barely felt the pain. He grabbed his attacker's hair, pulled his head forwards and freed himself. The thief caught him, trapping him against the hand-rail, and, seizing him by the waist, slowly hoisted him up. Joseph squirmed and wriggled as the man tried to push him over. A hundred and fifty feet below, the square dotted with people, the metallic ribbon of the Canal Saint-Martin, the two fairs and the Faubourg Saint-Antoine danced in Joseph's vision. He grabbed the thief's shoulders and pushed with all his might.

He did not see the man fall. Months later, when the recurring nightmare dragged him again from sleep in a sweat, he would be astonished at having visualised the interminable plunge that ended with the man lying broken at the foot of the column. His descent into hell was always played out in slow motion.

Kenji regained consciousness, but all he could see was a bluish grey haze.

'Monsieur Mori! Monsieur Mori! You can't do this to me! Wake up! It's me, your assistant, Joseph!'

Kenji's head was buzzing, but he tried to stand up. A sharp pain made him bend double.

'Thank you, Joseph, I owe my life to you,' he said feebly, one hand pressed against his abdomen. 'Help me to stand . . .'

'Boss, it's terrible . . . I . . . I've killed a man! I pushed him, and he fell to his death. I recognised him from his tinted glasses! He's the bloke who left me Monsieur du Houssoye's calling card . . . My God, I'm a murderer!'

'Dear Joseph, don't worry. It was self defence. What about the goblet?' breathed Kenji.

'It's not here. He must have held on to it.' Joseph looked reproachfully at Kenji. How could he worry about the goblet when Monsieur Legris might be dead?'

Charles Dorsel's crushed body, face down on the road, seemed to beg for divine mercy. John Cavendish's goblet had burst from his coat pocket and smashed to smithereens as it hit the ground. The obsidian face of a cat rolled over to a little girl, who picked it up and stuffed it deep into her pocket, just as her mother starting yelling hysterically that she was to come immediately. It will be my talisman for ever, the little girl promised herself.

CHAPTER 16

Wednesday, 20 April

INSPECTOR Lecacheur looked around the bedroom as if he were merely there to evaluate the décor. He paused at the roll-top desk, caressing the mahogany, lingered in front of the glass-covered prints of Fourier's phalanstery, then moved on to look at the little painting of Tasha, her breasts bare. Victor, propped up in bed against two pillows, observing the inspector's pent-up fury, half expected to see him metamorphose into a wild boar that attacked without warning.

Finally, having swallowed down a handful of lozenges, the inspector came to a halt by the bed. Victor had to stop himself from recoiling and let out a groan as his muscles contracted.

'Are you in pain, Monsieur Legris? I wouldn't complain if I were you. He who plays with fire gets burnt.'

'You sound like Kenji; making up proverbs is his speciality.'

'And another trick of his is keeping quiet when he's interrogated. However hard I try, I can get nothing out of him when I ask him what he was doing at the top of the Colonne de Juillet. All he says is that you summoned him there, along with your devoted assistant, who's also as mute as a clam.'

'He's still in shock.'

'As well he might be! He can count himself lucky that he's not been charged with homicide. No one forced your loyal right-hand man to administer justice! In the future he had better save his adventurous zeal for those serials he writes for the rags. As for you, I hope that injury will teach you a lesson. It's a miracle you survived.'

'Allow me to contradict you. It has nothing to do with miracles. The bullet was diverted by the nickel chronometer my father gave me on my seventh birthday to teach me about punctuality. I had stowed the family memento away at the back of the drawer, but I dug it out when I was going through my things: I decided I would be punctual once more!'

'How dare you speak to me with such insolence! That you are all over the front pages with your ridiculous exploits that put several lives including your own at risk and ended with a man's death, I can just about accept. I can even accept that you reneged on your promise to stop your covert sleuthing, probably complicating a criminal investigation that would otherwise have remained the preserve of the police. But that you should make fun of me, Monsieur Legris: that I cannot accept!' Inspector Lecacheur thundered, his moustache bristling with indignation.

'I would never dare make fun—'

'That's enough! Do you know where I have just come from? From 28 Rue Charlot, where your and your assistant's repeated visits were the talk of the servants! I spoke at length to Madame du Houssoye, but I was none the wiser for it. Her explanations were flimsy to say the least. Unfortunately I can't prove her duplicity, but instinct tells me that to put all these crimes down to insanity only clarifies part of the imbroglio. The lady, however, is sticking to her story: the assassin was unstable and possessive; he could not stand the maid's infidelity and after bumping off her lover, shot her before dumping her body in the Seine!'

'The maid . . . Lucie Robin?'

'Stop acting the innocent! Don't you think Inspector Pérot remembers you going to the station in the sixth arrondissement at precisely the moment the body of a woman with a ladybird tattoo had been found in the Seine? The woman was identified as Lucie Robin by Madame du Houssouye at the morgue the following day, after I asked her to attend, having heard from Bertille Piot about the maid's disappearance.'

'Well, the enigma is solved, a sordid *crime passionel*,' remarked Victor, regretting his flippancy, which was immediately challenged by the sight of an object the inspector had been keeping hidden behind his back.

'And what do you make of this, eh? We found it near the broken body at the foot of the column. What, in your opinion, is it for? A declaration of eternal love?'

Feigning surprise, Victor considered the dented tripod the inspector was holding up.

'I don't know . . .'

'Your pretence is getting on my nerves. Do you also maintain that you do not know Fortunat de Vigneules?'

'Of course not.'

'I also showed this object to him. His daughter had already assured me she did not recognise it, but he jumped when he saw it and invoked a treasure hidden underground by the Knights Templar. He told you about the treasure. According to him, this was part of a cursed goblet hidden inside an old cabinet by . . . have a guess.'

'I give up.'

'By the Grand Master of the Knights Templar himself, Jacques de Molay! When I mentioned your name, Monsieur de Vigneules embarked on a confused discourse in which he asserted that you had provided him with "Pharaonic posteriors" – those were his words – in exchange for information about the goblet. Bertille Piot, the cook, confirmed it by telling me that she had taken a letter from her master to a photographer in Rue des Saints-Pères. Do you deny that you are that photographer?'

'Not at all.'

'So you also won't deny having being told of treasure that you set about tracking down?'

Victor unconsciously imitated Tasha's tick, nibbling his thumbnail as he made up his mind. Finally he spoke.

'I don't deny it. It's the truth.'

'Liar! Rogue! Hypocrite!' yelled the inspector. 'I don't believe in this treasure. Fortunat de Vigneules has a screw loose. It's true you were looking for something – you, your associate and Joseph – but that something was stolen from you in a break-in! Raoul Pérot reported it to me.'

'Inspector, although Kenji was upset to have had his *French Pâtissier* and *The Book of Manners* by the much esteemed Baronne Staffe stolen, I swear to you that . . .'

'I forbid you to swear! I am closing in on you. I'm certain that if this murky affair has tickled your fancy, it's because, in some way or another, you are personally linked to it. And once again I meet a wall of silence when I talk to your entourage. Their lips are sealed, and that includes your associate's daughter and your girlfriend. Even that obsequious cousin of Madame du Houssoye won't say a word without first asking her permission!'

Inspector Lecacheur stowed the tripod in one of the pockets of his braided hussar's jacket. He wore the philosophical resignation of one who knows he's beaten. But Victor was not fooled and anticipated a counter-attack. He managed to keep calm when, suddenly bending over him, the inspector shouted, 'Achille Ménager!'

'A relative of yours?' Victor enquired, without batting an eye.

'A bric-a-brac merchant on Rue de Nice in the eleventh arrondissement. An anonymous telephone call was made to Raoul Pérot – him again, although it's not his area of jurisdiction – informing him that Ménager had been slain by a bullet just like the other two victims whose deaths I was investigating. The man's apartment had been ransacked from top to bottom, and his shop had also been scoured. Since he possessed only worthless baubles, what could the intruder have been after?'

'I can't imagine, Inspector. Has he been apprehended?'

'We've arrested a young Neapolitan girl, an organ player who was the victim's tenant and who left her lodgings suddenly and moved into the Latin quarter where she was easily picked up. Unfortunately for us, at least a dozen students and other Bohemian types were dancing the *sardana* around this Anna Marcelli on the day of the crime . . .'

'Not the *sardana*, Inspector, you mean the *saltarelle*.'

'Don't interrupt, for crying out loud! When I mentioned you to the Italian girl, she became flustered. But of course she gave nothing away. Damnable girl – she's concealing something!

Do you by any chance use a potion to cast a spell on women?'

'Nothing more than my natural charm.'

The inspector wagged a threatening finger.

'I will get to the bottom of all this, you hear? And then you'll have an uncomfortable quarter of an hour!'

He jammed on his fur toque, headed for the door, thought better of it and returned to look Victor up and down.

'Are you in a lot of pain?'

'No, only when I laugh.'

'In that case I hope you have cause to split your sides.'

'You're very kind, Inspector. By the way, are you still after a first edition of *Manon Lescaut*?'

The inspector softened. 'Why, do you have one for me?'

'Not as far as I know, but I'll find out.'

The door slammed. Victor closed his eyes. The trial of strength had exhausted him. He weighed up what the inspector had said. He hadn't mentioned two of the murders — Lady Stone's and Léonard Diélette's. So Bertille Piot had not mentioned Joseph's interest in Cité Doré. The puzzle was still incomplete, because neither he nor the police had yet discovered the significance of the goblet. Only one person could perhaps provide the missing pieces: Gabrielle du Houssoye. Through a series of painful contortions, Victor had managed to sit up, throw back the covers and swivel his legs round when the door opened softly.

'I knew that would happen. No sooner has that policeman been here than you are ready to rush out in spite of Dr Reynaud's strict instructions.'

Victor let himself sink back on to the pillows again.

'I wasn't going to do that. I just needed to move around a bit. I'm stiffening up.'

She adjusted the covers; her hand reached out to touch his cheek. She was torn between tenderness and rage.

'You could have been killed! Why do you behave like that? Do I mean so little to you that you would put yourself in danger without considering my feelings?'

She had never spoken to him in such a stern voice. He suppressed the emotion aroused by her words and replied as calmly as he could.

'You are deluding yourself. I am not really that important to you. If I died, you would soon get over me. No doubt I am going to disappoint you, but . . . I read this.'

He spoke composedly, his eyes fixed on the folded piece of paper in his hand.

'My God! The letter.'

She was terrified. What must he have thought?

'Victor, you're going mad,' she murmured.

'No, my darling, I'm just seeing things the way they are. You spend your time with many artists, some of whom have been very important to you. It's normal that you would have retained your links with them . . . Hans, for example.'

'Hans! What's he got to do with us?'

'As I've said before, you are free to act as you like. I've changed and, even if it is hard for me to admit, I am aware that I have no right to . . . Tasha, are you all right?'

As he had been carefully expressing himself, weighing up every word, she had smiled then laughed. Now the laughter was more like sobbing.

'You've changed! That's a joke,' she exclaimed between two hiccups. 'Your jealousy knows no bounds! At first I was proud to inspire that incessant worry; I told myself it was proof that you loved me. Now after two years of living together . . .'

'Living in parallel,' he corrected

'It's the same thing! I'm upset that you still don't trust me.'

'And I'm upset about this letter,' he replied.

She went over to him and pulled out an old leather wallet from under her shawl. She took out a photograph and showed it to him. A dark, svelte man of about fifty with a handlebar moustache and a bowler hat stared intensely from the picture. She turned the photograph over and Victor saw a few lines scribbled in pencil.

Tsu dir, mayn ʒis-lebn, tsit dokh mayn harts.[1]
I'm sending you a picture of me in Berlin in my bourgeois get-up. I will soon send you more detailed news.
    Your loving father, Pinkus.

Victor gulped. He recognised the writing from the letter.

'It's true. I did lie to you,' Tasha admitted, putting the photograph back in the wallet. 'There was no exhibition in Barbizon. My father had made me promise not to tell anyone where he was, even you. The Tsarist police are looking for him and he is suspicious of everyone.'

'Tasha, I am so sorry; forgive my stupidity. I should have had faith in you.'

She shrugged her shoulders and nibbled her thumbnail for a moment.

'It's in your nature not to have faith. But you're going to have to stop living in fear of losing me or you will drive me away.'

'Darling, I swear to you it's finished. From now on I . . .' he began, reaching out to her.

She silenced him with a gesture.

'Hang on, because now your faith in me is really going to be tested. Victor, I am leaving.'

'Tasha, no!' he cried.

'My mother, Djina, is in Berlin. She's ill. She had been living with my Aunt Hannah but the poor woman has just died. My sister Ruhléa is married in Krakow and my father is going to America. Djina is all alone. I'm going to look after her. I don't know how long I will need to stay before we both come back here. I'll . . . I'll need you.'

He twisted round and managed to take her by the hand. He kissed her passionately. 'I've been an idiot. How do you say that in Russian, a *dourak*? You can have anything you want; I'll pay for the journey, for your stay in Berlin, for your mother's lodgings in Paris, and for your father's ticket to America. I only ask one thing: that you return to me.'

They embraced again and didn't notice the door opening. Someone coughed.

'I hate to interrupt such passion, but it's time to go back to the hotel,' said a grave voice.

Tasha pulled away from Victor, blushing. The two men stared at each other. Pinkus was exactly like the bourgeois in the photograph, but now he wore a cap, a tunic and velvet trousers.

'So it's you who's turned my daughter's head! You have an

irritating propensity to stir up trouble, and you attract the police like a dog attracts fleas, so it's better if I take my leave.'

'Tasha told me you want to go to the United States. I would be happy to contribute to the cost of your passage.'

Pinkus exchanged a look with his daughter, who reddened slightly. 'I see. That way you will be rid of me more quickly.'

'Father, for the love of God, stop behaving like a child! In this life if you don't ask you will never get what you want.'

'The heavens are deaf to what happens on this earth. I don't want anything from anyone. I have always managed on my own. You are trying to bribe me to win me over.'

Victor managed to get out of bed. His chest hurt, but he found a way of expressing himself clearly. 'This conversation is ridiculous,' he said. 'It's time I took things in hand. So not another word; I'm going to make the decisions. I'm not trying to win you over. It's quite simple. I love Tasha and you are her father. That should be enough.'

'You are just as she described. Very well then, I accept your offer despite the dubious origin of your funds.'

'Are you really that naïve? What can you do without money these days? Starve to death? What is it you want me to justify? Let's see, I do possess a portfolio of shares left to me by my father, it's true, but I would never speculate on the stock exchange. I'm a professional bookseller, which allows me to earn my living and which is perfectly honourable.'

He turned to Tasha. 'Tasha, I have rarely demanded anything of you, but from now on it is me who calls the shots and you're going to listen. No more each of us going our separate ways.'

Tasha smiled at him and he felt serene. The balance was tipping in his favour. He was no longer afraid to be firm with her.

Pinkus looked at them mockingly. He sounded amused. 'In that case, Monsieur Legris, I will pay you back as soon as I am able. In truth, I had hoped to be able to manage without asking for my daughter's help, because as they say in Yiddish, "When a father helps a son, they both smile, but when a son has to help a father, they both cry." '

'Papa, please drop your cynicism,' exclaimed Tasha.

Pinkus patted her on the head. Although he was dark and she was a redhead, there was a strong resemblance.

'She's annoyed with me for having deserted my family, Monsieur Legris. I left Russia in 1882, after a particularly violent wave of pogroms, and it was several years before my family heard from me. My socialist beliefs put my family in danger and I love them too much to harm them, so it was better that I disappeared. I went to Vilna, where I helped organise the Jewish workers' strike.'

'A miscreant like you welcomed like a prophet in the Jerusalem of Lithuania! I can hardly believe it,' declared Tasha, laughing. She was clearly very proud of her father.

'Do you support the bombers?' asked Victor, suddenly alarmed.

'No, I can assure you I condemn the bombings. I would have nothing to do with those murderous demonstrations. You cannot defend the oppressed by such means. I aspire to a society founded on principles of justice, but not all socialists do. In Russia, the Tsar instigated the most barbarous and repressive policies towards the Jews. Even women and children were not spared. The intention was that a third of Jews would convert, a third would die and a third would emigrate. In these past ten years the streets have run with blood in Jitomir, Kiev, Odessa and twenty other cities. The civilised world was outraged. When these massacres began, a committee was created to aid the Russian Israelites, presided over by Victor Hugo. I helped by organising a fund to help feed the most needy. But eventually I was traced to Vilna by the Tsar's secret police and had to flee again, this time to Berlin. That's where I met up with my wife, Djina, again. I wanted to support her and make sure she was all right. But,' he concluded, avoiding Tasha's eye, 'she insisted I should get myself to safety.'

He sighed, turned and took a rose from a vase. He sniffed it delicately, as if the scent might banish his regrets.

'Sometimes my emotions run away with me,' he murmured to himself.

He took a newspaper from his pocket and held it out to Victor. '*La Libre Parole*,[2] what's that?' Victor asked.

'It's a new extremely nationalistic rag aimed at stirring up anti-Semitism. I warn you, Monsieur Legris, unless you feel affronted by these views, don't take up with my daughter.'

'What do you take me for?!'

'For a man in love. In France there isn't discrimination yet, or beatings, but since the dawn of time people have felt the need for scapegoats to exorcise their own demons.'

'Papa, that's enough. We are in a democracy, in a republic, where the rights of man and personal liberty are respected. That sort of thing would never happen in France.'

'You don't think so?'

'I'm sure of it,' she retorted, before leaving the room.

An embarrassed silence fell.

'Have you read the legend of Mélusine?' Pinkus asked bluntly.

'I've read some of it. It's the story of a fairy that changes into a creature that is half woman, half serpent.'

'Yes, only on Saturdays. She married Raymond, Lord of Lusignan, and implored him not to try to see her on Saturdays. Alas, his curiosity got the better of him and he caught sight of his beloved bathing naked, her serpent's tail swishing in the water.'

'I'm impressed by your knowledge of French mythology.'

'In my youth I liked to paint scenes inspired by the legends of different countries. Do you remember her downfall?'

'I think I remember that Melusine gave a heart-rending cry and disappeared for ever. I see what you are implying, but I am no Raymond.'

'Be careful. Tasha is her father's daughter. She needs independence or she will take flight.'

'And yet that's what is going to happen, apparently. And you can see that I am not standing in her way.'

Pinkus shook him by the hand. 'I do see that, Monsieur Legris – Victor – and when she returns I want you to promise me that you will persevere. And in any case one thing is certain: thanks to you she has been able to pursue her art in the best possible conditions and she has made remarkable progress. I can't thank you enough.'

Pinkus went to join Tasha, leaving Victor to savour those

last words while massaging his hand, which had been crushed by the rather vigorous handshake. His satisfaction at being complimented was succeeded by a niggling anxiety at nearly losing her and a sense of sadness at his own failings. He was about to give in to his misery at the prospect of solitude, but he pulled himself together and sprang out of bed, ignoring the searing pain across his chest.

Gabrielle du Houssoye stood in the middle of the drawing room in which Victor and Kenji had previously interviewed her and Alexis Wallers. She was clutching an exercise book that she put down on a side table.

'I was sure that you or your friend would come before too long, Monsieur Legris.' She gestured towards an ottoman and sat down opposite him. 'The inspector told me about your injury. How are you?'

'Oh, it's nothing serious. The bullet only grazed me.' He gazed appreciatively at her low-cut lavender blue dress that complimented her olive skin and dark hair plaited into coils over her ears before continuing. 'That poor inspector . . . he showed me what remained of the goblet. A meagre bounty that failed to satisfy his sleuth's appetite.'

'And what about your sleuth's appetite, Monsieur Legris?'

'I have quite a considerable advantage over the police. I know what the object looked like. I saw it and almost died because of it. But my problem is that I can't for the life of me think what that goblet signified.'

'It signified possible fame and fortune for my husband. But

mainly it represented a way out of his troubles,' replied Gabrielle de Houssoye.

'I can hardly believe that such an ugly goblet made from the skull of . . .'

'Permit me to tell you a tale that might help you to understand. As long as I have known Antoine, he has been passionately interested in evolutionary theories. He travelled several times to central and western Africa to study gorillas and chimpanzees who Darwin suggested are our distant ancestors. Are you aware of that hypothesis?'

'Vaguely. The monkey descended from the tree, and man descended from the monkey.'

Gabrielle du Houssoye smiled despite herself. 'I suppose you could put it like that. Antoine was also interested in other types of primate. Because he was a specialist in the study of orang-utans – in Malay that means men of the trees – he went several times to Java, Sumatra and Borneo. During one of his trips to Java in autumn 1889, he heard about Eugène Dubois, a lecturer in anatomy at the University of Amsterdam, who had begun palaeontological excavations and who had just unearthed a skull in Wadjak that was very different in structure from a contemporary human skull. Antoine was unable to learn more, but when he returned to Paris he carefully reread the work of the German professor of zoology, Ernst Haeckel, who had confirmed the existence of a morphological intermediary between the most evolved monkeys and man. Haeckel had even named this intermediary *pithecanthropus*. That is to say "monkey man". Are you following me?'

'So far, yes. But why look in Asia rather than Africa?'

'Ernst Haeckel was struck by the astonishing resemblance between human embryos and those of gibbons, and the East Indies are home to the gibbon. Eugène Dubois believed Haeckel's theories and so he decided to ask for a transfer to the colonies as military doctor, in order to see if he could verify them.'

Gabrielle rose and rummaged in a cupboard. She filled a glass with cognac and offered it to Victor, then began to pace about the room.

'I was happy to see that Antoine was dropping his veneer of the blasé scientist and reverting to the enthusiastic researcher I had first met. Our relationship was waning, but his renewed interest in the origins of man made life bearable again. Antoine soon came to suspect that Dubois was researching the *pithecanthropus*.'

'I think I can guess what's coming.'

'Antoine kept pestering the museum to be allowed to go on a new study mission to the East Indies, and permission was finally granted last summer. The official subject of the study was unchanged: the life of the orang-utan in its natural habitat. I insisted on going along too, and was authorised to do so, along with my maid, Lucie Robin, Alexis Wallers and my husband's secretary, Charles Dorsel, who had been taken on in Java in 1888 and lived under our roof ever since.'

'The protagonists of the drama were assembled,' murmured Victor.

'Two of them only played a minor role, Monsieur Legris. This time, Antoine arranged to meet Dubois and pressed him to reveal what he was aiming to find, aided by our secretary, who spoke fluent Dutch. Eugène Dubois had moved his dig near to a village called Trinil on the River Solo, a rich source of fossils containing sediments from the Tertiary period and the Pleistocene period.'

Gabrielle sat down again and leant towards Victor, affording him an excellent view of her plunging neckline.

'Shall we continue, dear sir?'

'Uh . . . yes.'

'In September 1891, a primate's upper molar was unearthed and then in October the skullcap of what Dubois immediately assumed was a *pithecanthropus* was discovered.'

'Palaeontology sounds just like a criminal investigation; you always end up with a corpse,' murmured Victor, looking away. 'Was Dubois willing to discuss his findings?'

'You must be joking! He agreed only to speak to Charles about the teeth of the orang-utan. So my husband decided to try to coax some information from the Malaysians working on the site by offering to line their pockets.'

'A tried and tested method I often use myself.'

'Antoine's dream was to be able to produce the missing link before Dubois; in other words he also had to lay his hands on a cranium that was too small to be human and too big to have come from one of the monkeys we were studying.'

'I see. Antoine thought he would win fame and prestige if he were the first to reveal the link.'

'At that point we had a stroke of luck. A young Javanese told my husband how his father, a bone sculptor, had dug up a cranium similar to Dubois's, and had mounted it on a little metal tripod decorated with diamonds and a cat's head to make an incense burner.'

'John Cavendish's goblet . . .'

'Pardon?'

'No, nothing. Please go on.'

'The incense burner had been given to a Chinese merchant from Surabaya. Antoine dashed off to see the merchant, who remembered having sold it to a botanical explorer staying at the Hotel Amsterdam. The explorer was completely taken in and, believing he was acquiring an antique, had paid up without negotiating. Antoine immediately scoured the hotel's registers, trying to identify the man.'

Gabrielle du Houssoye leant closer in a deliberately provocative manner. 'It was indeed John Cavendish,' she murmured.

'Your husband told you that?' asked Victor, looking at his shoes.

'I was his only confidante. He distrusted Alexis, who had always lived in his shadow and was desperate to emulate him, and he didn't tell Charles Dorsel either. But he had the unfortunate habit of writing about his findings in a notebook. As soon as we returned to Paris that December, Antoine wrote to John Cavendish who was living with his sister, Lady Frances Stone. She replied that her brother had died in Paris in 1889. So he decided to take advantage of a conference in London to visit Lady Frances Stone.'

'But he was spied upon, and the lady was killed after he left her, having been given Kenji's name.'

'You already knew that? So you will know that Lady Stone's murderer also murdered my husband,' said Gabrielle du Houssoye.

'And Lucie Robin, Léonard Dielette and Achille Ménager. And he almost murdered me and Monsieur Mori. Was it ambition that drove Charles Dorsel to commit these crimes?'

'Oh, no; far from it. At first I suspected Alexis. It was only the appalling sight of Lucie's body that gave me pause – she had after all been Charles's mistress. I hesitated to intervene; I feared for my life and for my family. But I wasn't mistaken – although Charles was very fond of my father, he tried to kill him.'

'So your father was right about that.'

'Oh, you know about that too? I'm impressed, Monsieur Legris – you are all-seeing. Yes, someone did indeed shoot at my father, but he was lucky enough to bend down at the right moment. The bullet embedded itself in the eye of one of his stuffed dogs.'

'You chose to remain silent even though your secretary was on a killing spree!'

'I regret that I endangered your life. I planned to alert the police the day before yesterday, but you beat me to it.'

'Investigating murders is one of my little hobbies.'

'The funniest thing about all this is that the goblet would probably have been useless to us anyway. Alexis confirmed that after I had filled him in on everything that had happened. Antoine thought the skull would have been enough to prove the existence of the *pithecanthropus* and establish his reputation. But he would have needed other bones as well, especially from the lower limbs, in order to prove that the skullcap belonged to a *pithecanthropus* and not a monkey. Besides, the cranium would almost certainly have been cut down and sandpapered to make the incense burner, so that I imagine the brow ridge was missing.'

'It was; I can confirm that.'

'Antoine was killed for nothing. And even after his death I clung to my false hopes,' she said bitterly.

'I understand now: you took over the quest from your dead husband. That's the real reason you kept silent! Did you really think you would be able to reason with a criminal?'

'It's easy to win men over, Monsieur Legris; they all have the same desires. You just have to use the right arguments,' she replied, languidly adjusting the front of her dress.

'Poor Lucie Robin wasn't able to.'

'I'm made of sterner stuff.'

'But Charles Dorsel could just have limited himself to obtaining the goblet. Why did he feel the need to murder everyone who touched it?'

'The key lies in his past. He was born in 1868, the eldest of three children, in a little town in Holland, Nijmegen. His father was an extremely puritanical Lutheran pastor and his mother, a Belgian immigrant, blindly obeyed her husband in everything. About ten years ago the family moved out to the Dutch East Indies to convert the natives. They moved to Tjaringin, a mission by the sea. Shortly afterwards Charles was sent to board with a pastor in Batavia in order to follow a course of religious study. On 27 August 1883 Krakatoa erupted and the entire Dorsel family perished in the tidal wave that swept the coast. Charles was traumatised.'

'That wouldn't necessarily turn you into a murderer.'

'No, but you have to take into account the added effect of the education he received. His tutor encouraged him to think of the catastrophe as an early warning sign of the Apocalypse. Charles was the product of a rigorous and puritanical upbringing. Later, when he was with Antoine and me, he pretended to laugh at it, but deep down it was still what he believed in. He was a gifted orator and wrote sermons, but feeling that this was not enough to fulfil him he joined the army. Later, he was introduced to Antoine at a dinner and was taken into his service.'

'You had no idea he was so unstable?'

'He was impulsive and would sometimes fly off the handle, but he also possessed great charm and was very attractive to the opposite sex. He was like a son to us. We were unaware he felt he was God's emissary. But he never got over the loss of his family and apparently thought he had been spared as part of a Divine plan. Given his education it was natural that he should abhor evolutionary theories. The implication that man was descended from orang-utans or gibbons was sacrilege to him – heresy. And to be employed by Antoine to demonstrate that lineage only heightened his fury. Yet he managed to contain himself. The turning point came on 27 March when he happened to witness one of those frightful explosions that have so terrorised Paris.'

'The explosion in Rue de Clichy on 27 March! It was horrifying – and must have given Charles an emotional jolt that revived a buried memory.'

'Exactly. Charles felt he had been called upon to act. Can I pour you another glass, Monsieur Legris?'

'No thank you, do go on.'

'Yesterday I searched through Charles's bedroom and found

his journal. He'd meticulously recorded everything he'd done from the point at which he followed Antoine to Scotland, but the journal also contained some more impassioned writing.'

She went over to the side table, gave him the journal and sat down again.

'Take a look at that, Monsieur Legris.'

The letters, in blue ink, ran into one another like a row of tiny octopuses.

27 March. This morning, the wrath of God resonated once more, piercing my eardrums and shaking my bones to the marrow . . .

2 April. We're leaving for London. The National Geographic Society Conference. I have read Antoine's notes without him knowing. Horror! God has severely taken me to task. I did not sleep a wink last night.

Victor slowly looked through the journal. On another page he read:

7 April. On the boat. It's done, the old woman has been eliminated; she did not suffer. I have the name and address of the owner of the abomination: Monsieur Mori, 18 Rue des Saints-Pères.

8 April. Monsieur Mori is abroad. Lucie thinks we are after a valuable jewel. Her greed will be her undoing.

Saturday 9 April. Success! I have the infamous object. Lucie believes the precious stones set into it are worth a lot of money. We hid the abomination in the cellar among the old furniture . . .

Tuesday 12 April. The scene at the morgue: Gabrielle grief-stricken, Lucie in tears — perfect. Alexis doing an excellent impression of a bereaved cousin bravely suppressing his grief, when deep down he was overjoyed, thinking, 'Now I'll have a free run at Gabrielle.' I'm sure God disapproves of their relationship . . .

A visit from the police inspector. He concluded the murderer was after money. Lucie took the old man by surprise; he dropped his neckerchief and Alexis put it in his pocket. Lucie recognised the material in which the abomination had been wrapped. We went down to the cellar: the thing had disappeared! Was Lucie trying to double-cross me? God advised me to get rid of the avaricious woman there and then. But she's so pretty and has pleased me so often...

The small cramped writing danced in front of Victor's eyes and he stopped for a moment before plunging back into the diary.

The old man told me he'd thrown what he thought was the cursed chalice of the Templars in the rubbish! I convinced him that the Templars would exact revenge if he ever mentioned our little trade. Farewell, Lucie.

Thursday 14 April. The associate is looking for Clovis Martel, second-hand merchant at Saint-Médard market. Thank you, God, for guiding me. I am scything your fields and gathering a renegade harvest that will populate the Kingdom of Satan and fill you with joy! No one will be able to take possession of that abomination . . . Oh, Lord, arm your emissary!

'The emissary was on your heels constantly, Monsieur Legris,' said Gabrielle, leaning over Victor's shoulder. 'He used a velocipede.'

'Now you mention it, I do remember that once or twice . . . a bicycle, yes . . . But there are so many of them nowadays. In fact I aspire to own one myself. I wasn't paying enough attention.'

'Charles was very cunning.'

'And yet you insist that his behaviour never gave you cause for concern?'

'He was a religious crank. But he had such self-control that he pulled the wool over our eyes. You know as well as I do that most people, while appearing completely normal, are, in one way or another, psychologically unbalanced. Charles Dorsel illustrates the malign influence of a narrow, bigoted religious upbringing. So, Monsieur Legris, do you feel you understand everything now? And do you agree with me that it would be best simply to erase the memory of that murderous insanity and everything that flowed from it?'

Gabrielle patted her hair with a delicate, rather seductive gesture. She glanced at Victor, smiling as if seeking his approval.

'Dear Monsieur Legris, what can the ins and outs of this affair matter now to the inspector? Wouldn't it be better if only you and your friends and Alexis and I knew the whole story?'

'Perhaps you're right. If you'll excuse me, I'm not feeling too well at the moment. I'm going to have to go home and lie down.'

'I'm so glad we are of the same view.'

She accompanied him to the door, saw him out and closed

the door. She did not see the figure barring Victor's way as he went along the corridor.

'Sycophant . . . I recognise you; you're my purveyor of voluptuous dancers!' exclaimed Fortunat de Vigneules. 'Have you come to replenish my stock of ample posteriors?'

'No, I just happened to be . . .'

'Ah-ha! You were having a rendezvous with the perfidious Gabrielle. Watch out, she would stop at nothing – not even patricide!'

'You're mistaken, your daughter never tried to . . .'

'I'm not the bumbling old fool she takes me for! And even though she got her doctor to drug me, I still believe she wanted to kill me!'

'It was Charles Dorsel who tried to kill you,' responded Victor calmly.

But, far from appeasing the old man, Victor's measured tone enraged him.

'Charles? You're blaming little Charles? He's the only one in this damnable house who had the courage to come to my defence! *Vade retro*, spawn of the devil! You may have taken on the body of a photographer in the hope of deceiving me, but I have seen through your disguise. You are the execrable Jacques de Molay! Don't rejoice too soon though – I'm not giving up without a fight!'

He ran off to a bedroom where, judging from the racket, he was barricading himself in. Victor sighed, concluding that the old man was locking himself in to escape being carted off to a psychiatric hospital, and resolved to send him a parcel of saucy, titillating photographs as soon as possible.

Fortunat de Vigneules, hidden behind the curtain, watched regretfully as his source of nymphs disappeared under the porch just as a black cat sprang out. Believing he had witnessed an incarnation of the devil himself, Fortunat fell to his knees before a portrait of Louis XVI, stammering imprecations against evil.

Victor was relieved to find that Tasha had not yet returned and would therefore remain unaware of his outing. He had just lain down when he heard heavy footsteps in the courtyard, and Euphrosine came in, weighed down by a basket of cleaning materials.

'Hello, Monsieur Legris. You've returned from death's door. This time you very nearly escaped this purgatory in which we are all mouldering. Poor us . . . the sooner we shuffle off this mortal coil the better!'

'Why so pessimistic?'

'I can't tell you; I can't tell anyone!'

'You can tell me – I'd like to know.'

'I've sweated blood and tears for twenty-two years to raise my son and now I'm going to lose him!'

'I didn't know Jojo was so ill!' Victor exclaimed in alarm.

'Oh, it's not his health. Although, of course, he is a bit shaken after grappling with a murderer at the feet of Le Génie d'la Liberté and tipping him head first over the edge. Since you don't seem to know about it, and in case you're interested, yesterday Monsieur Mori gave him your sister's hand in marriage in recognition of the debt he owes him for killing his attacker,' Euphrosine intoned, rather as if she were reading an obituary.

Forgetting his injury, Victor sat up, letting out a cry of pain. 'Joseph and Iris are getting married?'

'They're to be engaged next year, just after my son's birthday, which is 14 January. The wedding will be six months later.'

'I can't deny I'm surprised. I think it's a little hasty and I don't really approve. But it is true that without Joseph Kenji would not be alive.'

'Of course it's true!'

'And, if I've got this right, you'll have fifteen months before the ceremony so you're not going to lose him immediately. And afterwards,' he added with a hint of regret, 'you'll still see him every day in the shop.'

'That's not what I'm worried about, Monsieur Legris!' she exploded. 'It's just that I would have liked to see him marry a real French girl!'

'Oh, now we're getting to it,' he declared. 'Iris is not French enough for your taste.'

'I have nothing against her. She's pretty, and educated, and everything. It's just . . . if they have children . . .'

'It's true they might look a little Japanese, but they'll sound Parisian. You yourself are originally from La Charente aren't you?'

'Indeed I am, Monsieur Legris. My family is from Angoulême.'

'In that case, permit me to point out that Le Comte d'Angoumois only attached himself to the French Crown under Philip the Fair. Angoumois was then ceded to England, taken back again, and given for a while to François I's mother, Louise of Savoie. That chequered past hardly entitles you to disparage my sister's origins.'

'I'm not disparaging them at all! It's something else . . .' Euphrosine burst into tears.

'There, there, pull yourself together. It can't be that bad,' murmured Victor, acutely embarrassed.

Euphrosine wiped her eyes and blew her nose several times.

'Joseph's father . . . He was married when we fell in love. And then after his wife fell ill, he swore he would marry me when she passed away. But he died a few months before she did. Thank God he had recognised Joseph, so my son is a Pignot. But the same doesn't apply to me, my name's still Courlac!' Euphrosine bellowed, waving her vast checked hankie about.

Victor suppressed a nervous giggle.

'That's what you're so worried about? You've never told Joseph, is that it?'

'How could I bear his contempt?'

'There's nothing scandalous about this. Joseph loves you and will quickly get used to the truth. Do you really want him to stay a bachelor all his life just so that you don't have to reveal the truth to him? Anyway, Iris won't care; it's Joseph she's marrying, not you!' The Lord be praised, he added to himself.

'Thank you, Monsieur Legris. You've taken a weight off my mind.'

'Go over to Tasha's; you'll find some vodka there. I advise you to pour yourself a little glass and lie down for a moment on her bed. Unless your love of country prevents you accepting an offer from an Anglo-Frenchman living in sin with a young Russian émigré . . .'

'Oh, Monsieur Legris, I'm ashamed of what I said! I deserve a slap!'

'Well, I'm too tired to slap you,' he groaned, closing his eyes.

She stole out and he immediately sank into sleep.

He awoke with a start, aware of a presence. Kenji was smiling at him from the foot of the bed.

'I would have come yesterday if the tigress guarding you had not sent me packing. How is your wound?'

'I can't wait to have these damned stitches out.'

'Be patient. A stitch in time saves nine.'

'Very witty. How are you?'

'I've a few inconveniently placed bruises.'

'Madame Pignot told me about the marriage.'

'I'm indebted to Joseph, but although I've agreed to his request I did try to slow things down a little. They're both as scatterbrained as each other, so I do worry about them. Still, birds of a feather stick together.'

'You and your adages . . . I went to see Gabrielle du Houssoye this afternoon, and now I finally have all the pieces of the puzzle. Would you like me tell you all about it?'

'I certainly would. I expect your account will have the name Eugène Dubois somewhere in it . . . I'd advise you to close your mouth now, lest you swallow a fly.'

'How do you know about Dubois?'

'When I read John Cavendish's letter again, I noticed a name: Trinil. It just so happens that in my youth, during a trip to Java, I stayed in that village and had the opportunity of looking at the fragments of gibbon skeleton that the inhabitants had retrieved from the banks of the River Solo. On a hunch, I rang a friend of mine at the National Geographic Society in London who knows South-East Asia well. He gave me some important information on Eugène Dubois, who had undertaken palaeontological digs. Very few people knew what his aim was. I thought that if Antoine du Houssoye was interested in my goblet, it was probably something to do with Dubois's researches. Over to you.'

'When I was small and I had seen something amusing in the street or the bookshop, I would long for you to return so that I could tell you about it and savour your amazement. But I was always disappointed because, by some devilish trick, you always knew part of what I was going to say!'

'Yes, but only part. For some unknown reason, I never knew the ending of your stories and you always had to fill me in. So we complement each other perfectly, I think you'll agree?'

Victor nodded reluctantly and prepared to deliver an account of events.

'You can't even tell me anything about it?'

'Not even you, Iris. I promised your father when he agreed to let me have your hand. I swore on Maman's head!' protested Joseph.

Iris pouted. Then she consoled herself with the thought that once they were married she would know all of Joseph's secrets.

'What I'm most annoyed about is that I won't be able to use any of the material for my next novel. Too bad, *Thulé's Golden Chalice* will have to be all about the Templars' treasure, which, after all, is better than nothing.'

'Have you been able to do any writing today?' murmured Iris, coming over to the counter behind which Joseph sat on his stool, looking in a melancholy way from the morocco-bound notebook his beloved had given him the day before to the finally empty shop. 'No, not a single word. I'm feeling a little out of sorts today. Iris . . . Do you think you will regain your respect for me?'

'My respect? You've got it wrong: the important thing is love, and I love you, Joseph!'

'Yes, but respect is important too. I'm a murderer.'

'No, you're not! The inspector keeps telling you: it was self-defence! My dearest, thanks to you Kenji is alive!'

'Your dearest, you mean that?' Their lips were almost touching. 'You should lock the door,' he murmured at the precise moment that the doorbell tinkled and Euphrosine, red-faced and out of breath, dumped down her basket and dusters and held out a large rectangular package wrapped in thick brown paper.

'It's an engagement present from Mademoiselle Tasha, because she's going away soon and doesn't know for how long. It would be best if you hang it up in your apartment for the moment,' grunted Euphrosine to Iris, before picking up her bags and leaving.

Intrigued, Joseph cut the strings. He spent his whole week packing up parcels for other people and was happy for once to be on the receiving end. A familiar sphinx-like face appeared suddenly out of the paper, complete with an ironic expression in the eyes, which were lined with crow's feet.

'Papa!' cried Iris. 'It's the portrait I admired at Tasha's. That's so kind of her!'

Joseph said nothing; he felt rather less enthusiastic.

'Don't you love me any more?' Eudoxie had been on the point of asking as she pulled on a negligée. She stopped herself just in time. There was no point in asking, since he had clearly demonstrated his incapacity to express anything other than physical attraction. So she said instead, 'Don't you desire me any more? Excuse me, you're probably tired. I'm going to let you rest and I'll go and have a bath.'

Kenji was stretched out on the bed, hands behind his head. 'It's not that, my dear, it's that . . . I'm unfit at the moment – I received a low blow. We'll have to wait a while,' he replied evasively.

'A blow? Were you beaten up?'

'It happens sometimes.'

'But you? I can't imagine . . . Are you in pain?'

'Let's not talk about it. Come here, I've a present for you.'

He stretched out an arm towards the bedside table and placed a little jewel case in the lace at the top of her negligée. Inside she discovered a necklace of tiny golden pearls that seemed to contain sequins.

'Amber! It's so beautiful, and very generous of you!'

'I though it would complement your dark colouring. You see, darling, I've had a bad experience that has made me appreciate life, and to want to give more than I receive. I know other ways of pleasuring a lover,' he murmured, slipping a hand under the black crêpe de Chine that barely hid Eudoxie's nudity. 'Could you postpone your bath a little? Come and lie down beside me. Make yourself comfortable.'

Victor was gradually drifting off to sleep. Already he was tipping over into a universe where the maddest adventures became logical and where reality was distorted. A hand lifted the sheets and covers, a cool body slipped in beside him, an arm embraced him. He hesitated, attracted by nocturnal chimeras.

'Wake up, my love, no, don't move, your dressing will slip, just relax . . .'

He groaned for appearances' sake and abandoned himself to Tasha's caresses, soothed by the hail that was battering the capital after the wintry day.

EPILOGUE

Tuesday, 10 May 1892

IN the dusk the glass awning of the Gare de l'Est had a bluish tinge. Clouds of steam billowed out from under it. Locomotives vibrated and processions of porters cut through the crowds. A murmuring grew louder – a regiment of sappers was setting off on manoeuvres. A cheer went up.

'Long live the army!'

There was a splutter of applause, muffled by the hiss of a locomotive.

Tasha hurried along the platform, navigating her way through the baggage trolleys, looking for her compartment. Victor followed, carrying her case. He had hoped that some mechanical failure would prevent the train from being there. But the flow of passengers swept them both along past carriages with lighted windows all ready to devour the miles. In ten more minutes she would be on her way towards Strasbourg, her first stop.

'Here it is.'

He glanced at the newspaper vendor hawking the evening papers.

'Do you want one?'

She shook her head. 'I have something to read.'

He hoisted up the suitcase. She froze, as if suddenly

308

understanding that they were about to be separated. A blast of military music mingled with the grinding sound of the axles. Victor frowned at the noise, which made him look even more strained. His face was already lined from several sleepless nights. She watched him anxiously, lightly brushed a stray lock from his brow, then ran her finger down to his lips.

'My love,' he murmured, pressing her to him. She closed her eyes, holding her breath.

'How will it be?'

'Everything will work out. You will go to your mother, nurse her better and bring her back. As quickly as possible.'

'Promise me to be good: no investigations.'

'That's your idea of being good? What about women?'

'You can see Iris and Euphrosine.'

He tried to smile, and helped her up into the carriage, supporting her under the elbow. 'Go and sit down. I can't stand goodbyes,' he muttered.

She suddenly got down from the train again. Their lips were about to touch when a large family, worried that the train was about to depart, knocked into them on their way up the steps. Victor pushed Tasha in behind them.

She just had time to shout, 'I'll write to you,' before the porter banged the door closed.

The whistle blew once, followed by a second more strident note. The carriage swayed slightly and began to slide away under the white clouds of the locomotive. Victor walked rapidly beside it, his eyes fixed on Tasha's blurred face; he could tell she was crying. He ran for a moment or two as the train gathered speed towards the green and white lights of the night. He stopped abruptly and wiped his eyes with the back of his hand before wandering slowly back to the ticket hall.

Now that Tasha was gone, his sadness returned. All he wanted was the oblivion of sleep. Finally he collapsed into a cab. Rocked by the swaying he sank back against the seat and dozed for a moment.

He jolted awake. The cab had come to a standstill, hemmed in at a crossroads. He could hear a woman singing in an Italian accent.

> *'Sometimes when my heart is heavy*
> *I go out and take a stroll*
> *In all the little streets and alleys . . .'*

He leant over and recognised the Neopolitan Anna Marcelli turning the handle of her organ that was propped against a Wallace fountain.[1] Near her, large and gawky, but standing straight, was the Gascon student – what was his name? Oh yes, Mathurin Ferrant. He opened his mouth and murdering the melody bawled.

> *'Children on the dirty pavements*
> *Playing hopscotch one-two-three'*

Just as he was about to call out, the cab set off again. Victor felt reassured by the sight of them. At least the sinister affair that had overtaken them all had served some purpose. That reflection made him think about Rue Charlot, where the day before he and Iris had taken Yvette and her donkey, who

Gabrielle du Houssoye had decided to adopt. He hoped they would be happy with her. He was sure it would be good for Yvette, who had suffered a terrible blow with the death of her father. As for Clampin, he would certainly have preferred to wander about in the hills of the Cévennes, following the example of his distant cousin Modestine, Robert Louis Stevenson's donkey,[2] instead of being stabled in the third arrondissement. His mind drifted to Pinkus, sailing to New York, and he pictured the enormous silhouette of the Statue of Liberty in the mists of the Hudson River.

The torrential rain of the preceding days had left many puddles in the uneven surface of the courtyard. He decided to go straight home. The sight of the sheets hanging on the line strung between the acacia tree and the second-floor window stopped him in his tracks. A breeze inflated them so that they looked like the sails on a three-master. An inexplicable wave of happiness washed over him. He imagined himself the captain of a ship dancing on the sea of life. He entered the studio and lit a lamp. The familiar disorder, embellished by the faint smell of *benjoin* calmed him. As he took off his overcoat and gathered up brushes and tubes of gouache, he made plans. He would buy a bicycle, go and potter about in Cité Doré, help Kenji put together their next catalogue, file away Yvette's photographs.

Without being aware of it, he began to sing softly.

> *'Sometimes when my heart is heavy*
> *I go out and take a stroll*
> *In all the little streets and alleys . . .'*

311

SOME HISTORICAL CONTEXT
TO *THE MARAIS ASSASSIN*

Anarchists

In the spring of 1892, a series of anarchist bombings brought fear to the streets of Paris. These bombings were acts of revenge for the capture and imprisonment of fellow anarchists. The bomber responsible was the notorious criminal, Ravachol.

On the eve of Ravachol's trial, there was another bombing at the Restaurant Véry, the scene of his arrest. At the trial, despite the public prosecutor's best efforts, Ravachol was spared the death penalty, and given a life sentence of hard labour. Two months later, Ravachol received the death penalty for a murder committed in 1891. He was guillotined on 11 July.

Ravachol was successfully arrested, tried and convicted thanks to the innovative method of 'Bertillonage'. Invented by the biometrics researcher Alphonse Bertillon, it used anthropometrics, the comparative study of the sizes and proportions of the human body, to create a unique profile for every individual that could then be applied in the detection of a crime. The British polymath Francis Galton, who worked out the potential flaws of the method, later went on to discover the forensic value of fingerprinting.

Java Man

In the late nineteenth century, the debate was raging between the creationist beliefs of the Church and its adherents, and the scientific establishment who supported Charles Darwin's theory of evolution.

The German evolutionary biologist, Ernst Haeckel, who had studied the theories of French naturalist Jean-Baptiste Lamarck, developed the idea of the 'missing link', a supposed evolutionary stage between the great apes and man. Struck by the similarity between the embryos of humans and gibbons, he speculated that the missing link might have lived in the locations where gibbons were still to be found. Inspired by Haeckel, Eugene Dubois, a young Dutch anatomist working as a military surgeon in Sumatra, made some extraordinary archaeological discoveries in Java in 1891. On the banks of the River Solo he unearthed a skullcap, femur and some teeth belonging to a hominid that became known as Java Man. The skullcap was too large to be that of an ape and smaller than a human skullcap.

This apparent discovery of *pithecanthropus*, an intermediate stage between man and the apes, caused much controversy and debate throughout the world. However, we now know that Java Man was not in fact the missing link, as his skeleton, though primitive, is that of a man of the Middle Palaeolithic era.

NOTES

CHAPTER TWO

1. French writer (1848–1917) Mathilde Georgina Élisabeth de Peyrebrune.
2. French author (1851–1922).
3. See *The Montmartre Investigation*, Gallic Books.
4. At 22 Boulevard Magenta.
5. 'Ravachol's Ballad' by Jules Jouy.
6. Serialised from 20 February to 21 July 1892.
7. Charles Nègre, 1820–1880, French photographer known for his architectural photographs of French cities; Charles Marville, 1816–1879, official photographer for Paris in 1862.
8. An event in which cyclists had to catch up or overtake an opponent, following a trail of papers dropped by them.

CHAPTER THREE

1. 1857–1908. Of Polish origin, she was a pianist and poet and part of the avant-garde movement of the 1880s. She was also one of the first proponents of free verse.
2. Berthe Morisot (1841–1865). The first woman to join the circle of French Impressionist painters.

CHAPTER FOUR

1. Ravachol set off his second explosion at Rue de Clichy on 27 March 1892. It was an attack on Solicitor-General Bulot. Twenty-seven people were injured.
2. Émile Loubet.
3. See *Murder on the Eiffel Tower*, Gallic Books.
4. Hubert-Martin Cazin, publisher and bookseller, 1724–1795. In Rheims he began to publish small books in certain formats, octodecimo or vincesimo-quarto, which came to be named after him.
5. Agnès Hellebick.

CHAPTER FIVE

1. *Encyclopédie des sciences occultes* (Edition Georges-Anquetil, 1925).
2. In order to appropriate the immense wealth of the Knights Templar and to destroy their power, King Philip the Fair (1268–1314) had them arrested. Following an unfair trial, the last grand master, Jacques de Molay, was burned at the stake, cursing the King and his descendants as he was executed.
3. Drama in prose by Alfred de Vigny performed on 12 February 1835.
4. Song by Pierre-Jean Béranger, French songwriter (1780–1857).
5. A work by Théodore Bénard (Paris, A. Colin, 1874).

CHAPTER SEVEN

1. One of the Paris toll gates.
2. Now known as Gare d'Austerlitz.

CHAPTER EIGHT

1. Nickname for Palais de Justice.

CHAPTER NINE

1. Gérard de Nerval '*Le Roi de Thule*' in *Lyrisme et Vers d'Opéra*.
2. Popular novel by Maricourt.
3. Absinthe.
4. It's so cold!
5. Song by Maurice Marc.
6. Coward.
7. Bastard.

CHAPTER TEN

1. A famous gold and silversmith situated on Boulevard des Italiens.

CHAPTER EVELEN

1. Old German saying.

CHAPTER THIRTEEN

1. 'I love . . . but my love is without hope'.
2. Situated on Place de l'Alma.
3. A reddish clay that takes the appetite away and can be lethal.

CHAPTER FOURTEEN

1. 'Darling' in Yiddish.
2. Little bird.

CHAPTER FIFTEEN

1. President of the Association of Latin Scholars.
2. Celtic warrior chief who resisted the Romans, popularised by the *Asterix* comics.
3. Metro line that encircled Paris with a single track.
4. Battle of 52 BC, between the Romans and the Gauls, and led by Vercingetorix.
5. The last major battle, in September of 52 BC, between the Romans led by Julius Caesar and a confederation of Gallic tribes led by Vercingetorix – the Gauls were comprehensively beaten.

CHAPTER SIXTEEN

1. My heart is hurrying towards you, my sweet girl. (Translation from Yiddish.)
2. In 1886 Éduoard Drumont published *La France juive*. He led a movement of neo-anti-Semitism that attracted numerous adherents. On 20 April 1892 he launched *La Libre Parole* whose views were also anti-Semitic.

EPILOGUE

1. Drinking fountains scattered throughout Paris, fifty of which were donated to the city by British philanthropist Sir Richard Wallace in 1872.
2. *Travels with a Donkey in the Cévennes* by Robert Louis Stevenson, 1879.

There is more mystery in store with
Claude Izner's bestselling Victor
Legris series, set in Belle Époque Paris

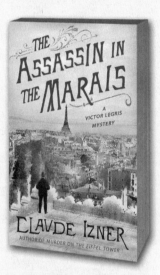

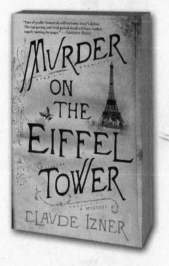

Don't miss *In the Shadows of Paris* on sale September 2012